LOVELAND PUBLIC LIBRARY

000539041

9/26/14
$16.99
938
B&T
JFIC

D0405954

The VOYAGE of LUCY P. SIMMONS

THE EMERALD SHORE

The VOYAGE of LUCY P. SIMMONS
THE EMERALD SHORE

BARBARA MARICONDA

KATHERINE TEGEN BOOKS
An Imprint of HarperCollins Publishers

Katherine Tegen Books is an imprint of HarperCollins Publishers.

The Voyage of Lucy P. Simmons: The Emerald Shore
Copyright © 2014 by Barbara Mariconda
All rights reserved. Printed in the United States of America.
No part of this book may be used or reproduced in any manner
whatsoever without written permission except in the case of
brief quotations embodied in critical articles and reviews.
For information address HarperCollins Children's Books,
a division of HarperCollins Publishers, 195 Broadway,
New York, NY 10007.
www.harpercollinschildrens.com

Library of Congress Cataloging-in-Publication Data
Mariconda, Barbara.
    The Emerald Shore / Barbara Mariconda. — First edition.
        pages   cm. — (The voyage of Lucy P. Simmons)
    Summary: "Lucy travels to Ireland in her magical house-turned-ship to
find the pirate treasure that will end the magical curse haunting her family
once and for all"— Provided by publisher.
    ISBN 978-0-06-211996-4 (hardback)
    [1. Orphans—Fiction.   2. Dwellings—Fiction.   3. Magic—Fiction.
4. Household employees—Fiction.   5. Aunts—Fiction.   6. Blessing and
cursing—Fiction.   7. Ireland—History—20th century—Fiction.]   I. Title.
PZ7.M33835Eme   2014   2014001885
[Fic]—dc23   CIP
                                                                    AC

Typography by Amy Ryan
14 15 16 17 18   CG/RRDH   10 9 8 7 6 5 4 3 2 1
❖
First Edition

For Thomas F. Lynch, of whom it's been said:
He's a strange blend of shyness, pride and conceit,
and stubborn refusal to bow in defeat.
He's spoiling and ready to argue and fight,
yet the smile of a child fills his soul with delight.
His eyes are the quickest to well up with tears,
Yet his strength is the strongest to banish your fears.
His hate is as fierce as his devotion is grand,
And there is no middle ground on which he will stand.
He's wild and he's gentle, he's good and he's bad.
He's proud and he's humble, he's happy and sad.
He's in love with the ocean, the earth, and the skies,
He's enamored with beauty wherever it lies.
He's victor and victim, a star and a clod,
But mostly he's Irish—in love with his God.

Loveland Public Library
Loveland, CO

1

JULY 1908

A sharp wind snapped the sails of the *Lucy P. Simmons*, and the chilling mist that swirled across Clew Bay dampened my face and hair. My overalls and sweater clung to my body like a cold, wet blanket. I shivered, then hugged myself tightly. Pugsley shook himself off and hunkered at my feet, stubby tail wagging despite the weather.

After a grueling ten months at sea trying to outrun the threat of the family curse—from Port Lincoln on the southern shore of Australia, across the Indian Ocean, past the great continent of Africa, drifting for the better part of a month on flat seas with not a breath of wind, roasting beneath the equatorial sun—the promise of arriving at our destination made the weather along the Emerald Isle feel almost welcoming. I pulled Father's spyglass from my pocket and pressed the brass-rimmed lens against my eye, searching for a scrap of green to indicate that Clare Island was in sight. I stared until my eyes began to water.

"Pull this around yourself, child—not bein' used t' Irish weather—you'll catch a chill, y'will!" Addie placed a thick shawl about my shoulders, draped her arm around me, and drew me in close. Her face was alight with excitement, despite the persistent, seamless gray gloom of sea, sky, and fog.

The ship's bell began to toll and Grady appeared beside us, his weaselly face screwed in a grimace. "Growin' up here I knows these waters like the back of me hand . . . but this"—he waved a thin, sinewy arm out before him—"this ain't no regular fog."

Walter ambled up beside me and took his place along the rail, his dark straight hair slicked to his forehead, the mist accumulating on his sweater like a fine white dew. "Aw, Grady," he quipped, a smile teasing his lips, "what is it this time? We've already seen more ghosts than I care to count, a disappearing specter ship, a deck of talking cards, not to mention—how should I put it?—the unusual characteristics of this ship. I was hoping we might finish this voyage without any more irregularities."

"It ain't funny," Grady muttered. "You kids gotta learn some r'spect fer whatcha don't understand." He adjusted his cap and stared out over the starboard side. A familiar feeling of dread slowly filled me, like cold brackish water seeping into the hold. It sloshed around and caused me to shudder.

"Look sharp!" Capt'n Obediah yelled. "Can't see my hand in front of my face! Tonio, sound the signal! Reds—you two watch well forward! Irish, I need you aft! Listen as well as look!" The crew scrambled toward their posts, each disappearing into the thick gray mist as the warning bell sounded—one ring, followed by two short clangs. This, to alert any other vessels of our presence.

I felt Annie's small hand slip into my own. She'd sidled up to me, her blond hair framing her face in dank ringlets, her blue eyes enormous with alarm. Her brother Georgie appeared on my left, so much more grown up than when we'd begun this quest— still small for ten, but during the entire adventure he'd managed to sprout considerably. Walter reassured his little sister and brother. "We've been through worse than this," he said.

"But are we gonna crash?" Annie whimpered. My heart did a flip inside my chest. It had been a day just like this, off the coast of Maine, when my life was first touched by the generations-old curse, as the little sloop in which I'd been sailing with Mother and Father capsized, leaving me the lone survivor. Though more than two years ago, the thought of it still had the power to blind me with tears.

"Of course we're not going to crash!"

I turned toward the confident voice of my aunt Pru. She was perched atop the poop deck, peering out beneath a visored hand, her long red hair so like mine, whipping about like the mane of a wild stallion. I took heart from her determined, regal profile, staring out into the unknown.

"Hmph!" Grady responded with his usual disdain. "Fools! Ye ferget that rocky headlands get their names from the ships they destroy!" He leaned forward, extended his skinny neck, pursed his lips, and sniffed at the air, once, twice, three times. "Ye smell that?" he barked.

We all inhaled, nostrils flared.

"Woodsmoke," he said. "Peat and ash."

Walter and I exchanged a glance. Pru turned our way, hair blowing straight back off her face. It was true. There was a peculiar burned smell, as though a fire of decaying wood had just been extinguished.

"The Grey Man . . . ," Grady whispered, his beady eyes narrowed, trying to penetrate the fog. Pugsley suddenly sprang up, the hair along his back rising in a bristly ridge. A soft growl rumbled from his throat. "Even the dog sees 'im," Grady muttered.

"'Tis nothin' of the kind!" Addie retorted, her face full of indignation. "Ye think yer the only one who knows Irish legends?" She extended a protective arm around the children, glared at Grady and then at the dog. "Sit, Pugsley, and stop yer belly-achin'!" The pup whined, circled around once, and lay back at my feet with a deflated *arrumph*.

"The Grey Man?" I asked. As if in response, a wave hit us portside, showering us with a sheet of cold water.

Grady seemed to take this as an affirmation. "An Irish fairy of the worst type," he said, pausing to nibble the inside of his cheek. "Sustains hisself on chimney smoke. Wherever 'e passes, he flings his cloak of gray mist over 'is shoulder, sheathing everything in 'is path with the pall of death. Shroudin' the coastline in smoky fog, then laughin' as ships are thrown into the rocks. On land, the Grey Man's presence causes potato rot, turnin' 'em to black mush."

Annie buried her face in the folds of my over-alls. Georgie puffed himself up. "Quaide told me how sailors use potatoes!" he shouted. "In the fog, keep a bucket of taters near the bow, and heave 'em one at a time in the forward direction. If they splash, proceed. If not, tack!"

Marni suddenly appeared, her long silver hair and pale green eyes blending with the seascape. "Sailing and potato heaving have little in common, as I see it," she said lightly. "And Quaide isn't here, thank the Lord. Let's all calm down. In Ireland, as I recall, the fog can roll in and out in the blink of an eye, isn't that right, Miss Addie?"

Addie, just as she'd done throughout the years she served as my beloved nanny, nodded with an air of reassuring confidence. "Ye got that right, Miss Marni! We Irish women know when foolish sailors take t' talkin' blarney, we do! That'll be all from ye, Grady! Whyn't ye jest focus yer attention on sailin' the ship?"

"Over there!" Pru shouted. "Off to starboard!"

We all turned and gasped. To the east there was a sudden break in the clouds. A scrap of bright blue sky appeared with a huge rainbow arching down toward the greenest land I'd ever seen. My heart swelled with a strange feeling of coming home, though of course I'd never been there before.

"Look, Annie!" I gasped. Marni closed her eyes for a moment, fingering the silver locket at her throat. Walter pounded Georgie on the back and, in an instant, threw his arms around me, lifted me off my feet, and spun me in a circle.

"There she is!" Capt'n shouted from the helm, one hand guiding the massive ship's wheel, the other pointing off toward the shore that had, moments ago, been veiled in fog. "Clare Island!" The *Lucy P. Simmons* seemed to ride the waves with a new confidence, her figurehead carved in the likeness of my ill-fated uncle Victor and aunt Margaret, reaching toward our final destination.

"Y'know what they say," Addie exclaimed, winking at me. "There's a pot of gold at the end of the rainbow, there is!" I nodded, offering a silent prayer that we'd find the treasure we were looking for here, and finally dispel the curse that had taken my mother and father from me.

Addie turned triumphantly toward Grady and retorted, "Guess the sunshine chased yer Grey Man away, it did!"

One last wisp of smoky mist swirled around the old seafarer, and a thin ray of sunshine cast his long thin shadow across the deck.

Grady chewed his bottom lip and shook his head, a faraway look in his eye. "Only time'll tell. . . ."

2

It was with tearful farewells that Walter, Marni, Pru, and I disembarked from the *Lucy P. Simmons*, anchored in the harbor at Clare Island. After all the months at sea we'd become like a family of sorts. There were the Reds—identical twins whose crooked smiles brightened many a day at sea—and Irish, with his mischievous blue eyes, all three eager to get back to Dublin. Bald-headed Tonio with the drooping walrus mustache was already making plans to head to Galway to secure a position on an Italian-bound ship. Rasjohnny and his son, Javan, shivering in the Irish chill, longed for their native

Caribbean, and would work their way back there in the galley of some other vessel, filling other bellies with their spicy island fare. I'd miss them all as I did Coleman—the quiet man with a paralyzing stutter who sang like a bird. He'd come ashore with us in Australia and decided at the last minute to stay on as a caretaker at Aunt Pru's ranch, perfectly suited as he was to life in the outback.

Equally difficult was saying good-bye to Addie and the capt'n, Annie, and Georgie, even though our separation would be only temporary. All had come to see Addie and Capt'n Adams as a couple, the two being drawn together more and more throughout our voyage. "The young ones are going to love Ballyvaughan," the capt'n reassured. It had been decided that Annie and Georgie would travel on to the capt'n's hometown and stay there for a time with Miss Addie. After all the months at sea Marni believed that what they needed most was solid ground under their feet, and a little break from all the adventure of the last two years. "My family has a homestead there, Annie," the capt'n continued, "with sheep, cows, ducks, and a couple of goats." Annie's eyes opened wide with excitement. Georgie looked longingly between his brother and the capt'n. "Not to worry, Master Georgie," the capt'n quipped. "I'll teach you to run the tractor and to shoe a horse. You can be both a sailor and a gentleman farmer—just like me!"

"But what about Walter?" Georgie asked.

"Lucy needs me here," Walter said. "But not to worry. We'll call for you the minute another strong pair of arms is required. With all that farmwork you'll be the fellow with the biggest muscles!" Georgie smiled and flexed his biceps, warming to the idea.

We cut our embraces shorter than we might have liked, not wanting to second guess a decision made in the little ones' best interest. Moments later we found ourselves aboard a small skiff, piloting us toward the island. There was little wind yet I watched her sails flap as though waving farewell. Then our beloved ship, and the figures of the capt'n, Addie, Annie, Georgie, and the crew shrunk from view. Once we were safely deposited on Clare Island, the rest would be spirited off to the mainland to go their respective ways.

"No worries," Marni murmured, patting my arm. "We'll be sending for them in no time, I'm sure."

And time was of the essence. With each day that passed, Pru and I felt the threat of the curse pressing in—the malicious pledge of the infamous pirate queen Mary Maude Lee, that had already stolen the lives of my great-grandfather, Edward the First, then grandfather Edward II, and finally the generation once removed from me, taking first Father and then Uncle Victor. Aunt Pru and I were the only ones left. Once we discovered that Marni was the daughter of Edward and Mary Maude Lee, it became clear she had a vested interest in unraveling the curse as well—and in locating her long-lost son, who also could be struck down by the powerful vindictive oath.

Then there was the matter of the missing treasure. Hopefully it would finally be recovered here in Ireland—at least that's where all the clues seemed to point. Just before we tied up at the pier, my fingers instinctively slipped into my ditty bag, retrieving the paper on which Coleman had scrawled the words of the ballad that spelled it all out. I stared at it for the hundredth time, the words nearly committed to memory:

> *This is the ballad of Mary Maude Lee—*
> *a Queen and a Pirate—the Witch o' the Sea.*
> *Tho' fair of face, and tho' slight of build,*
> *many a seafarers' blood did she spill!*
> *A la dee dah dah . . . a la dee dah dee,*
> *This is the ballad of Mary Maude Lee.*
>
> *She fired her blunderbuss, torched their tall sails,*
> *Laughing as mariners screamed, moaned, and*
> *wailed.*

Off with their silver! Off with their gold!
Off with supplies lying deep in their holds!
A la dee dah dah . . . a la dee dah dee,
This is the ballad of Mary Maude Lee.

Her coffers grew fat, till Edward, that gent,
Escaped with her booty, and then off he went.
She swore her revenge against that sorry traitor,
Placed a curse on the sons of the cuss who betrayed
    her!
A la dee dah dah . . . a la dee dah dee,
The sons of his sons would all die in the sea!
A la dee dah dah . . . a la dee dah dee,
This is the ballad of Mary Maude Lee.

Mary Maude Lee said, "I'll spit on their graves!"
Then drew back and spat in the white churning
    waves.
And each generation of menfolk that followed,
Into the sea they'd be chewed up and swallowed!
A la dee dah dah . . . a la dee dah dee,
This is the ballad of Mary Maude Lee.

The only real way that the curse can be broken
was revealed in the last words that Mary had
    spoken,
"If not in my lifetime, then to my descendants,

Hand over my treasure and appease Mary's
    vengeance!"
A la dee dah dah . . . a la dee dah dee,
This is the ballad of Mary Maude Lee!

As always, Father's flute, tucked in my pocket, began to vibrate and hum on the repeated refrain . . . *A la dee dah dah . . . a la dee dah dee . . .* bolstering my confidence that its magic wouldn't fail me.

"Mind yer step!" Grady called, ushering Marni, Pru, and Pugsley across to the wooden dock. I quickly folded the paper, thrust it back in my bag, and waited my turn. When next, I grabbed hold of the thick rope twisted around the piling to hoist myself ashore. Suddenly another pair of hands took hold of mine.

"Lemme help ye, miss! It'll take a wee time fer yer sea legs to adjust t' land. Wouldn't wantcha taken a header overboard and mussin' that lovely head o' hair!"

I looked up into the bluest eyes I'd ever seen, set in a face framed in light brown curls. A smile played on his lips, his eyebrows raised in some rambunctious thought. His face was totally arresting, and it stopped me midway between skiff and dock. I lost my footing, my face flushing scarlet.

Walter snapped, "She doesn't need any help!"

He was so close behind me I could feel his breath on my neck. "Have you lost your head?" he whispered. Walter put his hands around my waist, and gave me a forceful boost to the pier, then jumped up beside me.

"Seamus O'Connor," the young man announced, taking no notice of Walter at all. "Saw yer unusual vessel and decided t' see fer meself who was aboard." He took my hand as though inviting me to dance. Smiling with his eyes, his gaze never leaving mine, he bent and ceremoniously kissed my fingers. I yanked them back, the thought of my dirty, rough, sunburned skin against his full lips causing me to blush for the second time in as many moments.

"We have a lot to do," Walter said, his voice gruff and edged with anger. Seamus seemed not to hear him.

Eyeing the three of us, Grady hopped ashore like a nimble squirrel. "Well, I'll be danged," he exclaimed. "If it ain't little Seamus, all growed up in the years I been gone! Still the charmer, I see." He turned to me. "Watch out fer this one." And to Walter, "I can see already ye don't like the cut of 'is jib." Grady laughed silently, shoulders rising and falling in amusement. "Time t' see me mam. As I told ye's, we can put ye up on the fam'ly farm. Got a few cottages, that is if Seamus here has done 'is job with the upkeep."

"Good t' see ye again, Grady," Seamus said, grinning ear to ear.

A large cart pulled by a pair of fluffy-furred mules stood waiting on the dirt road that ran along the shore. "I'll help ye's t' row yer bags in the back," Seamus said. "Come on, man, give me a hand, wouldja?" Walter glared at him and single-handedly hoisted the largest trunk onto the cart.

But Seamus didn't notice—he was staring at me. "I didn't get yer name, lass. . . ."

"Lucy" was just about forming on my lips when Walter stepped between us. "Where's your trunk, Lucy? I want to make sure it's safe." I grabbed the handle on one end of my trunk and Walter took the other. As we lifted it off the ground Seamus stepped in and relieved me of my end, flashing me another smile.

"Lucy, eh?" Seamus exclaimed. "A grand name it is!"

"Can we stop all the blatherin' and just get the cart loaded?" Grady muttered.

In a matter of minutes everything we owned was stacked in the back of the old wooden cart. Marni, Seamus, and Grady were seated on the rickety bench in front. Seamus flicked the reins and the cart jolted forward. Walter, Aunt Pru, and I walked behind. I found myself watching Seamus, impressed by the way he took control and asserted himself with ease. The confidence he exuded, along with his good looks, almost prevented me from noticing his threadbare, though carefully patched, clothing. I was intrigued, in spite of myself. He and Grady led us on, Pugsley running alongside, nose to the lush green grass, sniffing out a new adventure.

"Over there," Grady called, pointing. "See it?"

An old boxy castle stood overlooking the shore, narrow rectangular windows cut here and there, and small lookout holes carved along the roofline. Two chimneylike towers reached from the top of the primitive fortress, and there were several slate-covered sections that must have once been sentry houses.

"The castle of Granuaile—the pirate queen Gracie O'Malley," Grady said. "Terrorized the high seas fer years. 'Twas her home base, right 'ere on Clare Isle."

Pru and I exchanged a glance, both of us, I'm sure, sharing the same thought—what better place for a treasure to be hidden but in the shadow of another famous female pirate's stronghold? It seemed it all, in some way, began here. My heart beat a little faster as I gazed at the ancient gray structure. As if reading my thoughts, Grady swept his arm across the landscape. "The Emerald Isle holds an enchantment an' mystery all 'er own. Some, the depth of their desires so grand, their oneness with the place so powerful—those few've been known t' channel 'er force, callin' forth every manner of magic." He leveled a glance at me, one that suggested his premise might apply, if not to me, I thought, then to my ancestors. The very idea made me feel as though I was walking on hallowed ground—or perhaps a land that embodied the curse itself.

The road hugged the shoreline and then veered to the left, over a patchwork of fields in many shades of green. Everywhere we looked there were flocks of sheep grazing, shaggy heads to the ground. Occasionally a group of them trotted across the road, oblivious to our party. They'd bleat and *baa* and take their time, forcing Seamus to bring our procession to a dead stop.

The cart bumped around still another bend, and Grady pointed. "Over there, on the knoll that drops off t' the water." There was a scattering of white buildings with thatched roofs, and more sheep dotting the pastureland. "Spent me childhood there, lookin' out t' sea, dreamin' of sailin' away. Still, it always feels good comin' home." He wiped the edge of his eye with his gnarled finger, revealing a softness in him I'd never seen before.

The two little mules seemed to know their way, turning off the road onto a narrow but well-worn path that snaked across the countryside toward the cottages. In minutes we caught up and found ourselves outside of the main homestead. It was a snug-looking little house, whitewashed and neat as a pin, the large wooden door painted shiny red. Up close the thatched roof topped the structure like a thick blanket of neatly woven hay. Window boxes overflowed with cascades of tiny blue flowers and white lacy baby's breath. A thin wisp of gray swirled from the chimney, bringing with it the distinctive smoky earthen smell we'd detected at sea.

A skinny black, brown, and white sheep dog with a wagging tail bounded around the side of the cottage. For a moment the scrappy hound and Pugsley circled one another, nose to nose, before the two rollicked off across the side yard. "Ah, Old Peader's little collie Miss Rosie'll show that imp around, fer sure," Seamus exclaimed.

"Lovely place, Grady," Pru said, "really lovely. Must have been hard to leave here."

"Well, when ye have the sea in yer blood the land can't hold ye fer long."

Suddenly the top half of the door creaked open and a strange figure appeared. The long face atop the tall thin body was ancient, wrinkled, and creased like a dried apple, the light gray eyes as sharp as those of a hawk peering out between the folds. Her features drooped at the outer edges, as though gravity had, over a hundred years, dragged them toward the ground. The woman's white hair was parted down the middle, pulled back severely from her face. She held a fringed shawl tightly around her torso.

"Mam!" Grady called. "I'm home agin!"

Seamus placed his hand on Grady's arm. "Just so's ye know, sir. Miss Oonagh's . . . not all she used t' be. There're times her mind gets a bit cloudy. . . ."

Grady shot him a black look. "What're ye sayin', boy?"

"Sometimes she talks a little . . . off, is all I mean."

Before anyone could exchange another word the door opened and Miss Oonagh stepped outside. She strode straight past Seamus and Grady, with a posture and carriage that seemed impossible for her age. Ignoring Grady's outstretched arms, she stopped directly in front of me. I felt myself shrink under the steady gaze of her riveting gray eyes, and the flute in my pocket began to vibrate and hum. Oonagh tipped her head to one side and stared from me to Pru, and finally to Marni.

"Ye arrived, fin'ly and not a moment too soon,"

Oonagh said, pulling her shawl closer. There was a clanging sound in the distance, sending a shiver down my spine—it was our ship's bell. The sun suddenly slipped behind a cloud and a misty fog drifted in off the water. With it, the smell of woodsmoke filled the air.

"Mam . . . ," Grady exclaimed, reaching toward her.

"Inside," she said, leading the way past him toward the cottage. The mist swirled between us in chilling furls. Was it always this chilly here in July?

"Mam . . . ," Grady began again.

Oonagh stopped short, turned, and pointed a long, gnarly finger at me. Her eyes seemed almost the same color as the fog. "Just the lass," she hissed. "I've been waitin' a long time fer the lass."

3

It took a few moments for my eyes to adjust to the darkness inside the cottage. Embers glowed in a large stone fireplace, providing the only light besides what little came in through the small windows.

"Sit, girl," the old woman directed, gesturing toward one of two rocking chairs positioned near the fire. "Sit!" I backed into one of the chairs and Miss Oonagh dropped into the other. She rocked forward and from a brass receptacle drew a long matchstick that she swiped briskly along the stone floor. The tip of the match burst into flame, lighting Miss Oonagh's face from below, giving it the withered look of a month-old jack-o'-lantern. She produced a small white clay pipe and a leather bag from her pocket, pinched a clump of tobacco, and in one practiced move stuffed the pipe, lit it, and puffed, her cheeks hollowing in and out like a pair of worn leather bellows. Once satisfied with her smoke, she settled back and stared at me—or, rather, through me.

"Oh yes, it's her all right, the one we've awaited."

I turned and glanced over my shoulder. It was as though she was addressing someone behind me. But no. The room was empty. "Who?" I asked. "I don't understand." The old woman continued to stare, trancelike, ignoring my words.

"Yep, felt it in the land itself, we did, in all the thin spaces . . ."

"Thin spaces? What?"

"Finally it all comes around, it does. And the one of the sea . . . sure, sure . . . waitin' for her even longer . . ."

"Who? Marni?" As if in response the flute in my pocket began to buzz, and something inside the ditty bag slung in my lap started to move. Miss Oonagh didn't miss this phenomenon—her eagle eyes riveted toward the bag as I pulled open the drawstring. Inside, my case of playing cards wiggled and twitched—the ones my great-grandmother had made, the illustrations on their backs providing the clues that had led us to Clare Island in the first place.

Miss Oonagh rose from her chair in a cloud of tobacco smoke and seemed to float toward me, eyes never leaving the scrimshaw box of cards I held in my hands. "Yes! Yes, I see ye now, I do, the whole bunch of ye's, inhabitin' them cards! Long time since ye's been here. Homecomin' now, 'tis, all comin' full circle."

As she spoke, the lid flipped off the box, and three of the face cards levitated before me. The queen of spades leaned forward and laughed, a wicked cackle. In response, the queen of diamonds, her bulldog jowls jiggling, retorted, "Back here at last!" The king of diamonds snapped up and hovered in the air between the queens. A sly smile spread across his lips.

With surprising agility Miss Oonagh slapped him down with one swipe of her hand. "Yer the cause of this tribulation! But it'll be over soon enough!" At her touch the cards dropped into my lap. I gathered them up and stuffed them back in my ditty bag. The energy had drained out of the old woman as well. She hobbled back to her chair and collapsed into it, blinking into the dim light. The brightness in her eyes was replaced by confusion.

"Grady!" she yelled. "Ye have some nerve keepin' yer old mam waitin'. Get yer arse in here!" She looked at me suddenly, as if just noticing my presence. "Who are ye, lass, and what're ye doin' sittin' by me fire?"

I opened my mouth to answer, but as Grady and Seamus made their way inside, her attention shifted to them. So I got up and tiptoed toward the door. As I passed Seamus he whispered, "Ye see what I mean?" He tapped his temple and rolled his eyes. Grady cuffed him off the side of his cheek and Seamus shrugged. I burst past them into the yard, where Pru, Walter, and Marni were waiting.

"What was that all about?" Pru asked.

Walter chuckled. "You one-upped Grady, that's for sure."

I groaned, suspecting I would pay a price for that. I was about to explain the old woman's strange ramblings when Marni spoke. "Miss Oonagh," she began, a faraway look in her eye. "She had the look of a cailleach."

"A c . . . c . . . cail . . ." I stumbled over the word. It sounded like "ka-lex."

Pru's eyes opened wide. "Oh, I've read of them," she exclaimed. "A kind of an oracle—a divine hag. These women have the gift of second sight—they see things the rest of us can't."

Marni nodded. "Her eyes . . . it was as though

she only saw you—not Seamus, not her own son—just you."

I thought of Oonagh's words—*And the old one, the one of the sea. . . .* "Oh no," I replied. "She saw you too, Marni. She called you 'the one of the sea.'"

Marni paled at the words and suddenly seemed even older than her years. Pru laid her hand on Marni's arm. "There's plenty of time for talk. Right now, why don't we try to get settled?"

"We're to take that cottage over there," Walter said, nodding in the direction of a ramshackle structure set on a grassy knoll behind the main house. "Said the door's open."

"Come on," Pru said. "We've had an incredibly long day. I'm sure we'll want to retire early this evening. Best to get the place ready." We exchanged a look, both of our minds on the same thought—something that happened with remarkable frequency. Clearly, there was some connection between Marni and Oonagh, and it was unsettling.

With an arm around Marni's shoulder, Pru led the way, Walter and I behind. "What happened back there?" Walter asked. I lowered my voice, so as not to upset Marni any further.

"Oonagh spoke, and my flute began to hum. Then the cards . . . I had them in my ditty bag . . . just like before. . . ."

Walter took my arm. "The cards haven't spoken since we were in Australia! What did they say?"

"Nothing much before Miss Oonagh silenced them. She said the king of diamonds—Edward the First—was the cause of all this tribulation."

"Well, it means something. Proof we're on the right track!"

I nodded.

"Here we are," Pru announced.

We pushed open the old wooden door to the place. Moss grew between its cracked and warped timbers. It creaked on its hinges, and as it swung open we were met with a musty smell.

"It'll be fine once we air it out," Pru said, with more confidence than I'm sure she felt. We squinted into the dark interior.

"I'll get a fire going," Walter volunteered. He moved toward the stone hearth, picked up a brush, and began sweeping a pile of ash to the side. Pru adjusted the dank window curtains to let in as much light as possible. I led Marni to a rocker, not unlike the ones in Oonagh's cottage. She sat back heavily and sighed, and I began to wonder if all the traveling had finally caught up to her. In a moment she was snoring softly.

The door suddenly squeaked open again. "I see ye found it okay," Seamus said. "There's a bedroom in the back fer the ladies to share. Ye might want to set yer cot in the main room, fella, so's ye can tend the fire."

"It's Walter." My friend scowled, turning his handsome face sour. "You want to tell me where we can find some firewood?"

"Firewood? Oh no—here we burn peat." The curve of Seamus's mouth told me that he enjoyed correcting Walter, and I felt a wave of irritation. "Firewood's scarce, so we dig up the peat—turf—from the ground. Can keep a fire burnin' day and night, it can." He reached into a box beside the hearth and pulled out a brick made of an earthy mix of soil and some kind of decaying plants. He arranged five or six of these on the stone and knelt to light them afire. In no time a swirl of smoke wafted from the peat. Seamus fanned it and coaxed a flame that flickered and stretched. Walter watched Seamus's every move, determined, I could see, not to ask for his help again. The unmistakable scent that Grady had associated with the "Grey Man" filled the room. "There," Seamus said. "It'll take the dampness out and cozy up the place, it will." He winked at me and Walter glared. I didn't know which of them to be more annoyed with. The edges of my aunt Pru's lips fought a smile—she was clearly finding the carryings on between them amusing.

"Thank you, Seamus," Pru said. "That'll do for now."

"Yes, ma'am," he said, bowing slightly. He pulled a tweed cap from his back pocket, put it on, and, with one last glance my way, ducked out the door.

"This will do nicely," Pru said, looking around, assessing the interior. "Amazing how a place can come to life once people inhabit it. And lovely country. Lovely."

"Why don't you ladies get yourselves set up in the back bedroom, while I have a look around the island?" Walter said. "Only six square miles. I can start to get the lay of the land."

"See if you can find Pugsley," I suggested. "He was off running around with that little collie."

He was out the door before I heard his response.

Pru was already rummaging through a cupboard, her wristful of bracelets jingling in a way I found reassuring. I'd come to associate the sound with her competence and determination. There was a confidence about her that never failed to elicit in me a sense of gratitude and excitement. After Mother and Father were lost at sea, I thought I might never find her, but here she was, bustling about our little cottage, preparing for the next stage of our quest together. I watched her with great admiration. There wasn't another woman I knew who self-assuredly wore khaki jodhpurs or trousers, tall leather boots, paired with tailored men's-style shirts one day, an Indian batik print blouse the next, a thick leather belt at her waist. She turned heads as she passed, her mane of long red curls as determined as she not to be tamed.

"Tea? How about it?" she asked. "Irish brew is as good as the English, maybe better!" She already had the kettle in one hand, a tin of tea in the other. We both looked around, and that was when I realized there was no sink—just a large basin with a bucket beside it. Pru grinned. "How about you grab that bucket and go outside and find the pump?"

I smiled. It wasn't what I was used to back in Maine, but the water would surely be fresher than what we'd endured all those months aboard ship. I took the pail and headed outside. What a magnificent view—for a moment it took my breath away. Completely opposite of the stark beauty of the red, gold, and brown landscape of the Australian outback, all the colors—lush green, brilliant blue, peaceful gray—were soft and cool. I thought again about Grady's words—there *was* something inherently magical about the place, as though the ancient rocks and fields themselves held secrets. A ways off, down a rolling hillside, I caught sight of Walter. I recognized the rhythm of his gait, the way he walked, head forward, full of resolve, hands tucked in his pockets. A flood of affection rushed over me—how fate, with Marni's help, had brought us together back in Maine, the unlikely paths of our lives coming together. Another thought crossed my mind—how back on the island of St. Helena . . . I blushed and covered my mouth with my hand. How close we'd come to a kiss . . . and how during all the following months at sea it was as if it had never even happened. I looked away, foolishly thinking that if he glanced back and noticed me watching, he might read my mind. I was grateful for the sight of the old metal pump, its red paint peeling. I strode over, plopped the bucket, and vigorously cranked the handle until the cold water sloshed.

In no time Pru and I were sitting at the rustic table, warming our hands around steaming cups of tea, the turf fire dancing merrily. Marni still sat beside the fire, her face strong and dignified even in sleep.

"Let's look at the cards," Pru suggested. I removed the box from my ditty bag and placed it on the table between us. With its rectangular, scrimshaw carvings on ivory, it had the look of a miniature coffin. The energy about it sucked some of the warmth and coziness from the room.

"Back at Miss Oonagh's—" I began. Before I could finish the sentence the lid of the box began to tremble. Pru raised an eyebrow. "Yes," I whispered. "The cards started acting up again." When I reached for the box, the lid shot off and clanked onto the table. As though shuffled by invisible hands the entire deck rose, then fanned out, facedown, before us. The cards slid this way and that, switching places with one another, until they finally came to rest in three neat rows.

"They've arranged themselves in order," Pru whispered. "Look!"

We took our time, studying the sequence of illustrations my great-grandmother had carefully drawn on the backs of the cards—two ships, tiny characters having a duel, a man making off with a chest. A woman waving a cutlass as the ship sails away. Men digging a hole on a hill beside a church—a grave? In it they place one of the large chests—or perhaps a coffin? The word CLARE is written in the clouds. And there were other depictions as well—the squarish fortress of Gracie O'Malley beside the shore.

My heart thrilled. Of course, I thought, we were exactly where we were supposed to be—it was all spelled out on the cards. My aunt and I exchanged a glance. "Right where we're supposed to be," she said uncannily, reaching across the table and patting my hand.

Suddenly the door flew open and a swirl of gray vapor wafted inside. Walter appeared in the midst of the fog. A wisp of smoke continued to drift about him.

"I discovered something," he said. His face was alight with excitement. "Grab your sweaters—come on!"

Marni opened her eyes and stood. "I'm going too," she announced. She appeared fully restored, her green eyes piercing, her movements decisive.

Without delay Pru and I scooped the cards back into the box, and the three of us set out behind him.

4

"What is it?" I asked. "What did you find?"
As fast as I walked it was hard to keep
up with Walter. Pru and Marni followed. We took
a dirt road that climbed uphill hugging the edge
of the sea. The countryside that had been green
and blue from my cottage vista was now veiled in
a clammy mist, turning everything a dull shade
of gray. It was as though a ghostly pall had been
cast over the entire land. And with it, the scent of
earthy smoke. I thought of Grady and his warnings about the "Grey Man." Shivering in the chill,
I tried to dismiss the notion. The smell of burning

turf was surely nothing more than the smoke from the hearth of some neighboring cottage. Still, I ran a pace or two ahead until I was at Walter's side.

"There's an old crumbling church set at the top of a hill. A graveyard beside it. You'll recognize it."

"From the cards . . ."

"Yes."

We continued to walk the dirt road along the rocky incline. To the left the land dropped steeply to the sea. From time to time I glanced back to ensure Marni and Pru were still behind us. I remembered that it was along a coast much like this, at home in Maine, where I'd met Marni in the first place—and how she'd been such a part of the sea, as she was even now. She must have felt my gaze, or perhaps she was recalling the same memory. Even from a distance I saw her sea-green eyes, the strong, chiseled face framed in straight silver hair. She nodded, fingering the pendant at her neck, as she did whenever she was pensive. What a sight we must have been—my beautiful, eccentric aunt, one-of-a-kind Marni, Walter, and me, still in our sailing clothes and smelling of ten months at sea.

We trudged on. How much wiser it would have been to draw a bath, wash our rank clothing, set up our beds, and rest.

"It's not far now," Walter said. "Just beyond the

next ridge and to the right."

The top of a rough, stone building became visible, its peaked roof stark against the white sky.

"Up here," I shouted, waving wildly to Pru and Marni. Walter and I ran ahead toward the ancient church. Sections of it had crumbled into piles of rubble. The homely structure had a number of small windows placed here or there with little regard for beauty or symmetry. A long, narrow pair of pencil-shaped windows along the back wall was its only decorative element. It was surrounded by a small cemetery, and a variety of headstones jutted crookedly out of the earth, as though the ground around them had quaked and shrugged, casting them this way and that.

A stone wall enclosed the whole of it, with an occasional opening through which visitors could pass. Walter went ahead and I leaned against the wall, waiting for Pru and Marni.

"Look," Walter called, pointing at the gravestones. "There's no doubt the famous Gracie O'Malley lived on this island. Look at all of them!"

Sure enough, this was the place where generations of O'Malleys were laid to rest, the O'Malley name carved into many a slab—likely all descendants of Granuaile, the pirate queen.

"There're other names here too," Walter said as

Marni and Pru caught up. "O'Gradys and Morans." He paused. "And then there's this. . . ."

We crowded around him to get a look at one small, nondescript headstone at the back corner of the graveyard. Just two letters in an old-fashioned script: E.S.

I recognized them—the same inscription as on the king of diamonds stacked in my deck of cards back at the cottage. My great-grandfather's initials.

Pru traced the letters with her finger. "Edward Simmons. It has to be. No small wonder he chose this place—he'd probably viewed it as a shrine to the pirate life and the values—or lack of them—that he lived and died by."

Suddenly I caught sight of a glass-enclosed placard affixed to the outer wall of the church. As I inched closer I saw a plot map of the graveyard. Something about it seemed familiar. I squinted at the grid, grasping at the slim straws of recognition teasing my memory. "Look at this!" I exclaimed.

Pru leaned closer. "Oh my goodness!" she exclaimed, turning toward me. "This matches the grid I discovered at Grandfather's homestead in Australia! There!" She jabbed her finger at the quadrant labeled J-3. "The spot he'd X'ed. It's all the proof we need."

Walter grinned. "Now all we have to do is . . ."

Marni interrupted him. "It does appear we've located the grave. And it will involve a bit of cleverness in order to unearth what we're looking for. But still . . ."

"Still what?" I asked.

"It feels too easy."

Pru and I exchanged a glance. Every other step in this quest had been riddled with complications. Was it possible our luck was changing?

No sooner did the thought occur to me than a wall of thicker fog pressed in, carrying with it a cold chill.

"There'll be a lot to plan," Marni said. "We can't very well just march over here with a shovel."

"No," Pru said. "We'll need to come at night. Wait until the moon has waned. A starless night. One of us as a lookout."

"There're supplies we'll need," Walter added. "Shovels. A cart. Rope for hoisting."

Despite our good fortune I suddenly felt weary. Anxious. The fog pressed in.

"Let's go back," I said, and to cover my anxiety, I added, "and make a plan."

"Good idea," Pru said. "This fog gets much thicker and it'll be hard to find our way."

I glanced out to sea and pushed back a wave of panic. Nothing at all was visible. It was like peering into a cloud. Again I was reminded of the day Mother and Father had been lost at sea—to me, the fog was a dire enemy.

We managed to find the dirt road, and painstakingly began to retrace our steps. It took all my concentration, eyes glued to my feet, to make certain I wouldn't trip and fall.

Suddenly I felt utterly alone—I had no sense of Walter beside me, or of Marni and Pru behind. "Marni? Aunt Pru? Where are you? Walter?" My voice bounced back and dissipated in the fog. An eerie silence enveloped us. My hands groped before me. Walter, I silently cried. Aunt Pru? Marni? A distant voice answered, pleading from some unreachable place. *Plant your feet firmly, darling. Don't move a muscle! Resist! You must!*

I knew that voice. Mother? My knees felt suddenly weak. Then, a sudden pressure on my arm.

There now, that's my girl. Steady! Steady! Inch your way back.

Father . . . Somehow, their voices empowered me to reinhabit myself, or at least regain some level of control.

Clang! Clang! Clang! Clang! As always, the warning bell of the *Lucy P. Simmons* roused me, and, with great difficulty, I riveted myself to the spot on which I stood. Slowly, slowly I edged my feet back.

As I did, a warm breeze curlicued through the fog, and floating on the welcome stream of air was the faintest hint of colorful glittering mist—the same that had transformed my home back in Maine and had swirled about the ship when the situation was most dire. As it wafted about me I felt the life force surge once again inside my veins, and at the same time the oppressive fog and acrid smoky vapor began to lift.

Exhausted, I sat down and closed my eyes. I was roused by a snuffling sound and a tugging at my sleeve.

"Pugsley!"

I gasped. My little dog was desperately trying to pull me back from the edge of a precipice where I was sprawled, just inches from where the cliff dropped into the sea. Not daring to get up, I scooched myself from the rim of the bluff on my backside, until I was far enough away to safely stand.

"Pugsley," I cried, "I don't see Walter, or Pru. Marni." Deeply shaken, my eyes scanned the cresting whitecaps, terrified that I might spy a rag doll of a body being cast about. Pugsley tipped his head, sniffed into the wind, and took off. Squinting, I followed him with my eyes and spied three rumpled forms farther up along the headland. I ran until they came clearly into view—Marni, Pru, and Walter, taken aback, but seemingly unharmed. The waves crashed below in a steady rhythm, and visions of our bodies being tossed against the rocky crag stole my breath away—the Simmons family curse, of course, once again nearly claiming me for the sea. I felt the familiar steely resolve rise in me. I wouldn't let Mother and Father down. No. I'd figure out how to find the treasure my great-grandfather had stolen, and somehow satisfy the conditions the wicked Mary Maude Lee had set forth. Then I'd make a pilgrimage back to Maine, to the place our home had once stood—this in memory of Mother and Father.

"Thank God, you're safe!" Pru threw her arms about me, and in a moment we four were locked in a single embrace, Pugsley yapping in circles around us.

"Do you realize how close . . . ?" Walter began.

Marni silenced him with a slight wave of her hand. "Close, perhaps, but safe nevertheless. This Irish fog is unpredictably dangerous."

"I told ye, didn't I, but not a one of ye's took me serious!" We turned to find Grady on the path, Rosie wagging her tail beside him. "I heard the Grey Man's steps, felt him suckin' the air outta the fog like he does. And I seen the bunch of ye fools settin' out, payin' no heed whatever. And now that ye seen 'is devilish handiwork firsthand ye won't be so quick to discredit me!" As if in response, the sound of the surf pounded against the rocks below. Grady jutted out his whiskery chin. "Could've taken ye's fer a swim, he coulda—last swim ye'd ever take, I daresay."

"I'd assert," Marni said, "after all the time you've spent aboard ship as our first mate, braving raging seas and roiling oceans—all of that has earned our respect. You do yourself credit, and we're grateful. Whether fog or the Grey Man, next time we'll pay you more heed."

"Hmph," he grunted. "Then ye's won't give me no lip about followin' me back to the cottage."

"We were just . . . ," Walter began. Grady silenced him with a sharp look.

"Plenty a time fer whatever yer schemin'. Been here but an afternoon 'n' already ye git yerselves in trouble. Fact is, it's me mam's summoned ye's back."

"What for?" Pru asked.

Grady had already turned on his heel. A brisk wind snatched his words and tossed them back at us. "A message. Says she has a message from the beyond."

5

A deep fatigue grabbed hold of me as we walked back toward the cottage. The day had felt never ending. Finally, the sun was dropping, the sky hanging over the sea striped in brilliant shades of blue, orange, and lavender, turning the distant hills to gold. Grady saw me stifle a yawn. "Dang fools fer settin' out at this hour. Almost nine o'clock now. I'm ready t' turn in meself."

Seamus sat outside Miss Oonagh's cottage whittling a chunk of wood in the dusky light. He handled the knife nimbly, a whorl of shavings curling from the blade. He looked up. "'Fraid the moment's passed. Hope ye didn't rush much."

Grady glared at him. "What're ye sayin'?"

"Miss Oonagh. She's . . . well . . . she's gone off again, she has. Sorry to say."

"We'll see fer ourselves, thank ye," Grady growled. "Be off with ye now." Grumbling, he pushed the cottage door open. "Thinks he knows everythin' . . ." Seamus stood to leave. "T'morrow's another day, it 'tis!" He caught my eye and winked. Walter put his hand on the small of my back and shepherded me inside.

It was hard to make out the huddled form of Miss Oonagh slumped in the chair beside what was left of the fire sputtering in the hearth, casting strange dancing shadows against the walls.

"Mam," Grady said, "I'm back with 'em, I am." He gently shook her arm. "Mam . . ."

With a loud snuffling sound the old woman lifted her head. Her mouth was slack, and she blinked slowly several times, giving her the look of an ancient lizard. Her eyes lacked the spark they'd held earlier, the strange, sharp intelligence replaced by a dull stare.

Grady knelt before her. "What was it ye had to tell 'em? They're here now. I brought 'em, jest like I promised." This was a tender tone I'd never heard coming from Grady before.

Oonagh licked her lips and swiped her mouth with the back of her forearm. She sat up a little straighter, and her hand went to her hair, patting and smoothing some imagined fancy coif. "Daniel," she said, a playful smile curling her lips. "You've come a-courtin'. Me father wouldn't approve."

The color drained from Grady's face. "It's me, Mam—Grady. Yer son."

Oonagh tipped her head, one hand cupping her cheek. "Don't be such a tease," she cooed. In her other hand she held a charred piece of tinder that slipped from her fingers to the floor. Her eyes closed and in an instant she was snoring quietly.

Grady gaped at her, and with his mouth hanging open the resemblance between them was arresting. Marni stepped forward and placed a hand on his shoulder. "It happens to the old ones," she said consolingly. "Daniel must have been someone she loved, for she saw him in your eyes."

Grady bit his lower lip, a frown screwing up his face. "Daniel was me da. Me father. Never forgave me fer makin' a life at sea."

"Oh no," Marni whispered. "Miss Oonagh saw a kindred spirit in you—you and your da as one and the same. That's because when we cross to the other side all the things of life are forgiven."

If it was true, I wondered, how could there

be such a thing as a family curse? The room suddenly grew darker, the sky through the windows now a deep navy blue. Grady knelt beside the fire, grabbed the poker, and jabbed at the smoldering turf, sending up a spray of angry sparks.

"Well," Walter said, "we should go. . . ."

Suddenly Grady sat back on his heels. "Lookie here," he said. He pointed the poker at the floor beside the hearth where the blackened kindling his mother had held had dropped. "Look!" He stood, quickly lit the lantern on the mantel, and bent it so that its light shone a buttery circle on the floor.

We leaned in, peering at the spot. On a smooth piece of stone was a primitive drawing that looked like a sun, with five uneven rays. "What is it?" Walter asked. "What does it mean?"

"A message," Grady said. "She musta written it there while I was gone for ye's." Pru had already pulled a pencil and small journal from her pocket and, peering intently, copied the primitive-looking symbol.

Marni squinted, her fingers drawing the pendant along the chain at her throat, a strange faraway look in her eye. "Yes," she whispered. "It means something, I'm sure. Something important."

Pru closed her notebook and slid it and her pencil into her back pocket. "Let's sleep on it. Tomorrow we can consider it, fresh." The gentle snuffling of Miss Oonagh's slumber reminded us all how exhausted we were. We bid our good nights, trudged back to our own cottage, and, with due haste, made up our beds.

I lay in the shadows listening to the sound of Marni's even breathing, a shaft of moonlight cutting through the window. "Aunt Pru?" I whispered.

"Yes . . ." Her voice, blurry and edged with sleep, caressed me in the darkness.

"Do you think it's true? What Marni said to Grady? About all things being forgiven . . ."

She sighed. "Once we cross to the other side?" Then silence. I thought perhaps she'd dropped off to sleep, but then she continued in a whisper. "I'm wondering the same thing myself." We were both quiet, and all we could hear was the sound of the waves in the distance, taunting us. "Maybe," she murmured, "in order to forgive, a wrong has to be acknowledged. Maybe we have to ask to be forgiven. . . ."

"But we didn't do anything. . . . It was Great-grandfather . . ."

"I don't know. . . . Maybe Mary Maude Lee needs someone to be sorry, to understand how she was cheated."

"It's not fair," I whispered.

"Most of life isn't," Pru ventured, her words soft as velvet. "Fair, that is."

Like an undertow, the murkiness of sleep began to pull me down, and amidst thoughts of curses and hurt, vengeance and forgiveness, I sunk into an uneasy but much needed sleep.

6

By the time I awoke I'd slept half the day away, roused finally by the bustling sounds enlivening the cottage. The others had, apparently three times already, heated, filled, and emptied the large metal tub dragged in front of the fire, each having taken their turn luxuriating in the soapy warmth that stripped away the grime accumulated from months at sea.

"You're next, Lucy!" Pru called. "No need to be shy—Walter's gone off exploring, and Marni and I've bolted the door."

I sat up, extended my arms overhead, and

yawned, stretching my back like a satisfied cat. The sun streamed across my bed. Fragrant steam rose from the tub, its lavender scent beckoning.

I gasped as I slipped one foot and then the other into the bath, the shock of the hot water turning my feet and legs lobster red. I dropped my bedclothes and slowly lowered myself. "Ahhhh . . . ," I sighed, sinking in up to my chin. I ran the thick bar of soap along my arms and legs, scrubbing away the layers of salt, sea, and sweat. Oh, how clean and tender my skin felt, the tingling joy of it!

Pru smiled. "Lovely, isn't it?" There was a knock on the door and I drew myself lower into the water.

"It's me," Walter announced, "but I'm not coming in. Just delivering one last bucket of hot water for Lucy."

With that I took a deep breath and submerged myself, running the soap through my tangled locks. When I came up for air, Pru helped me rinse and pull the comb through my hair until it squeaked. She held a thick towel out for me and I wrapped myself in its welcoming warmth. Clean clothes had been laid out on my bed—a long A-line skirt and white tailored shirt, a thick leather belt, and a pair of lace-up boots. I looked at Pru and she smiled. "They were mine—thought you might like them," she said. "Try them on!"

After toweling my hair and pinning it up, I slipped into the outfit. Immediately, the sleek, fitted cut of the clothing made me feel so much more mature and worldly. Womanly, like my aunt. Confident.

Marni looked my way approvingly as she set a tray of tea and scones on the table. "That bath washed away the girlishness to reveal quite a stunning young woman." Even Pugsley wagged his tail and sniffed at my boots, as though greeting a brand-new person.

I blushed with pleasure as I joined them at table. Over breakfast Pru and Marni decided it would do us all well to take a day to relax and adjust before we began our quest in earnest. I, however, had other ideas. I wiped the crumbs from my face, dabbed the jam at the corner of my mouth, and finished the last of my tea. I tucked my flute and spyglass into my leather bag and went to have a look around the island, making certain I paid close attention to the shoreline, should the ominous fog roll in again. Pugsley trotted along behind me, nose to the ground. This time I headed in the opposite direction, back toward the bluffs behind the dock area, where the boxy fortress of Gracie O'Malley stood overlooking the harbor. As Pugsley and I navigated the path, Rosie came bounding across a field to join us, leaving her sheep behind without a backward glance. The two dogs ran circles around one another, tails wagging wildly.

I lifted the edge of my skirt as I traipsed through the tall, wet grass surrounding the castle to a high point just behind it. There I found a spot to sit that would allow me to see our ship anchored offshore. The sight of her familiar silhouette against the brilliant blue sky and water bolstered my confidence. When I brought Father's spyglass to my eye, our ship jumped into view. As though the *Lucy P. Simmons* sensed my mood, her bell began to clang, and in response, the flute in my satchel hummed. I lowered the spyglass and took up the flute. How long had it been since I'd played Mary Maude Lee's song—the one that provided the clues about the curse? And wasn't it appropriate, after all, to play the ballad of one pirate queen at the castle of another?

I brought the flute to my lips and sounded the first phrase. Pugsley and Rosie tipped their heads and joined in with a strident *ah-oooooh.*

As the last strain sounded, a faint puff of colorful glitter rose from the flute and followed the melody out to sea. I lowered the instrument and watched the magical mist—it was just as enthralling as it had been before, back in Maine, and throughout our voyage to Australia. Enthralling, but concerning, as it had always signaled trouble of some kind. The beguiling cloud drew my eye across the harbor toward the *Lucy P. Simmons*. I stood, hand above my brow, and peered at the glimmering swirl of energy now encircling our ship. Pugsley growled, a low rumbling in his throat, the hair along his back bristling. Rosie pawed my leg and whined.

I returned the flute to my bag and gazed again into Father's spyglass. It brought the *Lucy P. Simmons* into clear view, the ship now fully encased in a sheath of colorful vapor. Two other ships appeared along the horizon, both familiar. One nearly transparent, more like a mirage with a shimmering aura around it—the specter ship that had shadowed us throughout our first voyage. And then, just to the right, the unmistakable silhouette of the black ship— the one I'd first seen in Boston that had pursued us nearly all the way to Australia. The ship on which the scrappy pirate and our former mate Quaide had sailed. I'd thought, or rather hoped, we were done with the black ship and its evil mariners—after the storm that had nearly destroyed the *Lucy P.* My prayer had been that the black ship had really sunk, once and for all. It had been blessedly absent throughout our sail from Australia to Ireland. And now, here it was again. All my senses suddenly piqued—I could swear the energy coursing through me lifted every hair on my head.

I stayed glued to the spot on which I stood, spyglass fixed on the unfolding scene. Both ships approached ours, the specter ship from the left, the black ship from the right. A small crew of ragged men worked the deck of the black ship. Aboard the phantom ship, bow to stern, a ghostly company of characters shone, their movements fluid, and difficult to make out, given the transparent nature of their bodies. Should I run back to the cottage and summon our group? The *Lucy P. Simmons* was unmanned and without protection, except for the colorful charged vapor. Would she be boarded? Pirated away? I nibbled the inside of my cheek. Once again the flute vibrated and hummed in my rucksack, initiating another rush of glittering mist that cascaded across the shore and billowed above the water until it, too, wafted around the *Lucy P.*

A movement in the water caught my eye. At first I thought it was a nimble seal, drawn by the spectacle of the dazzling force traveling across the sea. I turned the spyglass in the direction of the far-off swimmer, magnifying the image.

It was Marni, moving swiftly through the harbor with long, sure strokes. She paused finally, head and shoulders bobbing as she tread water, her face turned toward our ship, hair flowing out behind her in a silky stream of liquid silver. What in the world was she doing out there? It was as though she belonged to the sea, or the sea to her. I followed her gaze, and gasped.

The black ship had pulled alongside the *Lucy P.* A number of ropes were being tossed from their vessel to ours. One scruffy man swung across like a monkey, grasping our anchor line and shimmying upward until he could throw a leg over the side. He seemed oblivious to both the shimmering aura surrounding the *Lucy P.* and the nearby specter ship, or perhaps he was undaunted by them both. Once aboard, he secured the lines, and perhaps a dozen of his mates streamed across like water rats.

Marni continued to swim closer to the black ship, disappearing underwater from time to time, remaining submerged for longer than seemed humanly possible. I held my breath each time she dived under, waiting for her to resurface, gasping for air before I spotted her again even farther out.

There was a sound behind me on the path and I spun around. Grady with Miss Oonagh, his arm linked through hers. The old woman moved in an agitated, jerky gait, her strange gray eyes darting frantically.

"Spirits all about, I tell ye! It's in the air, it 'tis! Trouble brewin'!" She stopped suddenly and lifted her face as though sniffing the air to pick up a scent. Her eyes closed, the line between her brows deepening.

Grady peered out to sea, his face ashen. "Almost cain't believe me own eyes," he muttered through clenched teeth. "More devilishness. That ship and its mates shoulda been fish food by now. Fodder at the bottom o' the sea. And here they be again. Those cusses are boardin' our ship, though there ain't much left to steal. Perhaps the specter ship'll pertect her."

Oonagh silenced him with a raised hand. "Is there a merrow about?" she rasped.

"Merrow?" I whispered. Miss Oonagh opened her eyes and squinted out over the waves.

"A siren," Grady said. "A mermaid." His eyes scanned the ocean. There was no sign of Marni.

"Lookie there," Grady said. "They're leavin' the *Lucy P.*!"

It was true. Apparently not finding what they were looking for, the men retreated back across to their own ship. Hands empty, they shook their heads, pointed toward land.

I focused the spyglass more carefully, watched the specter ship hover protectively behind the *Lucy P. Simmons*, while the black ship collected her crew of marauders. The colorful mist began to dissipate, and for a brief moment the water around the ship glowed, until the effervescence slowly sunk to the depths of the sea. But where was Marni? The water where she had been was still, no sign of her at all.

A firm grip on my arm drew me from my musings. Miss Oonagh bent so that her face was directly in front of mine. Her hawkish eyes were open so wide I could see the white around her irises. "There's no time to waste," she hissed. "Do what ye must, the sooner the better!"

Grady stepped between us. "Ye never told me what exactly it is ye're seekin'." He paused. "But whatever it is, if ye need my help, ye know ye got it."

I nodded. It had taken almost two years to gain his respect. "Thank you, Grady." And we surely would need all the help we could get. "Perhaps after you get your mam home you could keep watch on that ship—let us know if anyone comes ashore."

"Ye got me word," he said, tipping his cap.

I nodded, and ran back toward the cottage. I didn't notice Seamus until I came right up upon him. He stepped off the path, bowed, and waved me along. "Lookin' lovely, miss," he called after me, "even better than yesterday, if that's possible! In quite the hurry then, are ye?"

"Yes," I called over my shoulder, "in a great rush."

"Yer friend came along ahead of ye, drippin' wet she was, and all wrapped in a blanket. Curious friends ye got, if I must say."

I stopped for a moment. "You saw Marni heading back to the cottage?" A wave of relief swept over me. It *was* curious. But it was something I couldn't bring myself to ask about—I knew she wouldn't welcome the question.

"Indeed. Water's awfully cold fer most. She's an odd one, she is."

"Thank you, Seamus. I must hurry!" I turned on my heel and dashed up the hill, feeling his gaze follow me. I needed to tell the others what I'd seen. What Miss Oonagh had said. Without delay we'd have to gather what we needed. Tonight was the night to unearth the grave and find out, finally, what secrets it held.

7

It seemed the sun would never set. We counted the hours, our collection of shovels, crowbar, buckets, rope, and a tarp stowed in the back of the cart, a pair of mules standing in wait. Eight o'clock, nine o'clock, nine thirty. Finally the sky along the horizon became awash with a lavender band that spread, tinting the sky first cobalt, then navy, and finally to the deepest purplish black. The moon shone, but a front of smoke-gray clouds inched across the heavens—with any luck they would float before the moon, providing us the cover of darkness we sorely needed. Grady and Seamus stood at the ready beside the O'Malley castle, prepared to warn us with three blasts of a whistle if there was any more activity around the black ship.

"Are you all dressed warmly enough?" Pru asked. "Summer evenings here are cooler than you'd expect." Clustered before the window, clad in our darkest denim, we nodded. Marni was particularly quiet, fingering the locket at her throat. I thought about the time aboard ship when that locket had broken free from its chain—how she'd come undone over it, frantic, until I recovered it. Its hinges open, revealing an intricate weave of blond hair—her son's hair, the boy who was lost to her all those years ago.

"It's time," Marni said. "We can't wait any longer. As Miss Oonagh told you, there's not a minute to waste. They'll likely come ashore tonight." As if in response the formation of clouds churned and stretched, one finger of dark vapor tickling the golden sphere of the moon.

"Let's go!" Walter said. We eyed one another, reasserting our resolve.

"Yes," Pru and I said together.

We silently slipped outside and made our way around the back, Pugsley at our heels. He would serve as a most effective lookout. The mules snorted and stamped their feet, impatient from their lengthy vigil. Walter took the reins and led the beasts along the path, the rest of us following behind the cart like mourners in a funeral procession. How apt a comparison—after all, if we were successful we might be returning with a coffin full of treasure. We'd already prepared a secret place in the cottage to camouflage the evidence until we could figure out a way to transport the booty back to the *Lucy P. Simmons*.

We moved quietly, the only sounds being the creak of the wheels of the cart and the gentle thump of hooves along the dirt road. Here and there we passed a cottage, lamps snuffed, windows darkened, the inhabitants tucked in for the night. As we walked our eyes darted skyward—the clouds had spread like spilled milk, puddling here and there across the surface of the moon. Pru and I exchanged a glance. We would need to make haste.

Up the hill, around the bend, along the shore we went, until finally the roofline of the church appeared. My heart quickened as the ancient abbey and the walls surrounding the adjacent graveyard came into view. The clouds filtered the moonlight, and the shadows of the tombstones stretched and retreated in a haunting game of hide-and-seek. Pugsley ran ahead, nose to the ground. Together, Marni, Pru, and I walked ahead to join Walter. "Take the cart around to the right," Marni whispered, "just beyond the break in the wall." We immediately saw the wisdom of that—the cart would be hidden from view in the unlikely case of anyone walking up the road, but close enough to Great-grandfather's grave to make the transfer of whatever we found swift and easy.

"Whoa," Walter cooed, patting our mules on the muzzle and handing them each a carrot. We unloaded our gear from the cart and, shovels in hand, tiptoed toward the grave.

"Wait!" Pru whispered. She stopped short, holding us back with splayed arms. "What's that?"

There was something on the ground at the foot of the grave. A crouched, hunkered-down, indiscriminate shape. Whatever it was, it was alive; there was no doubt about it. I could sense it turn our way, could see the glint of a pair of eyes in the dark. Before I could stop him, Pugsley darted forward.

"Pugsley, no!" I shouted, and immediately clamped my hand over my mouth, as though doing so could take back the sound. The beastly thing guarding the grave rose. Walter grabbed my arm, preventing me from bolting after Pugsley. Suddenly there was a chorus of barking, enough to wake the dead. For a fleeting moment a moonbeam broke through the clouds, illuminating the scene.

"It's Rosie," Walter said, releasing his stranglehold on my arm. We ran forward and the little collie met us halfway, tongue lolling, turning from us to the grave, and back. It was as though she'd been waiting for us.

"Hurry," Pru said. "We've probably already awakened half the farmers along the hillside!" Within seconds we flanked the gravesite, Pru at Great-grandfather's head, me at his feet, and Walter and Marni on each side. Rosie pushed her way between us and dug furiously with her front paws, throwing a shower of dirt into the air. Pugsley began to whine and pant, circling around and around, pawing the ground.

"Get back, Rosie!" Pru commanded. "Down! Pugsley, you too!" Rosie whined and began digging again, until Walter took her by the collar and pulled her out of the way. Reluctantly she lay down but continued to inch forward. Pugsley harrumphed and flopped down beside her.

Finally, the dogs under control, we prepared to dig, placing the pointed edge of our shovels into the earth, our feet along the blades, giving them a good push to get started. Strange how easily the ground gave way.

"This isn't right," Walter whispered. He dropped to his knees and I did the same, both of us patting the ground with open palms. Where yesterday there had been sod, there now was only soil. I leaned forward in the darkness and my hand plunged at least six inches through the loosely packed earth. Rosie whined pitifully.

"It's already been disturbed," Walter said. Pru gasped and a sound something like "no" escaped her lips.

"Keep going," Marni urged. "I feel we should keep at it." Rosie barked, as though approving the idea. We began to dig, furiously. We dived onto our bellies, scooping up huge armfuls of earth, then Walter and I lowered ourselves into the hole. We began again in earnest, Marni and Pru keeping watch above us, Rosie and Pugsley whimpering at the edge of the pit. I felt the tip of my shovel hit something solid, confirmed by the sound of Walter's spade connecting with wood.

"Dig along the side of it," Walter whispered. "We'll need a place to stand for leverage." Walter and I knelt on top of the coffin and hollowed out a space beside it, just wide enough to plant our feet in. Once we were positioned, Pru lowered the crowbar and helped us angle it into the crevice between the lid and the top of the casket then paused. "Are you sure you don't want me to do this?" she asked. "What we find inside might not be pretty."

"It's been three generations," Walter replied. "Worst we could find would be an old bag of bones."

It was true. I felt no emotional attachment whatsoever. Pru nodded. I'm sure she felt the same way.

As we prepared to leverage the bar and push, the clouds drifted from the moon, and the hole was flooded with light. Rosie lifted her snout and howled, and for a moment I thought she might jump right into the hole. "Now!" Walter cried. Together, we thrust our weight onto the iron bar.

The lid flew back and a ravaged figure sprang up, like a deadly jack-in-the-box, wild sunken eyes flashing, its skeletal head shining in the moonlight. The ghoul's mouth was tied with a gag, its gangly arms bound at the wrists. There was screaming, besides my own, and the zombie joined in with a strangled "AAARRRRGH . . ." Walter and I frantically tried to climb out, sending torrents of soil over the three of us. The dogs ran around the edge, barking and panting, tongues lolling.

Pru grabbed my hands and yanked, but the weakened walls of the grave continued to collapse. The ghoul moaned and writhed. Walter and I fought for a foot- or handhold. But the earth crumbled, and with it our hope of escape. Walter grabbed me around the waist and shoved me toward the surface. A vice grip on my wrists. Up, up, until I felt the ground beneath my belly. Somehow Walter shimmied up beside me. Marni and Pru dragged us back from the rim. In an instant Walter was on his feet, wielding a shovel over his head, eyes blazing, nostrils flared. He inched toward the gaping grave, in which the phantom man twitched about. Rosie sprang toward Walter, teeth bared, hair bristling along her back. Walter took aim, adjusted his swing . . .

"Wait!" Marni yelled.

"AAAARGH!" The half-dead remains of my great-grandfather convulsed, eyes popping, straining against his bonds, chest heaving. His nearly transparent deadly white skin glowed in the moonlight. Marni and he locked eyes. The moment stretched on and on.

Finally Marni commanded in a quiet, steely

tone, "Take hold of him, Prudence. Lucy, Walter—we have to get him out of there."

The goblin nodded furiously and made another garbled sound. "ERRRRRGH!"

"What?!" Aunt Pru exclaimed, her eyes fixed on the ghoul. I knew what she was thinking. What evil powers did he possess, and how would touching his corrupted body endanger us?

"If he was going to harm us," Marni reasoned, "he would have already done so. We can't just let our imaginations run wild. Walter, get in there and help him out. Lucy, hop in and assist Walter."

Pru, Walter, and I stood, dumbfounded.

"We don't have all night," Marni muttered, and before we could stop her she slid into the grave, wove her fingers into a stirrup, and nodded to the ghoul. He wobbled over and attempted, unsuccessfully, to raise a foot.

"All right," Walter said, dropping the shovel, and lowered himself back into the grave. "I can handle this," he said, as if to convince himself, taking his place beside Marni.

"Wait," Pru said. "I'll get the rope. Wrap it beneath his arms and we can pull." She disappeared, and in a moment a length of rope dangled into the hole like a long, black snake. Walter grabbed the end and the ghoul cooperated, raising his bound arms before him. Walter ran the rope around his thin torso.

"Here," Walter called up to me. "Grab the other end."

I gingerly extended thumb and index finger and attempted to pluck the rope from Walter's hand, avoiding all contact with the ghoul.

"Just take it!" Walter commanded. Again the ghoul nodded encouragement. Pru and I grasped the rope.

"Okay, on the count of three," Marni said. "One . . . two . . . three . . ."

We hoisted him into a standing position—a spooky scarecrow figure, so thin his clothing hung as though there might not be any body inside at all. Maybe all that was left of him was a disembodied head and long matchstick arms. The moonbeams highlighted a map of bluish veins just beneath the skin covering his skull. A meager tuft of white hair blew over the dome of his head.

"Heave!" Walter cried. Pru and I threw our whole bodies into the effort. I imagined his mummified body coming apart against the pressure of the rope. Between our nerves and our overexertion the almost weightless body flew up out of the grave with great force, knocking us both to the ground. I recoiled as his stone-cold, skeletal legs flailed against mine. Pru and I scrambled aside while he thrashed about on the ground like a fish on a line. Walter and Marni climbed out of the pit and I was vaguely aware of them hustling our catch to his feet. It was only then that I thought about the treasure.

Breathless, I crawled toward the edge of the grave and slowly lowered myself back in. Was it possible that the half-dead spirit of my great-grandfather had lain in his grave all these years protecting his loot? That he'd managed to scare off whoever had unearthed the grave before? Ignoring the hushed voices overhead, I dropped to my knees. Hands placed firmly on either side of the coffin, I leaned forward. Blinked.

Aside from a sprinkling of dirt the coffin was empty.

The treasure was gone.

For several moments I stared into the empty receptacle, a hollow feeling in my gut. As I took hold of the lid to close the casket, the clouds danced away from the moon, and once again the grave was bathed in light. Otherwise I might not have noticed the words carved into the hinged cover:

*To Edward, Darling Husband, Liar, and
Cheat,*

To death do us part, or so I thought,
Did you really believe you wouldn't be caught?
That I'd give up with a big boo hoo?
Now I'm a rich woman and the joke is on you!

8

Walter held fast to the rope that restrained the ghostly man while Pru scrawled the message from Molly to Edward into her notebook. What did it mean? Perhaps the ghoul could tell us. We quickly refilled the hole and tamped it down as best we could. The end result was a sunken patch of earth without a scrap of grass—an obvious sign that the grave had been unearthed. Marni hastily dug up several rosebushes growing wild along the hillside, planted them on top of the gravesite, and threw a bit of straw beneath them, trying to pass off the desecration as a bit of well-intended planting. It was better than nothing.

With trembling hands we marshaled the half-dead remains of my great-grandfather toward the cart. There was no way he could get away, bound as he was, Rosie jumping up and running circles around him. I cast sidelong glances his way as he traipsed along beside us. Strange—the more I looked at him, the more he resembled something human—old, terrified, and filthy, but human none-theless. "Maybe we should ungag him," I ventured, "so he can explain—"

Walter cut me off. "And take the chance of having him alert half the village?" he whispered. "Get arrested for grave robbing?" I shrugged, avoiding Walter's eyes. We stowed our captive in the back of the cart and arranged the tarp over him. He writhed beneath it, moaning and groaning unintelligible sounds.

All this upset the mules, who began to curl back their mouths, whinny, and neigh. Pugsley whined. Rosie leaped onto the cart, throwing herself on top of our ghoulish cargo. "Good girl, Rosie," Pru said. "Don't you let him out of there."

A loud snapping noise brought us all to attention. We spun around to find Marni holding a large branch from a nearby hedge. "Use it like a broom," she said, "to erase our tracks!" I grabbed it and as we walked, swished and swept it along the road behind us, trying to wipe away the hoof and wheel marks. We retraced our path, every moment feeling like an hour, praying we wouldn't be followed. Each time a strangled utterance emanated from beneath the tarp, Pru gave the rumpled form a good poke, and Rosie nudged him with her pointy snout.

It was a miracle we made it back to the cottage undetected. As quickly as we could we unloaded the tools, unhitched the mules, and led them to the stable. Then we pulled back the tarp, took the ghoul under the arms, and spirited him into the cottage, his bare feet dragging along the ground, head flopping about. His eyes rolled wildly, and garbled sounds came from his gagged mouth. Once we were inside, Marni secured the door, Pru lit the lanterns, and Walter and I arranged him on a chair. For a moment we all collapsed against whatever surface was nearest—a wall, table, piece of furniture—the tension, fear, disappointment draining from us, leaving us weak. Even the ghoul slumped against the back of the chair, the lids of his googly eyes fluttering. Walter muttered what we were all wondering. "Now what?"

Before we could answer, the door began to rattle and shake.

Knock, knock, knock . . .

We exchanged furtive glances. The ghoul tried to struggle to his feet.

Bam! Bam! Bam!

Marni walked slowly to the door, hesitated, then lifted the latch.

It was Grady, peering into the cottage. "What in the devil—"

The ghoul leaped from the chair. "ERRRRRGH . . . ARGHHHHH!" Rosie ran back and forth between the ghoul and Grady, yapping incessantly.

"Good god in heaven, whaddya doin' to Old Peader?" Grady demanded, striding across the room toward the ghost of my great-grandfather. He pulled down the gag, revealing the gaping mouth, his lips sucking air like a fish out of water. Before we could intervene, Grady had pulled out a jackknife and cut the bonds at the spectral creature's wrists. Rosie danced around the two of them, tail wagging.

"Old Peader?" Walter asked.

"Saved me, they did," he wheezed, "but why they kept me bound is beyond me!"

I started to open my mouth, but Marni silenced me with a look. "Tell Grady what happened. . . . Old Peader . . ."

Old Peader . . . I'd heard that name before, but I couldn't quite place it. I stared at him, the gag hanging around his long wattle of neck, the angry red marks from the bonds on his wrists.

Old Peader flopped back in the chair, ran his long knobby fingers through the tuft of feathery white hair atop his head. "Was in me cottage and heard somethin' out by the abbey, me an' Rosie did. Just as the sun was settin', when nobody had any business t' be there." He paused, opened and closed his jaws as though trying to determine if they still worked.

"Go on," Grady said. Pru was already putting on the kettle, setting up the tea, one eye on this Old Peader, the other on Grady.

"I snucked up, thinkin' it was a few lads busted out some whiskey and sneakin' a few smokes. Hid behind the wall, and what do I see but three men diggin' up and desecratin' a grave!"

Pru and I gasped. Somehow, they'd gotten there ahead of us.

Grady tipped his head and narrowed his eyes. "Grave robbin'?" he asked, his face dark with suspicion.

Old Peader went on. "Without thinkin' I called out, 'Hey, you there, whaddya think yer doin'?' Me girl Rosie ran and grabbed the big one by the seat of 'is pants, and the ruckus begun. Drug me over there, they did, cursin' and swearin' some nonsense 'bout the treasure bein' gone." Old Peader shook his head and blinked, as though seeing it all again. "Thought I'd stolen their treasure! Drug me to me cottage and tore it up pretty good, a-searchin'." He laughed, and the chuckle turned into a great rheumy cough. When he recovered he said, "Imagine 'em turnin' over me cupboards lookin' fer a treasure chest? I told 'em they'd do better chasin' leprechauns fer a pot o' gold than findin' treasure in me cottage. They didn't take kindly to that, and two of 'em—the big beefy one and the straggly pirate—bound me up, they did, drug me back to the grave, and threw me in! Nailed shut the lid. All the while the third one protestin'. But they paid 'im no mind."

He stopped, blinked, and wiped his eye. "Have to say I's glad there weren't some old skeleton bones in there with me! 'Twas empty, it was. Gave up me fussin' after they shut the lid and nailed it tight. Heard the dirt pilin' up and their voices fadin'. Figured to close me eyes and go to sleep, and hopefully the good Lord'd take me sooner rather 'n' later. Thought I was dreamin' when I heard the scritch of the shovel, and you folks up above. The lid popped open and I seen the lass. Thought she was an angel, I did. And then me faithful Rosie, there she was a-waitin' fer me."

"We came upon Rosie," Marni explained, "making quite a fuss. I daresay your loyal companion saved you."

Pru picked up the thread of the tale, crafting a story that would render us innocent. "As we got closer we could see that the grave was fresh. Then, a muffled sound. There was nothing else to do...."

"You saw no one out there?" Grady asked. "And dare I ask what ye's were doin' there in the first place?"

"We have reason to believe the grave was Lucy's great-grandfather's, Edward Simmons's."

Old Peader's eyes became two shining orbs. "Edward Simmons was yer great-granddad? Oh, the stories 'bout that one . . ." His eyebrows pushed halfway up his forehead.

"I know the stories," Grady said. "Now I'm puttin' two 'n' two together." He peered at me and Pru. "So these brutes thought they'd discover the supposed lost treasure—ahead of old Edward's kin?"

"These three men," Marni interrupted. "What did they look like?"

Old Peader licked his lips, considering. "One

big thug, thick faced and dull, but meaner than a bagful of snakes, he was. And once he took to lookin' for 'is treasure he was like a one-eyed dog in a meat factory."

Quaide. Of course. Pru and I shared a dark look.

"And a straggly pirate, a crossways scar clear from one side of 'is swarthy face to the other." I shuddered—this was the very same culprit who'd tried to kidnap Georgie and me at the docks back in Boston as we prepared for the first leg of our voyage.

Pru jumped in. "Let me guess . . . and a green-eyed man, more reserved than the other two, a little more genteel—he was the one in charge, but kept his hands clean."

"Indeed, he was there, he was!" Old Peader nodded furiously. "Just as ye say! The one tryin' to dissuade the others from sealin' me fate."

Grady caressed his chin, thoughts flying across his face. "So, let me get this straight . . . the four of ye's head out fer to do what—venerate Ol' Man Simmons's grave—ye happen t' hear some smothered sounds, ye see ol' Rosie carryin' on, and ye's dig up a grave? Is that whatcha expect me t' believe?"

"That's what I'm tellin' ye," Old Peader said, bobbing his wobbly head. "Dug me up, they did!"

"Wait a minute, Grady," Walter said. "You

promised to be on watch. What are you doing here?"

Grady opened his mouth to answer, but was cut short by three shrill blasts of the whistle. We froze, then grabbed the lanterns and ran for the door.

9

Seamus met us beside Gracie O'Malley's castle—the four of us, plus Grady, Old Peader, and the dogs. "Was keepin' watch fer men leavin' the ship," Seamus explained, "and instead I spied three approachin' it. Figured it might be important." He pointed seaward, our eyes following. "Over there, ye see 'em?" The moon illuminated a golden pathway across the water on which a small rowboat traversed, clearly heading toward the black ship. And Father's spyglass confirmed what we already knew—Quaide and the pirate were at the oars, the green-eyed man seated at the stern.

Marni took the spyglass, brought it to her eye, squinted, and adjusted the focal point. After a few moments she lowered the instrument and stared out to sea, fingering the locket at her throat.

Grady studied Seamus through narrowed eyes. "Hard t' believe ye didn't see 'em launchin' their skiff. Would've had to pass this way."

"That's right," Walter asserted. "How did they get by without you noticing?"

Seamus shook his head vehemently. "Nope. Not a soul passed this way, I swear it!"

Judging by their distance from shore, the men had been rowing for a while. Perhaps Seamus hadn't been as vigilant as he claimed. "Hmph . . ." Grady's eyebrows raised and lowered several times. "Well, they made their getaway, empty-handed."

"Thank goodness for that," Pru said.

Walter frowned. "Sure, it's good they didn't find what they were looking for. . . . But then, neither did we."

"And what would that be?" Seamus asked.

Walter silenced him with a black look. Our eyes followed the rowboat as it moved determinedly toward the black ship. As we watched, the clouds shifted and wandered before the moon, obscuring the path of light shimmering on the sea. At the same time a sinister dark gray fog gathered along the shore, carrying with it the unmistakable scent of woodsmoke, accompanied by a soft but rhythmic thumping sound.

"Ye hear that?" Grady asked. "Fairy footsteps. Don't any of ye's move," he warned. "Remember what nearly happened the last time."

"Fog's rolling in," Pru exclaimed. "Link elbows. Quick! If one of us falters the rest hold tight!'"

We huddled closer, creating a human chain, Walter to my left, Seamus to my right as the brooding swirl of fog began to envelope us. I shivered as its chill wrapped around one ankle, then the next, felt my legs and arms turn to gooseflesh. The ominous fog rose around our torsos, then circled our necks with damp chilly fingers. My eyes smarted as the smoky vapor misted my face, forcing my lids closed. With the fog, the cunning Grey Man ushered in a feeling of isolation. I no longer felt my arm entwined with Walter's or Seamus's, and a sense of overwhelming loneliness coaxed me in a direction that seemed inexplicably comforting. Toward a place where I was supposed to be. Though my legs had grown heavy I forced myself to take a step, and yes, that felt right. I dragged the other foot along, and as I did, a desperate instinct took over that continued to propel me forward.

A distant voice buzzed in my ear. A distraction.

I ignored it and pressed on. Again the voice, more insistent this time. "Be strong! Fight the urge!" Familiar, but far away. Something dragged on my arm, encumbering me. I resisted, the urge to move ahead being so much stronger.

Another voice now, this one closer, penetrating the edges of my brain. "Stand yer ground! Don't let go o' yer mates! Pull back, I tell ye!" An inkling of something tickled my brain, slowing my steps. Grady? Where was I? What was I trying to do? Blurred and sluggish thoughts fought their way to consciousness. Something about a boat, a buried treasure, a coffin? Jumbled images. Confusion. I struggled against the hands determined to hold me back, heard a groan escape my lips.

A sudden thrust, and I was yanked from the whirlpool of energy that held me bound. As the fog lifted a rush of fresh air filled my lungs. "Lucy! Lucy!" I turned toward the voice. Two voices. One with a brogue.

"The lass had the strength of two men, she did!"

"Never mind that! Just pull her back!"

Walter took me beneath my arms and Seamus grabbed my feet, rendering me helpless. "P-put me d-down," I stammered, thrashing about, trying to get my feet back on the ground. There was Grady,

Pru, and Old Peader looking once again like a ghoul, his mouth gaping and eyes popping.

"She's safe now; the culprit's drifted off to sea. Put 'er down there." Following Grady's instructions they set me on my feet, just a stone's throw from the shore. It had been another close call. My eyes met Pru's. But instead of relief on her face there was panic.

Pru turned right, then left. "We've lost Marni!"

We fanned out around the castle, calling her name. Old Peader stood like a pillar, eyes peeled. Grady's mouth was pulled into a grim line, and he shook his head. It seemed she was gone without a trace.

Pugsley and Rosie ran down the slope to the water's edge. Refusing to give up, I followed them with Father's spyglass and focused out to sea. The lens brought the water up close. There the black ship, the rowboat beneath its bow. I could make out the silhouettes of Quaide, the pirate, and the green-eyed man. Within feet of the rowboat I spotted something in the water. A porpoise, or maybe a seal. But even as these logical thoughts surfaced I knew it was neither. It was another kind of sea creature. The one who had saved me from drowning several times already. I suddenly heard Miss Oonagh's words again—*Is there a merrow about?*

"Maybe she went back to the cottage," Pru suggested. But the look on her face told me she didn't believe it. No one else did either. I thought about telling them that Marni was fine, that I thought I'd spotted her swimming all the way out by the black ship, treading water behind the rowboat. But I hesitated. I still wasn't ready to believe that she was a merrow, wasn't sure how that revelation might affect who we all were together. All I knew was that more than anyone I'd ever met, Marni had been drawn to the sea. More than my father, the sea captain. More than Capt'n Adams back in Ballyvaughan with Addie and the children. And even more than Grady, who'd left his father's farm for a life at sea. A merrow? How would they make sense of it? I felt a peculiar loyalty to Marni. As though we shared a secret I was bound to keep. At least for now.

I felt Grady's wary eyes on me. He'd been suspicious of Marni from the start. I looked up and then away, hoping he couldn't read my thoughts.

"Pru's right," I said finally. "Let's go back to the cottage. I feel sure she'll be there." My voice sounded hollow, falsely bright. They stared at me, perhaps with pity at what they saw as my wishful thinking. All but Walter, who'd been with Marni the longest, after all. He nodded, eyeing me thoughtfully.

We walked back in awkward silence.

Seamus sidled up to me and whispered, "Ye don't think the ol' gal's gone and drowned, do ye? Seemed t' be quite the swimmer, she did. But what with the Grey Man about, ye can never tell."

I avoided his eyes and quickened my step. I felt his hand on my arm.

"Pardon me, Lucy. Have I gone 'n' upset ye? Jest worried for ye, is all."

"It will be all right," I said, and realized that I meant it.

Grady and Seamus agreed to take Old Peader back to his home, to put it back in order after the ransacking and tuck the old fellow into bed, his loyal Rosie following behind. He'd been through way too much for one day. Pru, Walter, Pugsley, and I took the turnoff to our cottage.

The snug little house was dark and closed up tight—even from a distance it was obvious no one was there. "I knew it didn't seem possible," Pru murmured, "that Marni would be here—but all the same I have this strong feeling that she's safe."

Inside we poked at the fire and lit the lanterns, all without a word. Pru watched me carefully, more kindly than Grady had, and I knew she could sense I was withholding something. My loyalty torn, I avoided her eyes.

"I . . . may have seen something out there," I began.

I could feel Pru's interest flare like one of the peat bricks in the fireplace. "Where?" she asked. "What do you think you saw?"

"In the water. It could have been a fish—a porpoise. Or maybe a seal." I hesitated. "But it might have been Marni."

"Marni does not look like a porpoise," Pru began.

"Swimming. What I saw was definitely swimming."

"Why didn't you say anything?" Walter asked.

"Because I didn't want Grady and Seamus to know." I knew they both understood.

The door suddenly swung open. There was Marni, slick as a seal. Our eyes met. "Are you going to get me a towel, so I don't drip all over the floor?"

In an instant Walter had a blanket wrapped around her. "Get out of those wet clothes," Pru insisted. Marni went into our room and quietly closed the door behind her.

In relief we exhaled. There would be no more questions tonight. As Pru and I settled into bed, we both took in Marni's slim form beneath the blankets, the gentle rise and fall of her shoulders. What a night it had been—we'd unearthed a grave, found an old man buried alive, and had almost been drawn into the sea by the Grey Man—or the curse. Perhaps Marni actually had been. But a part of me knew she hadn't been lured at all. She'd jumped into the sea, and swam as close as she could to whatever it was she'd needed to see. I only hoped she'd tell us what that was.

Though exhausted I knew I wouldn't soon fall asleep. And the same nervous energy that buzzed in my head was flowing from Aunt Prudence as well. It moved like a current between us, and the atmosphere in the room felt like the air before a thunderstorm. Tingling. Electric. Unsettled, with the potential for danger.

"Tomorrow," Pru whispered, "we need to look at everything we know. Put the pieces together. Make a plan."

"Yes," I murmured. I didn't voice the thought that crept up behind those words . . . *Before it's too late.*

10

Four of us sat at the table and spread the deck of cards before us. Side by side we laid out our clues. "We have to be missing something," Pru said. "Something so obvious we're not seeing it."

I hunched over the display, searching for some scrap of significance we may have overlooked. Walter frowned in concentration. Marni, however, seemed distracted, distant. She went through the motions of considering this and that, but her mind was elsewhere. I gazed at her, undetected, and wondered what was going on behind those sea-green eyes of hers. A mystery, as always.

Pru tore several pieces of paper from her note-book. "Let's review what we know." She licked the tip of the pencil, reading each word aloud as she wrote, looking to the three of us for confirmation:

1. *Great-grandfather E.S. and pirate Mary Maude Lee had a child—Marni!*

We glanced at Marni. Then, as if to prove the point, Pru unrolled and smoothed the scrolled document portraying the Simmons family tree. We stared at the branches illustrating how we were all connected to one another—and to the curse.

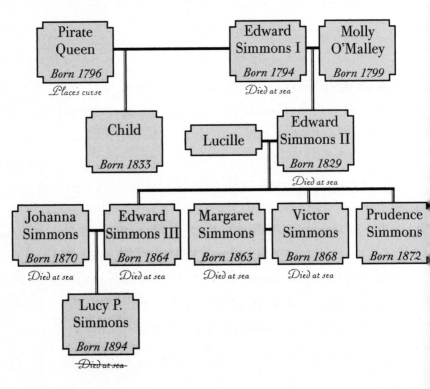

Pru penciled the next clue:

2. *E.S. stole Mary Maude Lee's treasure and M.M.L. placed a curse on all the Simmons men, killing three generations thus far.*

"Not to mention the loss of your mother and Aunt Margaret," Marni added. "And the close calls all of us have had. It seems no one related to the family is safe." She paused for emphasis, then pointed toward the lyric sheet. Pru wrote:

3. *The ballad explains that the treasure must be returned to Mary Maude Lee's kin for the curse to be lifted.*

Pru and I exchanged a knowing look. Three of the once-famous female pirate's relatives sat around this very table—Pru, Marni, and myself.

4. *E.S. had fled to Australia, but we didn't find the treasure there.*

Walter laughed. "I'll never forget all those holes you dug out there in the outback looking for 'J-3'—only to find it here on Clare Island."

Pru smiled ruefully, waving one hand under our noses. "I still have the callouses to show for it—and little else!" She bit her bottom lip and went back to her list.

5. *Another group is desperate to find the treasure—Quaide, the pirate, and the green-eyed man.*

Walter nodded. "They've been tailing us every step of the way. The question is, are they just treasure hunters following the rumors of Edward's exploits? Or are they connected in some other way? What do they know that we don't?"

"Good question," Pru said, tapping the pencil on the table before going on.

6. *The cards my grandmother—your great-grandmother—Molly O'Malley designed depict the treasure being buried in a grave on Clare Island. But the treasure is gone.*

"And," I added, "besides Old Peader, there was no corpse in the coffin. Either it has been removed or it was never there to begin with."

"Good point," Pru said.

"Maybe your great-grandfather faked his death," Walter suggested.

"And buried his treasure in his own grave!" Pru scribbled furiously:

7. *Edward's wife, Molly, carved a message on the coffin—suggesting she'd stolen the treasure to double-cross him.*

With that, one of the cards flipped up from its spot on the table and hovered around us. Before I even looked I knew which card it would be—the queen of diamonds, Molly O'Malley. My great-grandmother leaned off the card, her jowly face raised defiantly, wagging her chubby index finger in the air. "Nobody deceives me and gets away with it!" she crowed.

My aunt's voice rose to a shrill cry. Her cheeks were flushed and her mouth pinched. "But Lucy and I are your own flesh and blood," Prudence cried. "Why don't you help us? Tell us what you know? Holding back has led to many deaths already—your own son, Edward the Second; my brother and Lucy's father, Edward the Third; my brother, Victor; not to mention Lucy's mother, Johanna, and Victor's wife, Margaret! When is enough, enough? You're no better than Mary Maude Lee! In fact, you're worse!"

The force of Pru's emotion caused the animated card to quiver and dip. I almost expected it to revert to being just a plain old card again and drop, lifeless, to the table.

But it flipped up again, the queen of diamonds's face like that of a spoiled child, her bottom lip petulantly rolled. "What makes you so sure I know where the treasure is?"

"Your message carved on the lid of the coffin!" Pru exclaimed. "The treasure was in there until you made off with it!"

"Brilliant, if I must say so myself," Great-grandmother Molly said, puffing up like a proud mother hen. "True, I dug it up, and hauled it off with me to the mainland. No small task, I'll have you know! But I figured it out and I did it! Then I used some of the money to build myself a little inn and tavern, set up a business fer myself."

"And . . . ," Pru urged, circling her hand in the air impatiently.

The queen of diamonds smiled, basking in the attention. She cleared her throat, stretching out the suspense. "I had a secret vault built into the foundation of the place. That's where I hid the treasure."

"Where is it now?" I asked.

"How should I know?" The queen of diamonds snorted. "Stolen out from under my nose. So you know as much as me. You'll have to use your wits for once!"

My aunt flew from her chair and in one swift blow smacked the card to the table. Pru stood, palm down, breathing heavily, nostrils flared. I could see the queen of diamonds's buggy eyes peering up between my aunt's slender fingers. Walter, Marni, and I held our breath. Another card rose, as though carried by a playful gust of wind. We stared at the dapper king of diamonds, his crafty smile spreading ear to ear. "Can you see how she made it easy to betray her?" he quipped. "The woman could drive a person mad!"

"You're even worse!" Prudence exclaimed, snatching his card from the air and holding it before her.

The queen of diamonds wriggled out from beneath Pru's flattened hand and flew back into the air, facing her king. "I may have lost the treasure," she taunted, "but at least you never found it!"

"Oh, I found it all right," he snarled, "and died trying to take it back!"

"How?" I sputtered. "Where?"

"How? Where?" he mocked in a high-pitched voice. "That's for you to figure out!"

Pru snapped up both cards, stuffed them in the box, and slammed the lid. An uncomfortable silence filled the room.

Marni shook her head. "I'll never understand how some parents can be so ignorant of the ways their decisions affect their children, and their children's children."

Walter's face clouded over, and I thought of how we'd all been let down by one ancestor or another—Marni betrayed by both parents, Mary Maude Lee and my great-grandfather, Walter, Georgie, and Annie, by their brute of a father. At least Pru and I enjoyed loving parents, although they were lost to the curse of the previous generations. If they'd taken the curse seriously, they might still be with us. I shook my head, dispelling the litany of what-ifs that traipsed through my brain.

My musings were interrupted by a knock at the door. "Comin' to see if Miss Marni made it back safe 'n' sound!" came a voice from outside. Pru quickly rearranged our clues and evidence into a neat pile and opened the door. A large wedge of sunlight spilled inside. Seamus stood framed in light, his curly hair sparkling as if on fire.

"I'm fine," Marni assured him, "after my skirmish with the Grey Man. Thank goodness I'm at home in the water." A little too "at home," I thought.

"Well, thank the good Lord," Seamus exclaimed. "Was hopin' fer nothin' less." His eyes wandered to the papers on the table. "What were ye's workin' at there?" he asked. "Looks like quite a pile o' stuff."

Walter swiped up the evidence and handed the collection to Pru. "Nothing," he said, his eyes boring into Seamus's face. His tone let Seamus know it was none of his business.

Undaunted, Seamus grinned. "Hurry out then! I've somethin' to show ye!" His enthusiasm was infectious, and even Walter, in spite of himself, followed Seamus outside.

The sky was bright blue, without a cloud, the moisture from an overnight shower still glistening in the sky. Seamus took me firmly by the shoulders and turned me about. I gasped.

Arching across the sky to the east, as far as the eye could see, was a rainbow, the colors brilliant and shimmering. It curved over the sea to the mainland like a luminous celestial bridge. One by one the others caught sight of it, and for a moment all thoughts of curses and clues were forgotten. "Couldn't let ye miss a glimpse o' this," Seamus exclaimed.

As we stood ogling the spectacle, Grady and Miss Oonagh climbed the hill to our cottage, arm in arm, eyes peeled skyward. It seemed the grassy knoll in front of our door provided the best vantage point. Grady nodded at Marni, as though not at all surprised to see her reappearance, and turned back toward his mother. "Nowhere in the world can ye find such heavenly finery, ain't that right, Mam?"

Miss Oonagh had her white pipe clamped between her teeth, her weathered face tipped skyward. She gave no indication that she'd heard him, nor did her expression reveal any trace of wonder or delight. Perhaps she'd seen many an Irish rainbow and was no longer impressed. The ancient woman puffed on her clay pipe, her eyes riding the crest of the rainbow, shore to shore. "'Tis the way t' take, I sees it clearly." She spit the words between her teeth, the pipe bobbing with every other syllable.

Walter chuckled. "You know what they say about leprechauns and rainbows—a pot of gold at the end. . . ."

"Don't be daft," Seamus said. "Cain't ye see Miss Oonagh's prophesying?"

Walter bristled. "It was just a joke. . . ."

"The rainbow leads to the mainland," Marni said. "Westport, or maybe even Galway."

Miss Oonagh raised a hand, silencing them. "Ballyvaughan," she breathed.

"Ballyvaughan!" Pru and I exclaimed at precisely the same moment.

"Where Addie, the capt'n, and the little ones await," Marni said.

"Why Ballyvaughan?" Walter asked. "What will we find there?"

All eyes were on Miss Oonagh. She inhaled deeply, plucked the pipe from her mouth, lifted her chin, and drew her lips into a small spout. Her sunken cheeks puffed in and out, sending several short bursts of smoke into the air. It was as though she willed the smoke to shift and change shape, like turbulent clouds on a windswept day. Fascinated, we watched the smoke rings stretch, separate, and take on a new configuration. With the rainbow as a backdrop, the wisps of smoke twisted and danced. Miss Oonagh inhaled and expelled another mouthful of smoke, her pursed lips opening and closing like the beak of a small bird, sculpting the escaping vapor into the strange symbol she'd drawn on the hearth—the uneven rays reaching away from a circle. Before I could point this out, the smoke dissipated and all that remained was the rainbow. The old woman removed her pipe and smiled, revealing one snaggly long white tooth, a large gap, and a golden incisor. "Ballyvaughan," she crooned, as though that explained everything.

"What about Ballyvaughan, Mam?" Grady asked. Miss Oonagh seemed not to hear him, and kept grinning foolishly, her pipe jammed between what teeth she had.

"Then Ballyvaughan it is!" Pru said. "Molly O'Malley's tavern is on the road between Bally-vaughan and the Burren—I know this from the last time I was here."

"I've been missing Georgie and Annie," Walter said.

"And Addie and the capt'n," I added.

"Best to take the ferry to the mainland, then go by land," Grady said.

His mother vehemently shook her head. "The *Lucy P.*," she hissed.

"Impossible," Walter said. "We don't have a crew to sail her. I agree with Grady. Take the ferry."

Miss Oonagh removed the pipe from her mouth, pointed a bony finger at Walter, and pronounced it slowly, deliberately, one syllable at a time: "The—*Lu—cy—P.*!" Walter took several steps back, buffeted by the intensity of her words.

"Look!" Marni exclaimed. A second rainbow crystallized before our eyes, arching even farther toward the western sea. Miss Oonagh nodded, turned, and began to walk to the west. Seamus shrugged and motioned for us to follow. We paraded like mice behind the Pied Piper, toward the edge of the island that faced the Atlantic. When the shore was finally visible Miss Oonagh stopped.

The second rainbow arched over the island and exploded in a glittering cloud around our ship. Seamus gasped at the sight of the *Lucy P.*, surrounded by a swarm of brilliant glittering particles at the base of the rainbow. Miss Oonagh's gray eyes shone in kind, like liquid silver. She made a sound, "Ah-ya!" affirming her assertion about the vessel. "Ah-ya!" she repeated. "Not today, no, but as soon as ye can, haul anchor and set sail!"

"But Mam, how kin I leave ye? I's just arrived!"

Miss Oonagh was already retracing her steps.

"Mam!" Grady hollered, and under his breath he muttered, "Dang confounding woman!"

"Me ears are fine," she retorted. "Ye think I

cain't hear ye? Get 'er ready t' sail. Now leave me be. I've packin' t' do!"

"Packin'?" Grady barked. "What packin'?"

"Always wanted t' sail," Miss Oonagh said. "And now I shall."

Grady opened his mouth to protest, but Miss Oonagh silenced him with a hawkish glare. "All of ye's better collect yer things," she said. "And prepare t' cross the sea to Ballyvaughan!"

11

We'd barely gotten settled on Clare Island and here we were gathering our belongings, preparing, once again, to sail. Unlike previous voyages, in which our launch was anticipated with confidence and excitement, the atmosphere this time was laden with anxiety. Our skeleton crew—Grady, me, Walter, Pru, and Marni—was worrisome, and although it wouldn't be a long journey, the Irish shore could be a challenge for the best of sailors. Miss Oonagh's insistence on coming brought another layer of concern.

Our trunks were laid open and the cupboards in which we'd carefully arranged our belongings, emptied. Plates and cups stashed back in the sidebar, the fireplace swept and tidied—all of this left the cottage stark and plain, the life we'd brought within its walls waning.

"Just when I was getting used to tea and scones," Walter said, tucking his oilskins into his seafaring chest.

I made an effort to be cheerful. "When we get to Ballyvaughan, Addie will make you the best scones you've ever tasted!"

"I'll bet Annie and Georgie have gained a few pounds," Walter teased, smiling at the thought of the two little ones.

The white lace curtains billowed, and the breeze carried in a whiff of smoke-tainted air. I raised my face and sniffed. The Grey Man's presence here unnerved me, and added to the worry about navigating these coastal waters. But this smell was different, not as woodsy. A bitter, greener smell.

"Like hay burning," Walter said, as if reading my mind. Marni's hand rose to her throat, fingering her pendant, a crease forming between her brows. Pugsley paced by the door, nose raised, whiskers twitching. The hair along his back bristled.

There was a knock at the door. Seamus burst in, his face smudged and glistening with sweat. "All hands," he yelled. "Bring all the buckets ye can! Old Peader's cottage is a-burnin'—the thatch caught fire!"

We dropped everything and ran up the hill, lugging clumsy wooden buckets that thunked against our calves and blistered our palms. Pugsley hightailed it ahead of us.

"As if the ransacking wasn't enough," Pru exclaimed, "now a fire!"

Halfway to the abbey we saw dark thick smoke churning up, blackening the sky. The sound of men's voices pierced the air.

We joined a line of islanders stretched between the pump and cottage, passing water pails to a crew desperately trying to douse the flames. Before we even began, I could see it was futile. The thatch atop the cottage roared like a bonfire, huge tufts of flaming hay falling inside. The whole thing blazed and crackled, puffed and belched, the acrid air smarting our eyes and taxing our lungs.

Old Peader stood to the side, his tall frame stooped, shoulders slumped, arms dangling by his sides. His face was black with soot, his mouth slack. For a moment I thought the old man was too stunned to actually realize what was taking place—until I saw the shiny tears running down his cheeks and chin. Rosie sidled up to him, nudging his motionless hand with her snout, whimpering softly. "Smelled smoke all night, I did, but danged if I could find the source," he mumbled. "Gone. Everythin' I own, gone up in smoke!" He shook his head, raising trembling fingers to his chin. "This is all that's left!" He gestured toward a pile of this and that—whatever he'd been able to grab and heave onto the lawn.

By now the chain of water haulers slowed. Old Peader was right. It was too late to save anything more, the dryness of the thatch and ferocity of the blaze proving to be unbeatable foes. Pugsley nosed through the small but precious collection of things Peader had managed to salvage. I arranged them neatly—a couple of shirts and a worn pair of trousers. A homely wooden box that probably held important papers or keepsakes. Rosie's old blanket and dish. A small pile of books. The well-loved Holy Bible, its spine broken and cover threadbare; a slight volume titled *The Wind Among the Reeds*—poetry, by the look of it; and a third, *Irish Myths and Legends.* This one I picked up, brushed off, and thumbed through the pages of small text and detailed line drawings of many a type of Irish mystical creature—fairies, banshees, leprechauns, and merrows. I stopped, flipped back to a picture of a merrow sunning on a rocky shore, and read the underlined caption:

> Legend has it that when a merrow comes ashore she must leave her cloak behind. A fisherman and others who frequent the seas, upon finding the cloak, might hide it in the thatch of a cottage, thus holding the beautiful sea creature captive onshore—the merrow can't return to the sea without it. Once she discovers it, however, the merrow's desire to return to the sea becomes overwhelming, and she disappears again, with her cloak, into the sea.

Old Peader glanced my way, and feeling like a snoop, I quickly closed the book and laid it down with the others. What a peculiar passage to underline, I thought.

One by one the volunteers left, offering condolences to Old Peader. "The wife and I can put ye up," one called. "Me son's gone t' the mainland, he has—his room is empty. . . ."

"We can clean it up and rethatch before winter,"

another called. But Old Peader waved them off, mumbling thanks. It was as though his spirit had been doused along with everything else. As the crowd dispersed, we stood together watching the pyre burn itself out. "How d'ye think it caught?" Grady asked. "'Twas one heck of a fire."

Old Peader snuffled and wiped his nose with the back of his hand. "When the marauders came a-lookin' fer their treasure, the big one took me broom and lit it afire. Waved it at the roof, he did. Thinkin' if I knowed a thing atall 'bout the treasure, I'd spit it out 'fore he set me place aflame. When it was clear I'd nothin' to tell, he shoved me burnin' broom into the hearth. Musta sent a spark flyin' up where it smoldered all night until . . ." His voice faltered.

Walter spit out of the side of his mouth and shook his head. "Wasn't enough to turn the place upside down, they had to burn it besides?"

Seamus muttered, almost to himself, "Had I known, I never would have . . ."

Walter looked at him sharply. "Never would've what?"

Seamus's face paled. He hesitated. "Left the old fella alone."

Pru and I exchanged a glance. Something about

Seamus's demeanor was unsettling—it was the same nervous energy he'd displayed the night he served as lookout, reporting the sighting of the rowboat later than he might have. At the same time I found Walter's accusatory tone distasteful.

Marni laid a hand on Old Peader's arm. "You have fine neighbors who'll be here for you. What can we do to help?"

Old Peader wept silently. "Been better if ye's hadn't dug me up," he said. "How much can an old man bear?"

Suddenly Miss Oonagh appeared. She must have arrived in the thick of it, unseen. She took in the scene with a sweep of her silvery eyes. "Stop yer bellyachin'," she said. "Day after next you'll leave this place. I sees it clearly!"

"I've nowhere t' go," Old Peader cried. "Too set in me ways to be stayin' at the neighbor's . . ."

His words tugged at my heart. I knew what it was like to lose everything. To have your home desecrated by ill will and greed. Without thinking the words burst from my lips. "Old Peader, you can come with us to Ballyvaughan! We set sail on Wednesday."

"But I'm a-scared o' the sea," he lamented. "And what about Rosie?"

"Rosie too," I said.

"How in the world am I supposed to sail a ship with a crew o' nothin' but elders and women?" Grady exclaimed.

Walter cleared his throat. "'S'cuse me . . ."

"Oh, forgive me oversight," Grady answered. "A crew of elders, women, and one experienced man, save myself."

Seamus stepped forward, his dark mood suddenly lifted. "Make that two men! I volunteer me service. 'Twill be grand!"

"What good will you be?" Walter demanded. "You don't know anything about sailing."

"Neither did you, Walter, if mem'ry serves," Grady retorted.

"A sailor needs to be reliable," Walter insisted. "Trustworthy!"

"If he can do it, so can I!" Seamus winked at me, ignoring Walter's objections.

"Frankly, Grady, I'm offended that you discount what we women have to offer," Marni said. "Pru, Lucy, and I can hold our own with the best of them, and you know it."

I linked elbows with Pru and Marni and nodded vigorously. "We're up for it!" I said, with more confidence than I felt.

Seamus broke in between Marni and me. "I'll be a thorn among roses!"

"You'll be a detriment," Walter muttered.

I found myself wanting him to prove Walter wrong.

Grady could see he was outnumbered. Or perhaps he was leery about disregarding his mother's premonitions. He shook his head and stared out to sea. "Better get packed," he said. "We'll need to go aboard tomorrow, set the sails, chart our course, gather supplies. Thank the good Lord it'll be a short journey."

Walter, Marni, and Seamus stayed behind to help Old Peader see if there was anything else left to salvage. There wouldn't be much he could bring to Ballyvaughan.

"At least he has Rosie," Pru whispered. My aunt and I walked back to the cottage in silence, then continued our packing in earnest.

Once my things were neatly stowed I looked about. Marni's trunk sat in the corner and she still hadn't packed. I lifted the lid of the trunk and then opened the cupboard where her clothes were neatly folded on the shelves. It wouldn't take long. While Pru tidied the hearth, I began to transfer Marni's things from compartment to trunk, one neatly folded pile at a time. Side by side, I laid them in the traveling chest, pleased that she'd return to find one more task completed.

As I slid the last orderly pile of garments from the cupboard, something caught my eye. Something at the far back of the shelf. I peered into the wooden chamber. A blanket? I reached in. My hand swept across something smooth and soft.

I pulled the hidden parcel toward me, the sleek coolness of it luxurious under my fingers. As I removed it from the shelf, it slipped against the polished pine surface and unfurled into my hands. A fur pelt, silvery gray, and fashioned into a cape. I gasped. Miss Oonagh's words resonated in my head: *"Is there a merrow about?"* That, and the words Old Peader had underlined in the book he'd saved from the fire.

"What is it?" Pru asked. I held the cloak before me, displaying the flowing length of sealskin. "Oh my," Pru uttered, stroking the fur along the grain.

At the sound of footsteps on the path, we hastily folded the mystical garment and shoved it back into the depths of the cupboard.

Marni and Walter came in, Old Peader between them. "Old Peader's collected what he needs," Marni said. He clutched a leather sack against his chest, as if it was the last thing he owned, and of course, it was.

"He's ready to sail," Walter added, in a voice meant to cheer. The old man shuffled in and threw himself into the chair beside the hearth, Rosie at his feet and his bag in his lap. Pugsley plunked down beside the little sheepdog.

"I packed your clothes," I said to Marni, avoiding her eyes. My voice sounded too bright. False. I could feel her green eyes boring into me. Without a word, she slowly walked to her trunk, knelt, and thumbed through the stack of folded clothing. She rose, shooting a cursory look into the cupboard before closing its door.

"Thank you," Marni said. "But I would have preferred to tend to my own things." There was an uncharacteristic tightness in her voice. Questions hung between us.

"Am I missing something?" Walter asked. "What's wrong?"

"Nothing!" Marni, Pru, and I answered, as if in chorus.

"Trouble in the henhouse," Old Peader muttered.

A peculiar feeling rose in my chest. I wanted there to be a logical explanation for the strange seal-skin robe. But Marni's behavior—taking inventory of what I'd placed in the trunk, her quick guarded glance into the cupboard—confirmed to me that her possession of the fabled cape was not something she had wanted to divulge. Her withholding felt like a betrayal, and her secrecy conjured all my old suspicions. Aunt Pru chewed her lip. I could imagine these same thoughts marching around inside her head. "Well then," Pru began. All eyes turned toward her and she stopped, as if unsure about what to say next. "I . . . um . . . Why don't I put on some tea?"

Relieved at the distraction, we each pulled up a chair to the table and busied ourselves unnecessarily, clinking spoons against cups, moving the sugar bowl here or there, folding and refolding a napkin. Only Marni neglected to join us, heading outside, fingering her locket.

We stared at one another as the door closed softly. I got up and went to the window, watching her stride down the path along the shore.

"Tea's ready," Pru called, but I remained at the portal, watching Marni's thin form moving, or perhaps pulled, toward the water. I found myself memorizing every detail of her person, eyeing her until she turned the bend and disappeared from sight. "Lucy, tea?" Pru asked.

I shook my head, kept my back to them, fighting the tears that suddenly threatened to spill. Perhaps I'd lose Marni to the sea as well. Maybe it had been fated since the very beginning.

12

"File the manifest 'n' we're set to sail," Grady
called, pointing toward the *Lucy P.* He jutted his long narrow chin in my direction. "Since
the ship's christened fer ye, ye should be the one t'
sign. Harbormaster's office is right over there."

"Where?" I asked.

"Take 'er over," Grady said, giving Seamus a poke.

Seamus grinned. "Let's go then, darlin'."

I glanced at Aunt Pru. "Come with us?" I asked.
Pru and I followed Seamus, our ship's documenta-
tion in hand. The harbormaster's bungalow, listing
dramatically in the face of a century of buffeting

westerly winds, was inconspicuously tucked at the very end of the pier. We pushed open the creaky door and entered a small, sun-drenched space, framed in windows with views of the water on three sides. The walls below and between were lined with shelves full of thick leather-bound volumes. A bear of a man, with the ruddy complexion of an Irish seaman, sat behind a tall desk covered with papers, several open ledgers splayed across the top.

"How can I help ye's?" he boomed, his white bushy brows dancing above blue eyes. A headful of white curls poked haphazardly from beneath his navy-blue woolen cap. Above one ear, a pencil was speared into his nest of wiry hair. He chewed on a fruitwood pipe, waving us forward with a large freckled hand. As he did, he knocked a precarious pile of paperwork onto the floor. The pages billowed and flew in all directions. We scrambled to collect the mess.

"Oh, sweet Lord, this is just grand," he bellowed, shaking his head, heaving himself from his chair, lumbering around the desk to collect his documents. "So, what is it ye's need?"

"To file our manifest," Pru began, "for the *Lucy P. Simmons.*"

"Ah yes," he said. "Unusual vessel, fer sure."

He shoved the papers into a pile, drew a thick volume from the shelf, plopped it on top, and opened it. "Right there's where ye sign. Then I give it me stamp—how's that then?"

I stared at the pages of surprisingly neat columns. *Name of Vessel. Date. Port of Embarcation. Port of Debarkation. Crew—Names in Full. Passengers. Cargo.* Pru began to fill in the blanks in her distinctive hand. An idea began to take root. "How long have these records been kept?" I asked.

The harbormaster laughed. "Long as ships've been lost off the western shore—which means darn near fer'ever."

"Can I look at some of the old ones?" I ventured.

"As ye like."

I could feel the prickle of Pru's attention, which heightened my own sense of excitement. Each volume, arranged in chronological order, had the dates embossed in gold on the spine. When would my great-grandmother have hauled the treasure to the mainland? I did some quick calculations, pulled out a century-old log, and ran my finger along the columns of passengers. "Who're ye seekin'?" Seamus whispered, his chin thrust over my shoulder, cheek nearly touching mine.

"An O'Malley," I said. "My great-grandmother, Molly."

"So, ye've O'Malley blood, have ye? Bein' seafarin' women I should've figured as much."

While Pru did the necessary filing, I pored over page after page. One O'Malley, then another appeared, but not Molly. Just as I was about to give up I spotted it—O'Malley, Molly S. She'd chartered a ship called the *Buccaneer*, an English vessel departing for Ballyvaughan before crossing to America. In fact, it was the sole entry I saw listing Ballyvaughan as a port of debarkation. Molly was the only passenger, in fact, with a crew of six men, their names listed in the same spidery script. Under cargo, a vague entry—ten sealed crates containing personal items and furnishings.

"That's it . . . ," I whispered. "I wish I could . . ."

Seamus mouthed, "Have it?" He smiled devilishly, dimples marking his mirth. He sniffed several times, glanced over his shoulder, inhaled . . . "Ahh . . . ahhh . . . ahhhh . . . CHOO!" At the explosion of his fabricated sneeze, he ripped the page from the book in one swift tear, no one but the two of us the wiser. His timing was impeccable. My mouth dropped at his audacity. He quickly folded the page and tucked it into my hand.

"Finished!" Pru announced, after having drawn out the process, engaging the old salt in playful conversation. She turned and I nodded ever so slightly.

"We'll be on our way then," she announced.

"Have yerselves a safe crossin'," he called. I quickly shoved the ledger back in its place.

"Will do," I responded, clamoring for the door, Pru and Seamus at my heels.

"What did you find?" Pru gasped.

"Show 'er," Seamus boasted. I sheepishly drew the pilfered page from my pocket.

Pru's eyebrows shot up. "Oh my," she said, her look of shock quickly replaced by an admiring gaze. She took the sheet, sharp eyes devouring the text. "There's something here," she said. "I'm sure of it." She handed it back to me. "Put it in a safe place—once we're sailing we'll have a closer look."

By the time we returned Walter and Grady had the *Lucy P.* prepared to go. "She's shipshape and Bristol fashion, all standing and ready to launch!" Grady called.

Looking out to sea, I wondered what had become of the black ship but convinced myself that Oonagh's insistence we depart on this particular day boded well. I quickly hid the manifest of the *Buccaneer* in my cabin, beneath the floorboard where the collection of documents and clues were stashed, then headed back up on deck.

A feeling of excitement surrounded the *Lucy P. Simmons*, her sails set, rigging neat. Pugsley scampered happily about, sniffing out familiar salty smells. Miss Oonagh resembled a scrappy seabird, the wind flipping her white hair like the ruffled feathers of a hunkered-down gull. Her expression was one of great anticipation—it was easy to see where Grady had inherited his love of the ocean. Seamus, too, looked especially eager, having changed into brand-new oilskins, a handsome leather ditty bag in hand.

Old Peader was another story. Feeling claustrophobic in his cabin below, he'd made his way back up, reluctantly taking his place beside Oonagh. "Got the willies down there," he whispered. "Dark. Dank. Full o' strange creaks and groans. Thought I saw somethin' lurkin' in the shadows, I did." His gnarled arthritic fingers clenched and unclenched the rail. Rosie positioned herself next to him like a bulwark.

"Just yer imagination runnin' away with ye," Seamus replied gently, patting the old man on the arm.

"A rat from the bilge is what ye saw," Oonagh cackled. "A great big rat! I sees 'im meself in me head!" She tapped her temple with a bony finger.

"Stop talkin' nonsense! 'Twas no rat I saw," Old Peader insisted. Seamus rolled his eyes. Between Old Peader's fears and Oonagh's visions, it promised to be an interesting crossing.

And then there was Marni standing beside

Grady, awaiting his next direction. Not a word had been uttered about the sealskin cloak. I found myself staring at her travel chest as Walter stowed it, wondering if she'd placed the cape inside. Had she had it all along? Or could it be that she'd retrieved it here on Clare Island and now her urge to return to the sea was all-consuming? These thoughts gave way to another. The book I'd found with Old Peader's things—*Irish Myths and Legends*, with the information about merrows underlined. Was there a connection between the fire that had destroyed Old Peader's house and the appearance of Marni's cape? I tried to imagine a young Peader, spying Marni, cloaked in sealskin, sunning herself on the rocky shore . . . Peader, mesmerized and love struck, creeping toward her, stealing away her cape, forcing her to stay on land. It seemed so unlikely— almost comical, and yet . . .

The winch groaned and strained, hauling up anchor. The plan was to set sail from the west of Clare Island into the North Atlantic and head due south, cutting a wide swath around the band of rocky islands off the coast of Clifden and the Aran Islands, just outside Galway Bay. At most, a half day's sail.

The *Lucy P. Simmons* danced over the waves west of the mainland, graceful and swift, her bow-sprit pointing the way. I was quickly seduced by the brilliance of sea and sky, the bite of salty air, and the calling of raucous seabirds. But the need to carefully study the manifest tugged at me. If only I could slip away, determine how the information about the *Buccaneer* might be helpful. . . . Leaning against the mainmast, arms hugging my knees, I closed my eyes and tipped my face to the wind, imaging the spidery script, the names of seafarers, long dead.

"Penny fer yer thoughts."

My eyes fluttered open to find Seamus sitting beside me. In the sunlight his eyes shone brilliant blue, flecked with hazel, framed with long lashes. His tangle of unruly curls backlit by the sun created a halo-like shimmer—this in sharp contrast to the mischief that still tickled his face. "No thoughts at all," I lied.

"Yer Walter's quite the sailor," Seamus said, squinting up into the rigging, where Walter straddled one of the yardarms.

Something about his turn of phrase—"yer Walter"—made me feel quite mature. Was he "my Walter," I wondered? And if so, what did that mean?

"Ah, I see the thoughts runnin' 'cross yer lovely face now, I do," Seamus proclaimed. "Ye cain't deny it!" He traced his index finger from my left cheek to my right, gently scaling across the bridge of my nose. I froze for a moment, then looked away to hide the blush in the wake of his touch.

"So, is he yer beau then, is what I'm tryin' t' figure?"

I opened my mouth and shut it again. Shrugged.

A smile tweaked the edges of his mouth as he pulled a small block of wood and carving knife from his pocket. He turned the whittled hunk this way and that and gazed my way before beginning to carve. His concentration allowed me time to study him, unobserved. I wondered about his home, his family—he'd never mentioned them at all. As outgoing as he was, there was something secretive about him. Something he camouflaged with charm and a quick wit.

"Nothing better to do than whittle the day away?"

Seamus and I looked up. Walter stood over us, frowning at Seamus. "Thought you wanted to be a sailor?"

I sprang to my feet. "We were just talking. . . ."

Walter's face held an expression I couldn't name, but didn't like.

"Stop yer yappin', all of ye's," Grady yelled. "We got us a ship t' sail!"

I took one last look at the diminishing coast of Clare Island before getting back to the tasks at hand—the tasks that all the Simmonses were born to do, and many had died doing. But, for the moment, it appeared they didn't need my help. Pru, Walter, and Marni were working as a practiced team, and Grady was busy coaching Seamus. Before anyone noticed, I slipped into the companionway and down the stairs toward my cabin. I hurried along the narrow, dark corridor, my hands nearly twitching with anticipation at the hidden clues the *Buccaneer* manifest might reveal.

When I approached the portal, I hesitated. The door was slightly ajar. I placed my hand on the knob. Instead of easing it open I tipped my head and peeked through the gap. "What do you think you're doing?" I cried, throwing back the door.

The scrappy pirate jumped to his feet, all of our notes and clues spread on the floor about him. He lunged toward me, a sinister sneer emphasizing the diagonal scar slashed across his cheek.

I turned and ran through the narrow corridor. "Walter!" I screamed, sounding the alarm. "Grady!"

The stowaway grabbed me by the wrist, yanking me back toward my cabin. I writhed against his steely grasp—it was just like it'd been on the docks of Boston, when he'd tried to kidnap Georgie and me. "Ain't nobody gonna hear ye down here," he snarled, clamping a filthy hand over my mouth.

Kicking and stomping, I slammed my foot into his ankle. I scratched and bit like a savage, finally managing to knee him in the groin. In the split second he recoiled, I twisted free. He was on my heels in an instant, spewing curses. I leaped toward the companionway stairs. Slash dived toward me, missing me by a hair, landing on his belly with a *whoomph!* I took the steps two at a time, burst through the hatchway.

"Slash," I tried to scream. "Slash!"

Alarmed, Walter rushed toward me. "Lucy, what is it?"

Before I could answer, Slash crashed through the door behind me. Walter threw a punch, bloodying the pirate's nose, then took another wild swing and missed, throwing himself off balance and onto his backside. Seamus attempted to throttle the interloper, toppling both of them to the ground. Eyes wild, Pru grabbed an oar from the lifeboat, wielding it like a club. Pugsley and Rosie entered the fray, snarling, teeth flashing. Grady pulled me to the wheel. "Steer 'er steady," he growled as he drew a long, fierce knife from a strap on his ankle.

Boom!

The gunshot brought the brawl to a halt. Slash rose, holding the pistol over his head, smoke curling around its blunt nose. The smell of gunpowder hung in the air. "Get back," Slash warned, "or I'll blow ye's all t' smithereens!"

I looked to Walter clenching his bloodied fist. Seamus sprawled on the deck. The pirate wiped his nose with his hand, spit blood from the side of his mouth. Pru gripped the oar, guarding Old Peader, who stood with eyes closed and fingers jammed in his ears.

"That's better," Slash hissed.

Suddenly Grady sprang from behind a pile of crates and wrenched back the brute's arm, whipping the blade within a hair's width of his throat. "Drop the gun!" Grady's knife glinted in the sunlight as it pressed against his jugular. Slash drew his long, skinny neck as far back as possible, teeth clenched, his beady eyes rolling around in his skull like a pair of bloodshot marbles. He squirmed like a worm on a hook and fired the gun in the air.

Grady didn't flinch. "Drop it," he growled, exerting pressure on the blade. Drops of the culprit's blood beaded along the edge of the dagger. Slash reluctantly released the gun. It thunked onto the deck and Grady kicked it out of reach.

"We checked this ship top to bottom," Pru said. "How did you slip aboard?"

Slash licked his lips, giving him a snakelike look. "I don't need t' tell ye nothin'!"

Grady drew the knife closer to his throat, as if to give the dirty cur a close shave. "Ye might wanna reconsider that answer."

Slash grimaced. "Stole away t' the hold while ye were still anchored. When ye checked below I slipped into the bilge, like a water rat."

Miss Oonagh looked triumphant. "Didn't I tell ye's I seen a big rat?"

"What else?" Grady said, lowering the knife a little.

"Cold and foul that water was. I stunk like a latrine by the time I got outta there."

"Ye still do!"

We turned toward Old Peader, who'd finally opened his eyes and unplugged his ears. He stepped toward Slash, a fist raised above his head. "'Twas you and yer mates who ransacked me cottage, shoved me in the grave, left me fer dead! Then ye's burnt me home to the ground! It's not yer clothes that reek of the bilge—it's yer miserable soul!" Rosie, sensing her master's wrath, sprang at the scar-faced man, knocking Grady off balance. Pandemonium erupted. The knife clattered to the ground, and as the pirate sprang forward Rosie sunk her teeth into his calf. He cried out and kicked her squarely in the ribs. Rosie howled in pain, Old Peader dropped to his knees to comfort her, tears running down his cheeks.

"That's enough!" Without thinking I rushed up to Slash. Stood my ground. "You and Quaide— nothing but a couple of bullies! Cowards! You pick on people who are weaker than you! Help yourself to what isn't yours! You . . . you . . . make me sick! A sorry excuse for a man!"

Slash's eyes narrowed. The next thing I saw was the back of his hand. *Crack!* He struck the side of my face so hard I was knocked to the ground. The world went hazy for a moment—I saw only darkness. Then a jumble of scuffling feet, a din of angry voices, the pop and crack of blows. Walter and Grady, in duplicate, pounding on Slash. Seamus straddling him. Aunt Pru, swinging the oar like a bat, connecting with the pirate's shins. Something small and dark hurtling across the deck. The gun?

Boom! Another shot.

Old Peader, hands shaking, pointed the smoking pistol.

"Jump!" he commanded, waving the weapon. Slash scrambled to his feet, mouth agape.

Boom! We ducked as another bullet shot over Slash's right shoulder, ricocheting off one of the masts. Old Peader inched forward, trembling hands still brandishing the gun. "Now JUMP!" he commanded. "Over the side!" His eyes popped and his lips curled back, giving him the look of a crazed skeleton. He cocked the pistol again.

Slash's gaze shifted past Old Peader toward the horizon.

"Ye ain't seen the last of us!" Slash muttered. To me he added, "Got what I came 'ere fer—what I seen—I seen!" He hoisted himself on his wiry arms, swung one leg over, then the other. He hung that way, only the top of his head visible, peering at us over the rail. "And you," he growled—to exactly who, I couldn't be certain—"far as Quaide's concerned, a deal's a deal."

Before anyone could ask what he meant, Slash slipped from view, and *splash!*

He was gone.

13

Old Peader slapped the tears that continued to leak from his reddened eyes. "What, in the name o' God, came over me's what I wanna know?" he wailed, face averted. He gently beat his fist against his chest in supplication, sniffled, and wiped his nose, all the earlier bravado drained away. "Forgive me, Lord, fer takin' the life of another—even though he's a worthless sinner!"

"Not too sure you need to beg forgiveness," Marni said, turning from the rail where she'd been watching Slash tread water. She nodded toward the horizon. "Look . . ."

The black ship inched into view around the far side of Clare Island. Slash swam in that direction, stopping every few strokes to thrash his arms in the air, signaling his mates.

Grady spit overboard. "Soon as we seen that scalliwag we shoulda known 'is ship'd be close behind. If he's lucky they'll spot 'im and strain 'im outta the sea."

"Oh, thank the good Lord," Old Peader said, blessing himself.

"Never in me life 'ave I seen such a whimperin' bleedin' heart!" Grady replied, glowering at Peader. "Right now we gotta check 'er again, bow to stern. Pump the bilge. Search the cabins. Make sure he was alone."

"Aye," Walter replied. He headed for the companionway, Seamus at his heels.

Grady nodded. "Jest a precaution. Then we gotta make time! Full sails! We can outrun 'em. Be done with the black ship and her rotten crew fer a while."

"Ah, but yer wrong, sonny," Miss Oonagh said, a faraway look in her eyes. "They's got somewhere t' lead us, they do. Ain't that right, Miss Marni?"

Marni looked at the old cailleach. "Where would that be?"

Oonagh snorted, as though the answer was

obvious. "To yer boy," she replied. "Where else? To yer missin' lad. He stowed aboard hopin' we'd give 'im the clues t' lead 'em to the treasure. Instead they'll be leadin' us to the lad! A whole diff'rent kind of treasure. Ain't that funny?"

The color drained from Marni's face. Her fingers flew to the locket at her throat—the locket that contained the weave of golden hair from the son she'd lost. She looked at Oonagh. "Please . . ." She took a deep breath. "Finding my boy—this is something you foresee?"

Miss Oonagh turned her attention back to sea. Marni persisted, "Miss Oonagh? What do you mean? Where will they lead us?"

The old cailleach leaned on the rail, her hawk-like eyes scanning the waves. "He'll have a good thrashin' about fer a while, he will. Tee, hee, hee . . ."

"All clear," Walter called. "Checked her top to bottom."

I felt an arm slip around me, and turned. Pru tenderly ran her hand along my cheek. "You're swelling up a little," she said. "I'll get you a nice cool compress."

"Found him in my cabin," I whispered, "pawing through our clues! We have to see if he took anything, figure out what he knows!" A parade of emotions ran across Pru's face. Surely she was wondering the same thing—could he have pieced together something that would lead them to the treasure ahead of us?

"They planted him on board to find out what we knew," she said. "Probably intended to jump ship to report back to Quaide before we launched, or hunker down until we anchored." She narrowed her eyes. "Let's go," she said, leading me back to my cabin. In minutes I was lying on my bunk, a cold, wet, salty cloth folded neatly across my cheek. Once I was settled Pru combed through the evidence strewn on the floor. "Everything's here, I think. More a question of what he saw that he didn't already know . . ." She held up the torn page we'd pilfered from the harbormaster. "Puzzle pieces we haven't put together yet. Problem is we don't know what pieces they might have that we don't."

The door opened quietly. "How's our girl?" Marni asked, studying me closely.

"No worse for wear," I mumbled from beneath the soothing cloth. I wondered suddenly about Miss Oonagh's prophecy. About Slash and his cohorts leading us to Marni's son. But if Slash should drown out there, what did that mean? That Marni's son was already a part of the sea, that the curse would eventually claim the rest of us as well? Reuniting us on the other side? I shuddered at the notion. Marni continued to watch me closely as I rested. Whatever she might have been feeling was closed off and locked away.

I began to feel restless, or maybe it was just a sense of urgency to get to Ballyvaughan well ahead of the black ship. "I think I need a little air to clear my head," I said. "I'm ready to go up top. Help sail this ship."

Pru nodded. "Will likely do you good," Marni added.

The air above deck whipped about, restoring my vigor and determination. In the course of a morning I'd pilfered the *Buccaneer*'s manifest, discovered a stowaway, surprised him before he was able to make off with valuable documents, dodged a bullet or two, confronted Slash, and witnessed Old Peader's shocking show of bravado. An amazing day thus far, if I thought about it in the right light.

Walter caught sight of us and hurried over. "Did he hurt you, Lucy?" he asked, gently reaching toward my cheek. Seamus ambled up behind him. Two pairs of eyes full of concern, one dark as night, the other blue as the sea.

"I'm fine now." I took my spyglass and squinted through the lens. Scanned from east to west and back again. No sign of Slash or the black ship. A smile teased the edges of my lips. As if reading my mind, Marni followed my gaze out to sea. "I might not count them out just yet," she said quietly. "Things have a way of not being what they seem."

Pru nodded, remembering, I'm sure, how many times we'd given Quaide the slip, only to have him resurface. "Perhaps this time is different. . . ."

"Yes," I said hopefully, enjoying the feeling of the wind in my face. "Right now I believe we can conquer just about anything."

"What d'ye have t' say about it, Miss Oonagh?" Seamus teased. We all turned toward her, waiting.

She was seated atop a huge coil of rope, looking like an ancient mariner queen, holding court from her nautical throne. What better place to channel prophesies from the deep? The old woman closed her eyes. Her mouth dropped open, head tilted back so that the sun shone on her face.

We all froze in anticipation. The old cailleach's lips began to twitch. We leaned forward so as not to miss a single word. I held my breath.

"K . . . k . . . k . . . k . . . k . . . puh . . . puh . . . puh . . . K . . . k . . . k . . . k . . . k . . ."

Was she speaking in Gaelic or some magical tongue?

No. She was snoring—long rasping inhales

punctuated by short bursts of exhalation. "K . . . k . . . k . . . k . . . k . . . puh . . . puh . . . puh . . . K . . . k . . . k . . . k . . . k . . ."

I caught the twinkle in Seamus's eye, glanced between him and Pru. She threw back her head and let out a hoot, and the group of us laughed until we cried, the sound mingling with Miss Oonagh's snuffles. The ruckus drew the two dogs, who joined in, yapping and howling. Old Peader flapped his hands to try, unsuccessfully, to shush them.

As our laughter finally subsided, the tension and exhilaration of the last hours drained from me, leaving me a little weak in the knees. I caught Marni, not a trace of levity on her face, staring at Miss Oonagh, probably weighing her earlier prophecy. How much she must have desired for it to be true.

I leaned back against the mast, watching our small crew work together—all of us driven by one desire or another, searching for whatever it was we believed would make us whole. Maybe that was what made sailing so fulfilling—the sense of striving together to get to a destination that would, once and for all, satisfy our hearts. I laid my hands to the sails and joined them, losing myself in the task, enjoying the familiar feeling of coursing over the waves.

Seamus called out. "Look!"

"Land ho!" Grady hollered. "Land ho!"

There was the mainland, just visible off portside. Before Grady could grab hold of the ringer to sound the sighting, the ship's bell began to clang. Old Peader blessed himself. Miss Oonagh snorted to attention, snapping her mouth shut and eyes open.

"Ballyvaughan." The word sighed from Oonagh's lips like a wispy incantation.

"Ready about!" Grady commanded. "We're bringin' 'er in!"

14

They must have spotted the *Lucy P. Simmons* as she entered the harbor at Ballyvaughan. By the time we'd anchored, Capt'n Adams and Georgie were piloting toward us in a small boat. The capt'n welcomed us with an energetic salute and Georgie waved wildly, creating such a commotion that their vessel bobbed, threating to dump them both into the sea.

When they were within a hundred yards, Walter stripped off his shirt, let out a whoop, and plunged over the side. Georgie jumped in as well, and splashed the rest of the way to his brother. You'd have thought we'd been gone for months rather than mere days. A chilly, watery reunion, but one that couldn't have been warmer.

"Drop a line," commanded the capt'n as the skiff pulled alongside us.

"We've a few extra passengers," Pru called. Seamus, Old Peader, and Miss Oonagh leaned elbow to elbow along the rail.

The capt'n quickly replaced his look of surprise with a smile. "A couple of trips'll do it. Send them first."

It took quite a lot of coaxing to get Old Peader into the harness and lower him into the boat. He hung like a fly in a spider's silk trap, eyes closed, body rigid, arms by his sides. Miss Oonagh went down with a wide-eyed "Woo hoo!" Seamus followed with Rosie in tow. The rest of us made it on the second run.

Annie and Addie waited on the stone jetty that pointed into the harbor like a long, curved finger. In one hand Addie held a basket and she shielded her eyes with the other. With the aid of Father's spyglass I watched her extend a hand to Old Peader and then Miss Oonagh, while Annie *ooh*ed and *ahh*ed over Rosie. Then they turned their attention to Seamus, who bowed deeply, and ceremoniously kissed each one's hand. I could see they were charmed. Who wouldn't be?

Anticipation made the wait feel interminable, but soon I was in Addie's embrace. "Oh lass, it's grand t' see ye, it is! Feels like it's been ferever!" After a good long squeeze she stepped back, holding me at arm's length. "Yer hair is a bit of a fright, and—oh—good heavens, is that a bruise formin' about yer eye?"

"Quaide . . . ," I began.

"Quaide?!" Her soft brown eyes flashed as she peered over my shoulder toward the ship.

"Not Quaide exactly," I said. "He planted one of his cohorts aboard the *Lucy P.* But we outsmarted him. It's fine, Addie, really." I sounded more confident than I felt.

"Ye can tell me all I need t' know over tea 'n' scones. And I'll prepare a poultice to take down the swellin' 'neath yer eye." She nodded toward Seamus. "We don't want t' mar yer complexion fer yer new admirer." My face flushed, surely accentuating the bruise.

Walter approached, Annie clinging to him like a little monkey. "We missed you, Addie," Walter said. "Could have used your able hands to help guide the *Lucy P.*" He pointed, thumb over shoulder, at Seamus. "Difficult with landlubbers pretending to be sailors."

"Say what ye will, Wally," Seamus countered, "but when Old Peader started shootin', I did me part, ain't that right, Miss Lucy?"

"Don't call me Wally. . . ."

"Shootin'? Did 'e say shootin'?" Addie asked, mouth agape.

I sighed. "We'll tell you about it over tea."

After piling our trunks on a small donkey cart, the capt'n led us along a main road lined with white thatched buildings, and down a narrow dirt lane that wound away from the sea through a meadow of gorse and wildflowers. Rosie and Pugsley dashed off across the lea, startling the lazily grazing sheep, nipping at their heels. The pastureland gave way to fields striped with neat rows of crops. Georgie pointed. "Our potatoes are over there. See the cabbages and carrots?"

We finally reached Capt'n Adams's homestead—a fine, white-washed, two-story structure topped with a snug woven carpet of golden thatch. A number of uppity chickens strutted around the yard until Pugsley and Rosie sent them scuttling off in a huff.

"Just as lovely as I'd expect," Marni said to the capt'n. "One who runs a tight ship always maintains the same high standards on land. The same could be said of your father, Lucy, don't you agree?"

Pru and I nodded in tandem.

"Nothin' like a place with a view of the sea," Grady said. Sure enough, beyond the fields and pastureland was an expanse of bright blue trimming the patchwork of green. Old Peader dabbed his eyes.

"There goes the human waterin' can," Miss Oonagh barked. "Always leakin' at the eyeballs!"

"You'd be mournful as well," Peader retorted, "if ye'd lost what I 'ave. 'Course it'd be unlikely ye'd even remember afterward."

Miss Oonagh ignored him and poked the capt'n with a bony finger. "So, when's the weddin' is what I'd like t'know? Don't 'ave a thing t' wear!"

Capt'n Adams cleared his throat and cast his eyes away. Addie blushed deeply. "Scones . . . tea and scones it 'tis," Addie sputtered. "I'll be layin' out the table, I will, so 'scuse me, all. . . ." Like one of the flustered hens with feathers ruffled, Addie retreated inside, wiping her hands on her apron.

"Time for tea then," the capt'n agreed, quickly ushering us inside.

Annie tugged at my shirt and whispered behind her hand. "They're in *love*. . . ."

"Does seem love is in the air," Seamus suggested. "Grand, it 'tis!"

Miss Oonagh grinned. "Sure—ye oughta know!"

she cackled. "With yer goo-goo eyes fer Miss Lucy, there." She spun toward Walter. "Ye better watch out! Tee hee hee!" Her shoulders shook with laughter.

I glared at the old woman as I retreated into the cottage, my face on fire. I joined Addie, laying out cups and saucers, fine lace napkins, spoons, and knives. Neither of us spoke, each sneaking sideways glances at the other, questions hovering in the space between us. The rest wandered in to the smell of warm scones scenting the kitchen.

We whiled away the afternoon, relaying all that had happened on Clare Island and then at sea, avoiding much mention of Quaide or the pirate in front of Georgie, who could be too easily impressed by tales of his former hero's swashbuckling. In the midst of my musing, day gave way to evening. Addie and Annie listened to our saga while preparing shepherd's pie with brown bread. The cheerful peat fire in the hearth lent light and took the dampness out of the air. How much I'd missed the feeling of home that Addie brought, how she made me feel grounded and safe. My mind wandered to the days when she'd cared for our family back in Maine. In fact, I couldn't recall a time when those strong, capable hands hadn't provided a sense of security for me. She'd been in my life even longer than Mother and Father, and I'd spent more time with her than with Aunt Pru and Marni combined. Oh, how I longed for the impossible—a real family to call my own.

I stared into my bowl so the others wouldn't notice my eyes welling.

But Addie somehow knew. She reached across the table and gave my hand a squeeze. "Glad t' see me hardy fare warmin' yer heart agin," she said. "Just as it should be!"

Our appetites sated, we gathered around the fire, pulling up chairs and benches, Annie and Georgie sprawling on the thick woven rug. Miss Oonagh pushed back in a creaky oak rocker, slipped her clay pipe and bag of tobacco from her pocket, and began tapping the pipe and blowing out any leftover ash, pinching a bit of tobacco, sprinkling it into the bowl of the pipe. She tamped it gently with her index finger, took a test draw, and repeated the process. Finally, she expertly lit the pipe, sucking air and aromatic smoke into puffed cheeks. I watched this ritual with great satisfaction, realizing it signaled a special kind of settling in together. By the time Miss Oonagh exhaled, Old Peader was snoring softly, his face slack with relief.

Capt'n Obediah sank into the comfortably worn wing chair. The fire crackled and snapped, calling us to order as we turned our attention to Capt'n

Adams. Our shadows danced in the flickering light, casting elongated silhouettes across the walls.

Suddenly Pugsley scrambled to his feet, curly tail wagging, ears perked. Bolting across the room, he skidded to a stop in front of a large cupboard.

Annie flew to her feet. "Pugsley, no!" He pawed the ground at the base of the cabinet, whining. Annie took hold of his collar and hauled him back.

"Dog mistakin' himself fer a cat," Seamus said. "Chasin' a mouse, is he?"

"It's not a mouse, silly!" Annie exclaimed. She dropped her voice to a whisper. "It's a fairy!"

Walter chuckled.

Annie confronted her brother, eyes narrowed. She shook her head emphatically. "*Never* make light of fairies," she warned. "You'll offend them! Tell him, Capt'n O!"

I expected the capt'n to humor her with a pat on the head. But there was no trace of a smile on his lips, no twinkle of laughter in his eyes.

"Annie's right," he said softly. "This house was built near a fairy rath—that cleft on the hill to the west. Discovered when my great-grandfather's cow turned an ankle in a deep burrow, actually an entranceway to their underground fort."

A chunk of turf in the hearth popped with a percussive *crack*, producing a sudden burst of sparks.

Old Peader flinched and sat up with a snort, eyes wide. "'Twas a shot I heard?"

"Course not," Addie assured him. "We're talkin' of the wee folk."

"Wee folk here?" Old Peader asked nervously. "They cause all manner of trouble, they can. . . ."

Miss Oonagh exhaled a burst of gray smoke. "Ye've domesticated one of them, eh? Or so ye think?"

"Exactly," said the capt'n. "We exercise a healthy respect for one another."

Walter shook his head. "You expect us to believe that some little sprite with gossamer wings is living under the cupboard?"

Addie, the capt'n, Annie, and Georgie cut him short with a collective "Shhhh!"

"Really, Walter, after everything we've witnessed, is it so hard to believe?" Marni asked. "I'd say we've glimpsed enough of the realm beyond to have earned a healthy respect for all manner of magic. Wouldn't you agree?"

Walter smirked. "Now it's fairies? What will it be next—leprechauns? Merrows?"

Marni's face hardened. "You shouldn't be so glib. . . ."

"Ow! Owww!" Suddenly Walter jumped to his feet, frantically shaking his hand. "Something bit me . . . or . . . or . . . stung me!" He splayed his fingers. The tip of his pointer finger began to swell. In a moment it inflated to twice its size and turned a nasty shade of red, then plum. It looked as though it might explode.

"Hit ye with a fairy dart," Miss Oonagh asserted. "'Tis the worst mortal offense to disbelieve in fairies. Punished ye fer yer arrogance, they did." Lifting her chin, she dispersed a smoke ring. It wafted up and shifted into the shape of a fairy, wings fluttering. Pleased with herself, she grinned.

"Oh, good Lord," Addie exclaimed, taking Walter's hand. "A fairy dart can cause a wicked infection. You'd best apologize. Make amends. Waste not a second!"

Annie was already collecting several small potatoes from the basket, and Georgie poured a petite stoneware mug of milk, another of wine. Together, they lined their peace offerings at the foot of the cupboard. "Say you're sorry!" Georgie ordered. "Unless you want your finger to shrivel and fall off!"

Walter scowled. "I will not!"

"Don't be a donkey's behind," Grady said. "Next time they might not hit ye in the finger."

Seamus laughed. "If I were you—"

"Well, you're not me!" Walter growled.

"I'm not the one with the digit resemblin' a sausage," Seamus said. "Doesn't do much t' improve yer looks!"

"Oww!" Walter moaned, blowing on his bloated finger.

"What'ye think the Grey Man is?" Grady fired the question at Walter. "Ye believe in him, don't ye? Jest another type o' fairy he is, after all. If ye believe in the Grey Man, why not the wee folk?"

"True," the capt'n said. "And the wee folk are not to be underestimated. They're capable of stirring the wind, raising the waves, drawing a fog. Blighting crops. Can make a sheep lame, dry the cow's milk. It's been said they can turn a man into an insect. Or a horse. Have you ever sneezed? Hiccuped? Tripped over your own two feet?"

We all nodded.

"Fairy mischief . . ."

Walter's face was screwed into a mask of pain. His finger looked like a violet cucumber.

"Stop being so stubborn!" I said. "Whether you believe it or not, just apologize!"

"Oh, but ye have to believe it!" Miss Oonagh asserted. "The fairy folk smell insincerity, they do! Sixth sense, they 'ave."

Sweat beaded along Walter's brow. "I believe it,"

he gasped, "and I'm sorry for not believing sooner. I was wrong."

Grady grunted his approval. Stood. "Ye must 'ave a vial of holy water about?"

"Well, o' course," Addie replied. She spirited a small bottle of water from the cupboard and presented it to Grady.

He unstopped the cork and poured a little into his palm. "Gimme yer hand," he said. Walter thrust his unsightly paw into Grady's and the old sailor sprinkled the swollen finger.

"From a stream on Croagh Patrick," Addie boasted, "the mountain o' the saint himself!"

"Now, bless yerselves and pray," Grady directed. Old Peader took the lead. "May God bless ye," he said, eyes lifted. Addie, as though struck by a sudden insight, turned to the table and returned with a plate of shepherd's pie, some berries, and a leftover scone. These she set at the base of the cupboard. "Delicacies! A peace offerin'."

"We've done what we can for now," the capt'n said. Annie and Georgie exchanged looks of concern. Walter stared at what used to be his index finger. The large clock on the wall ticked loudly.

Miss Oonagh blew another smoke ring into the air. It wafted into a fairy shape and levitated, wings pulsing, before floating across the room. In front of the cupboard the hazy sprite stretched and spun into a single thread of smoke, descended, and like a snake, slithered beneath the cupboard.

15

Bone tired, I settled into bed. Pru was asleep almost as soon as she laid her head on the pillow. I snuggled into the down feather bed, Addie's linens crisp and sweet smelling, as always. But despite my exhaustion, sleep evaded me. I could hear Walter in the next room, tossing and turning, trying, I'm sure, to find a comfortable way to lay his swollen finger. And then there was his bruised ego. . . .

But that wasn't all. A feeling of urgency pressed in on me. What had Slash learned that might give the pirates an advantage? What did Quaide know that we didn't? Was there a crucial connection we were missing?

Restless, I drew back the covers, quietly slipped out of bed, and tiptoed down the stairs. There I could sit and ponder without disturbing Addie. In the parlor the burning peat still glowed merrily in the hearth, its warmth welcome in the dampness of evening.

"Thought you'd be fast asleep by now."

Startled, I turned to see the capt'n seated in the wing chair, a glass of amber spirits in his hand. "Just having a midnight libation, enjoying the feeling of a full household again." He smiled, lifting the glass. "Cheers!" he said. "What is it keeping you awake?"

I shrugged. "Just trying to make sense of things. On Clare Island I came across a ship's manifest from long, long ago. My great-grandmother was aboard. It listed all kinds of information about the crew, the cargo, the passengers. . . ." As I spoke, an idea sprang into my head. "Capt'n—when you hired our crew back in Boston, you must have had to fill out a manifest?"

"Of course."

"Where would that document be? In Boston?" My brief excitement waned. Boston was a long ways away.

"Yes, filed with the harbormaster." He took a sip of his drink. "Why do you ask?"

I considered for a moment. "I'm not sure exactly. . . . I guess I don't know what I'm looking for until I find it."

The capt'n nodded. "It's that way with a lot of things. But once you see it, you realize it was what you were looking for all along." He smiled and I wondered if he was thinking of Addie. Then his expression changed. "You know, as captain, I kept a log of every voyage. If time permitted I often made note of the information filed on the manifest."

"Oh, Capt'n, could you . . ."

"Find it? Of course." He stood and walked over to a large book cabinet and opened the glass doors. "Let's see. . . ." He withdrew a thick volume. The linen cover was warped and faded—evidence of the way the sea had so many times overtaken us. He hesitated for a moment. "My log is like a journal, a diary. Its pages hold many of my most private thoughts. What you're searching for is a record of our setting sail, correct?"

"Yes, Capt'n! I wouldn't intrude on your personal entries. Perhaps . . ."

"Let me have a look. . . ." He pulled a pair of wire-rimmed glasses from his pocket, arranged them on his nose, and flipped open the book. "Ahh, yes . . ."

"What did you find?"

"Right here—list of crew, description of vessel, port of embarkation . . . dates. Cargo list." He perused several pages, considering.

It took every last bit of restraint not to move closer and peer over his shoulder. I waited. The clock ticked.

"Well then," he said, "let's do this." He strode to his desk and removed a pair of angry-looking scissors. He splayed the journal open and carefully snipped, slicing out several pages of tidy notations. "Here you are, Miss Lucy. I pray you'll find whatever it is you seek."

"Thank you, Capt'n!"

"I'll leave you to it then. Just snuff the lamp when you're through." Capt'n Adams downed the remains of his drink and left me alone. I took his place in the wing chair, its sturdy arms enveloping me, and leaned into the light. I scanned the page, running my finger through the columns of familiar information—the names of our little party, an accounting of foodstuffs and nautical equipment, intended ports of call. I turned the page over and paused. In Capt'n's neat script was a list of our hired crew, which I read with great interest. Though these men had become as familiar as family, I realized I'd never learned their last names.

There had been no need.

James O'Grady—I blinked. Grady? His first name was James? Padric Carolan must have been the given name of the man we called "Irish." Coleman Thayer—dear Coleman, who we'd left behind in Australia. I read on, as though being introduced to these men for the first time, which I was, in a certain kind of way. There, at the end of the list, was the name I was seeking: Quaide Coogan. "Coogan . . . ," I whispered. Something about the name struck a chord in me. Or maybe it was just a visceral reaction to my deep disgust for the man. I frowned, feeling suddenly let down. It was all interesting but didn't reveal the elusive clue I'd hoped for. Stifling a yawn I extinguished the lamp and tiptoed back upstairs, the capt'n's generous but likely futile contribution in hand. Without a sound I slid the box from under my bed and stashed Capt'n's log pages in with the rest.

Following a night of fitful sleep the morning seemed to dawn sooner than expected. I dragged myself down to breakfast, where the mood was somber. Walter's finger was still swollen and had ripened into the color and size of a small eggplant. The slightest touch sent waves of throbbing pain radiating through his hand and up his arm. Addie's home remedies did little to alleviate the swelling or discomfort. The capt'n had already sent for the village doctor, an elderly fellow with a curt way of speaking and no bedside manner. "Soak it," Dr. O'Leary said. "Epsom salts t' draw the poison. Keep it elevated," he instructed. "If that doesn't do, we might try a leech t' suck the bad blood."

Annie's eyes opened wide. "Put a bloodsucker on his finger? Ewww!"

Walter grimaced. "What if none of that works?"

The doctor rubbed his chin, considering. "If infection in a finger or limb begins t' affect the rest o' the body, the prudent thing would be, lose the finger, save a life."

Walter's face paled.

"That's quite serious," Marni said.

"Indeed," the physician replied. He removed his spectacles, huffed on them, drew a soft cloth from his pocket, and concentrated on giving the lenses a good polishing. He arranged them back on his stubby nose and leaned in to see Walter more clearly. "So, boy, I'd suggest ye do as yer told unless ye care t' be known as ten minus one."

"Enough!" Pru exclaimed, glaring at the old man. "A little sensitivity would go a long way!"

The capt'n took Dr. O'Leary by the arm. "I think we're done here," he said, whisking O'Leary to the door.

"Oh, sweet God in heaven," Old Peader began, voice trembling. "If I could, I'd stand in yer place, Walter. Me, an old fella, what do I need ten fingers fer? But yer young . . ."

"B'fore ye start leakin' from the eyes agin," Miss Oonagh warned, "ye might consider shuttin' yer trap! That fairy might hear and shoot a dart yer way too! Right in the arse! Heeheehee!"

"It isn't funny!" Walter shouted. For a moment he looked as though he might cry.

"I'll heat the water and Epsom salts," I said. "Before it's lukewarm we'll have the next batch ready. And how about I rig a line from the ceiling that will pull your arm up to keep it elevated?"

He nodded, sat back, and closed his eyes. Georgie inched over and patted his brother on the shoulder.

"Knock it off!" Walter cried, shrugging Georgie's small hand away.

"It's all right," Marni said, reaching for Georgie. "Your brother appreciates your concern, I know. Everyone's nerves are rattled. You and Annie go on out and check the sheep. Collect some eggs from the hens. Let us tend to Walter."

Addie, Pru, Marni, and I spent the afternoon caring for him as best we could. I strung a winch and a line to help keep his hand above his heart, but he balked. The soaking bath was either too hot or not hot enough, the Epsom salts stung. The tea I made that was "too strong," the scone "too dry." After several hours, Addie retreated to the kitchen to prepare a meal, while Pru gathered her notebooks and map of Ballyvaughan and headed upstairs to her room. Marni took Miss Oonagh by the arm, led her outside for a walk, leaving us alone.

"I thought I might make a poultice and wrap it in a bit of cheesecloth, like a bandage," I ventured.

"Did you hear what the doctor said?" he cried. "Did he say to use a poultice? No! Do you want me to get better or not?"

"Of course I do, but—"

"Then stop making stupid suggestions!" He slammed his good hand on the table, upsetting the bowl of salty water and spilling it all over himself. "See what you did!" he yelled, jumping from his seat, his pants soaking wet. It was all I could do not to take the empty bowl and hurl it at him.

At that moment the door opened and Seamus stepped in.

"Heard a commotion, I did. Makes me think Miss Lucy might need t' take a break from playin' the nursemaid." He shot Walter a look. "Seems as if ye've gone and wet yerself. . . ."

"Out of here!" Walter shouted. "Get out!"

My heart was pounding. I wasn't sure what I felt the most—anger, pity, fear, or indignation. Not to mention that his unfortunate encounter with the fairy was already interfering with our quest. "Suit yourself," I hissed, narrowing my eyes. I wanted him to see how put out I was. But he was already trudging toward the stairs to his room. I glanced at Seamus as we headed out the door. "Did you really need to mention his wet pants?" I asked. "Adding insult to injury?"

Seamus shrugged. "He was actin' like a baby, pickin' on me best girl after all ye did fer 'im . . . so 'e had it comin'!"

I almost protested. But Seamus gave me an affectionate squeeze. "The thought of havin' a lovely gal tendin' to me every need is enough to make me swoon." Holding his chest he collapsed on the path, throwing himself at my feet. "Oh," he moaned, "m' heart is breakin' and the sight o' ye made me knees weak! Can ye help me, sweet?"

"Oh, Seamus, stop!" I fought a smile. "Get up," I said, extending a hand.

He took my hand, drew it to his lips. Stared up over my knuckles at me. His eyes twinkled. I felt his lips brush the tops of my fingers. "Worth it, 'twas," he said. His breath on my hand felt warm and moist. A tingling feeling spread from my fingertips and it was a second before I got a hold of myself.

"Stop your nonsense," I scolded, yanking my hand away and turning to hide the color that had crept up my neck to my cheeks.

He scrambled to his feet, beaming. "Come on then," he said. "'Ave somethin' to show ye!"

Before I knew it, my hand was in his again, and we were running across the field together, laughing. It felt good to be out of the dreariness of the cottage, to feel the wind in my hair, the sun on my face. Seamus had brought all that with him—fresh air and light. We slowed when we reached the dirt road that led into town. He didn't release my hand, and I didn't pull it away. "Wait till ye see," he said.

Up ahead, at the edge of the town center, stood a peculiar old tree, with a number of thick, graceful branches that dipped gracefully. It was as though they were bowing to us, inviting us closer. A bench sat in the shade beneath it. "Ever seen such a tree?" Seamus asked.

"No, never."

"Ye can climb up in 'er boughs 'n' escape the world. Perch like a bird, out o' sight!" He hopped the bench and easily scaled the branches, his brown boots disappearing into a cluster of greenery. "Will ye be gracin' me with yer presence?" he coaxed.

After climbing ratlines and traversing yardarms

aboard ship I knew this would be easy. In seconds I was sitting beside Seamus in the crook of a thick, curved branch, enveloped in a veil of delicate leaves. Peeking through the foliage provided a view of the street below, and off in the distance, the harbor. Here, in the confines of this hidden sanctuary, Seamus's presence seemed to fill the space. I was suddenly tongue-tied, shy. And grateful for the distraction of whomever it was approaching along the road beneath us. "Shhh!" Seamus whispered. He grinned. "Look who's comin'. . . ."

Marni walked arm in arm with Miss Oonagh. "I'm takin' a load off," Oonagh said. "Me feet are painin' me!" I was about to call down when Marni spoke up.

"The other day—you started to tell me about my son. You said Quaide and his cohorts would lead me to him. . . ."

If there'd been a moment when we could have revealed our presence, it was past. The intensity of Marni's words, the longing in them made it impossible. Seamus and I exchanged a look.

"Miss Oonagh . . . fifty years I've been searching for my son, drawn, by instinct, from one place to another. And I've never felt closer than these last months."

As always, her fingers caressed the locket at her

throat. "Miss Oonagh?" Marni repeated.

Oonagh looked at Marni and blinked. "Ye have a son, do ye?"

"Yes, you told me. . . ."

"Where's 'e live, this boy o' yers?"

Marni's shoulders slumped. "That's what I'm trying to find out."

"Ye don't know where yer own lad lives?"

Marni sat back and stared straight out across the harbor. "He was only seven when his father kidnapped him—stole him away for a life at sea. You told me—"

"Must be mistakin' me fer someone else," Miss Oonagh said. "Don't know no Quaide. And who are ye, anyway?" She stood, looking this way and that. "Where's me Daniel? Gotta find me man!" She took a step, stopped. Pointed. "Oh, there he is!"

Grady walked toward his mother, and nodded to Marni. "Went into town t' pick up some things. What's wrong with the two of ye's? Both look like ye seen a ghost."

Marni rose. "Better take your mam home. . . . "

Miss Oonagh linked arms with Grady. "Daniel," she scolded, "it took ye long 'nough!" With a wry look Grady tipped his cap at Marni and led his mother back toward the house.

Marni watched them go. An intense desire

emanated from her—I could feel it pressing on my chest. She ran a hand through her hair. Tipped her head slightly, listening to something we couldn't hear. Seamus and I scarcely breathed. She lifted her chin and turned one way, then the other, like a greyhound sniffing the air, trying to pick up a scent.

I wondered if she sensed us hiding up there above her. But, instead of looking up, she took a deep breath, exhaled, and set off in a westerly direction. I felt suddenly ashamed—for eavesdropping on her need. For only seeing her as strong, as being there for me. All the while she took her loss in stride, shouldering the pain of it. Could it be that Oonagh had been right—right in the sense that Marni's son was gone—dead at sea, and that Quaide followed him there? And that ever-present attraction of hers for the ocean depths was actually some sixth sense or mother's intuition that pulled her toward her boy? I felt a lump in my throat, words of regret on the tip of my tongue. I turned, and Seamus's face was right in front of mine. Before I could speak he cupped my chin and kissed me.

"But . . . ," I sputtered, caught in a tumult of feelings.

"But what?" he asked, his eyes lazy and very blue, a smile tweaking the edges of his mouth.

"Marni . . . ," I began. It was all too confusing.

I took a deep breath and slipped down to the next branch.

"Lucy, wait!"

"I have to go!"

"But why? Lucy!"

I peered up at him. "There's something I have to do!"

My feet touched the ground. Marni was crossing the field, moving like a ship through the waves of wildflowers. And I followed.

16

I tracked Marni from a distance, keeping her just in view. She'd walk for a while, then stop, stand absolutely still, and rotate slowly in a circle, as though waiting for some invisible clue to direct her course. Whenever she'd pause I'd slip behind a stand of trees, or duck behind a stone wall, wondering if she could sense my presence. If she did, she didn't let on.

She continued, across fields and meadows. Where was she going? A building, set on a hill, came into view—an imposing stone structure. It appeared to be some kind of institution—perhaps a hospital or asylum. She quickened her steps, proceeding toward it. On closer inspection I realized it was part of a compound spread across several acres—a low block spanned one side, a three-story main building behind it, and a number of wings connected by a central hall. At the western side of the site stood another stark two-story construction. There was an air of deprivation about the place, with nothing in the way of embellishment, no flower box or garden bench, no statuary or ornamentation. The windows were deep narrow slits, suggesting an interior dark and dank.

A door opened and twenty or thirty girls about Annie's age filed out, all wearing uniforms—dark smocks topped with full white aprons. They trudged in line, a dour matron marching beside them wielding a hickory stick, barking orders and delivering blows to any girl who moved out of step.

Even from where I stood I could feel Marni's outrage, and, at the same time, her restraint. She collected herself and strode toward what appeared to be the front entrance. Once she disappeared inside I moved closer. A placard hung beside an entranceway: BALLYVAUGHAN WORKHOUSE.

The sound of a cry turned my attention back to the formation of girls and their warden. The woman grabbed one sorry child by the hair, yanking her out of line. "Ye know there's no jabberin' on the way t' work! Wastes time better spent gettin' t' the task at hand! What ye need is the slothfulness beat out of ye! Learn the value of work!" She savagely whacked the cowering girl with her switch.

"Stop that!" I cried. "What do you think you're doing?"

The line of girls gasped and gawked at me. The matron froze, and slowly, deliberately turned from her sprawling victim. Her eyes widened at the sight of me, and then narrowed. The ire that screwed up her features melted into a cruel smile. "What do we 'ave 'ere?" she asked, tapping the switch against her palm. "An indignant do-gooder? Protestin' for the rights o' the poor?"

"There's no need to beat a child!" I cried. The gaping girls straightened up a bit and stared at me as though I was some strange, never-before-seen creature.

The matron's nostrils flared. "Here's what ye don't understand, missy. Pauperism is bred into 'em. Suckin' off the system fer generations. They need t' learn to be God-fearin' and productive, they do. That's me job. I'd suggest ye take yer fancy privileged self offa the property, before I call t' have ye removed."

I blinked, realization dawning. It was a poor-house. A work camp for those of no means. The little girls lowered their eyes. Their shoulders slumped. Acid rose in my throat as I stared at the self-righteous bully.

"I'm waiting for someone," I said, stubbornly holding my ground.

"Is that right?" The matron sneered. "So if I were t' announce ye to the warden he'd vouch fer ye?"

I hesitated.

"Jest as I thought. Be gone with ye then, before I alert the guards."

Frustrated, I turned and hurried back the way I came, my thoughts jumbled. What had led Marni there? What was her purpose? Did she think her son, now a grown man, was an inmate? Or had she been drawn to the parentless children, in the same way she'd been led to Walter, Georgie, Annie, and me, just when we needed her most?

I found myself back in the meadow surrounding the capt'n's farm, with no recollection of the route I'd taken—such was the extent of the anxious thoughts knocking about my brain. Not only about Marni and her quest, but of my own quest as well. When would the curse assert itself again?

And why was I plagued by the feeling I was missing something right before my eyes? I was surprised to nearly stumble over Annie, crouched before a small raised mound of earth. She was so totally immersed in whatever she was doing that she failed to notice me, despite my close proximity. Her attention was focused on the ground before her. She was speaking quietly.

"I know he made a terrible mistake. But he's an American, like me. We didn't know about these things—until we got here. And, besides, he's a boy. You know how they are."

Was she talking to herself? Or perhaps she was praying? She paused and there was a buzzing sound, similar to that of a bumblebee, except the high-pitched hum varied in tone, with a dipping and rising inflection.

I inched closer and my mouth dropped open. In Annie's open palm sat a tiny sprite—she was clothed in greenery, a delicate leafy frock, her shoes and belt crafted of tree bark. A necklace of miniature blossoms adorned her neck. The mystical creature's iridescent wings were the size and shape of a dragonfly's. Her face was surrounded by brown curls, and atop her tumble of hair sat a hollowed-out acorn cap. I realized that the buzzing was actually the sound of her quick and frenzied speech.

Itdoesn'tmatterwherehecamefrom.Heinsultedmeand mykind.

"Oh, but he learned his lesson—it will never happen again! Please, please, Nessa, give me the antidote! You trust me, don't you?"

Imightgiveittoyoubutifheoffendsmeagainhe'llbesorry!

"He won't, Nessa, I know this, for certain! I promise!"

Nessa rose from Annie's hand and began to flutter toward a small hole in the ground. Abruptly she pivoted in midair, and hovered. When she noticed me she let out a torrent of fairy buzz, so quick and agitated that I couldn't understand a word.

"Lucy!" Annie gasped. "What are you doing here? Fairies don't like to be surprised!"

Nessa tucked her wings in close, then sprang into flight. Like a bolt of light she made a beeline for the hole in the ground, and disappeared inside.

"Nessa! Nessa! Please, come back. Please! It's only Lucy! Lucy believes! Tell her, Lucy!"

"I . . . I believe in fairies," I mumbled. "I believed even before I saw you." I looked at Annie for help. She nodded vigorously, and I went on. "Had already met the Grey Man . . ." Annie shook her head. No! No! "But I know you're of a different class of fairies than he. . . ." Annie nodded encouragement. "A more . . . refined class of fairies . . ."

I heard the hint of a buzz and saw her peek out of the burrow. I ventured on. "In fact I have the greatest respect for all manner and members of the world we mortals can't usually see. And I too apologize for Walter. Ignorance was what it was, not rancor or disdain."

Nessa edged farther out of her lair, resting her elbows on the ground. She peeked between tall blades of grass, chin resting in her hands.

HowdoIknowyou'retellingthetruth?

I considered this for a moment. "Annie can vouch for my trustworthiness. She and I have faced many challenges together, and I believe she'd say that when I give my word, I mean it."

"Yes! Yes, Nessa, it's true! Lucy is brave and strong and isn't afraid to stand up for what's right! I love her very, very much!"

The sight of Annie speaking so passionately, with such conviction, brought me, once again, toward tears. Her face so earnest—eyes wide, lips pursed, her cheeks rosy with resolve.

Nessa slipped from her tunnel and zipped into flight, hovering just inches from my face. She peered at me, tipping her head this way and that, considering.

IfyoucanproveyoubelieveinmagicImighttrustyou. . . .

Before I could respond, Father's flute, in its usual place in my pocket, began to vibrate and hum, a sound not unlike her own fairy speech. The pixie's eyes opened wide and she cupped her ear. The flute nosed its way out and levitated toward her. She flitted around it, reaching a tentative hand toward the tone holes. As she touched it, a burst of glitter cascaded from it, riding the wave of the familiar melody—*a-lah-di-dah-dah-a-lah-di-dah-di*. . . .

Ohmygoodness!Itsbeenyearssincelheardthattune!

"You've heard that tune before?" I asked, incredulous.

AnoldmelodyfromtheislandIthink.

"You see!" Annie squealed. "I told you! Lucy believes in magic just like you! And so does Walter—he forgot for a moment, that's all! So you'll give me the antidote?"

Firstyouhavetogivemesomething!Somethingmagical!

She eyed the flute in the most covetous way and I felt a flash of anger. Fairy ransom! I couldn't possibly part with Father's flute! Nessa flew along the length of it, over and around, running her hand across the surface. I had the urge to grab the magical instrument and shove it back in my pocket. Annie watched me, wide-eyed and hopeful. And then the memory of Walter's infected finger. What had the horrible doctor said? Ten minus one? Was keeping the flute worth all that? I was ashamed at my selfishness.

Suddenly I had an idea. "The flute is magical, for sure, but wouldn't you prefer something smaller and lighter that you could easily carry? Something less weighty and cumbersome?"

Nessa zipped to a stop before me, her wings pulsating so rapidly they appeared as a sparkling blur.

What?Whatisit?

"A talking card."

Ooh!Showittome!

Annie looked at me anxiously. We both knew that the cards performed amazing feats at random, and spoke only when they felt like it. The rest of the time they lay in their ivory case like the bunch of musty old cards they appeared to be. And they often provided important clues about the past, about the treasure. I was regretting the offer already. Which card could I possibly part with?

Sensing my hesitation, Nessa became even more excited.

Yes!Yes!Amagiccardfortheantidote.

"Give us the antidote first," I demanded. "Then I'll give you the card."

Ifyoudon'tI'llshootWalteragainandshootyoutoo!

I didn't doubt for an instant that she'd have her

collection of fairy darts at the ready. Extortion is what it was, pure and simple. I would have enjoyed giving her a good swat! But Walter's health was at stake. There was nothing else to do but comply. "Agreed," I said. "Now, the antidote?"

Tonight,underthecupboard.Avialoftonicforhimtodrink.

"Good. Once we have the vial of tonic, we'll slip the card under for you." And, I thought, once Walter was well we could, once again, concentrate on the treasure.

Yes!Yes!Justkeepthatsnufflingbeastaway!

"Pugsley scared her," Annie explained.

"We'll be sure to keep him away," I said, shuddering at the thought of what havoc fairy darts in the snout might cause. "So we're in agreement? The antidote for a magic card? Tonight? After supper?"

Yes!Yes!UnlessIchangemymind!

17

We hurried back toward the house to share our news of Nessa's antidote.

"Look!" Annie pointed. "Someone's visiting!" A horse and buggy was tied to a post in front of the cottage. My heart dropped. Having visitors would complicate things. I was bursting to explain to Pru what had happened, and to figure out how to select a card from the deck for the antidote exchange. It had to be done by evening. And I still wondered about Marni visiting that horrible workhouse.

"Do you know who it is?" I asked, hoping against hope that whoever it was wouldn't further thwart my efforts to find the treasure and dispel the curse.

Annie shook her head.

"Whatever you do, don't say anything about Nessa in front of company," I warned.

Annie sighed. "I'm not a baby!"

"I know that—I'm just reminding myself." Which was true.

We pushed open the door. The sound of excited chatter poured out. "Oh, there she be!" A girl about my age bolted toward me. "Oh me gosh, Lucy, I know ye though never I've laid eyes on ye! Read all me mam's letters, I did, from the time I was just a wee one, hearin' tales of Aunt Addie's adventures in America!" Excitement lit the girl's delicate, heart-shaped face. Her long-lashed eyes and shoulder-length, thick hair were the color of honey. A sprinkle of freckles across her nose made her beauty a little less intimidating. Before I could respond she grasped my hand and pumped it in a hearty shake. "I'm Brigit, and this here's me mam, Aunt Addie's sister."

"Patsy," the older woman said. I studied Brigit and her mother, an older, less refined version of my Addie. Patsy grinned at me, revealing horsey teeth and an open, merry face. "Brigit ain't exaggeratin'. We two read every correspondence, followed yer adventures. Rooted fer ye every step o' the way, we did, from clear across the Atlantic! So when we heared Addie'd come t' Ballyvaughan we made the trip from Dublin t' see 'er fer ourselves. And t' meet the famous Miss Lucy!"

Addie beamed at her sister and niece, dabbing her eyes with a hankie. "Does me heart good to see all the womenfolk I love in one place!" she gushed.

Aunt Pru nodded. "I know the feeling. Family ties are stronger than steel." She threw an arm around my shoulder and pulled me close. Brigit and Patsy could barely contain their curiosity, scrutinizing Pru and me. I could understand their fascination with Pru. Without intending to, my aunt wore her worldliness—the stacked exotic bracelets, her Australian jodhpurs and white tailored shirt, the tumble of wild reddish hair, and the confidence that came with it. I was suddenly so proud of her, and grateful to be linked to her as family.

"Come! Sit down then, all of ye," Addie said. The table was already set for tea. "Wait, let me give dear Walter a hand," Brigit cried. "What with that terrible wound he's suffered. Very brave, he is, and so uncomplainin'!"

"Uncomplaining? Ha!" The words burst from my mouth. In all the excitement I hadn't noticed Walter sitting in the capt'n's wing chair. At Brigit's words he was already on his feet, eager, smiling, making a liar of me.

Brigit raised her pretty eyebrows for a second, then turned and took Walter by the arm, propping his swollen hand on her shoulder to keep it elevated. His finger lay there like a giant, overplump earthworm. I was suddenly out of sorts with both of them—Walter, miraculously transformed from the ornery, demanding person he'd been just hours before, and kind and understanding Brigit, who seemed a saint in his eyes. Saint Brigit! Reading my sour thoughts, Addie leveled a cautionary look—the one she'd reserved for times when I'd been on the verge of sassy. I glowered. Patsy looked away. What a first impression! I was making a fool of myself, and embarrassing Addie. And to make matters worse, the edges of Pru's mouth curved up in a smile, as if this was somehow funny.

I plunked myself into the chair and drew it up to the table. I hadn't intended for it to screech along the floor—it was as though the wretched seat was expressing my own sentiments. Everyone glanced up, then quickly away. Addie, in particular, was staring at me as though I was someone she didn't recognize. "Sorry," I blurted, and forced a smile.

"She's just clumsy," Walter said.

I glared at him and he laughed.

"Oh, what a tease ye are, Walter," Brigit said. "Lucy can sail a ship, an' ride a camel! How clumsy can she be?"

"I'm *not* clumsy," I said emphatically, reaching for the teapot. In my haste I knocked my cup on its side. It wobbled, rattling against the saucer.

"What's gotten into ye, child?" Addie asked. Brigit covered her mouth with her small white hand and giggled. Walter shrugged, a grin spreading across his face. I shot him a hateful look. When I realized Brigit was watching me, I tried to replace it with a neutral expression. My mouth twisted strangely with the effort. Beside petite, graceful, and polite Brigit, I must have seemed a fright— scowling, dirty overalls, a dark line beneath each of my nails, hair disheveled. With a clink and a clack I righted the cup, folded my hands in my lap, and stared at my plate.

During tea I said little, concentrating wholly on projecting poise and confidence. Walter managed to wolf down a couple of scones without moaning or groaning, despite his purple swollen finger. Perhaps the pain was decreasing and he wouldn't need the antidote after all. But if I went back on my word, Nessa would surely retaliate. So now, because of Walter we both had a fairy problem! It was all his fault!

The clock chimed—*bong, bong, bong, bong!* Four o'clock. Out of the corner of my eye I noticed a swift flash of light beneath the cupboard. Pugsley took off. Annie and I flew from the table, my chair toppling behind me with a bang.

"Who said she wasn't clumsy?" Walter quipped, making a big show of righting my chair.

"No, Pugsley!" Annie and I shouted in unison, dragging the eager pup away from the fairy hideout.

The smile was suddenly swept off Walter's face. He waved his hand. "Oh, ow! *Ow!*" he shouted, jumping from one foot to the other.

Brigit's eyes opened wide. "Oh dear," she said. "How can I help ye?"

"You can't," I said. "What he needs is an anti-dote, and I'm working on getting it. But then again, I might be too clumsy to manage that. Might be better that he try to arrange it himself." I crossed my arms and shot him a look.

"Aw, Lucy, come on. . . . Don't be that way!" Walter cried. He blew on his finger. "I was only teasing. . . ."

"All right, I can see we've enough high emotions fer one day," Addie said. "Whyn't ye put the dogs outside, and all of ye's head t' yer rooms to relax fer a bit while Patsy and I'll prepare fer the evenin' meal?"

"Good idea," I said, giving Annie the eye. We marched upstairs, collected the box of cards, and slipped into Pru's room.

"Tell her!" Annie said.

Before I could respond, the ivory box began to tremble. The lid rattled and flipped, sending a shuffle of cards catapulting into the air. In an instant three of the face cards hovered between us, all talking at once. "You're not sendin' *me* with some scheming little fairy," the queen of diamonds growled. "Get stuck in some musty underground burrow for the next three centuries? Forget it!"

"I don't know why you're worried," the queen of spades retorted. "Unless your power is so much less than that of a wee sprite."

Molly O'Malley, the queen of diamonds, shot back, "Then why don't *you* go—after all, you're the high and mighty pirate queen! Or so you think!"

"Why not let the fairy choose?" the king of diamonds interjected.

"Y'only say that because, given your history with women, y'know she won't pick you!" Molly said. The king of diamonds laughed wickedly. The two queens, Mary Maude Lee and Molly O'Malley, each leaned forward off their cards, viciously swiping at the man who had betrayed them both. It was hard to believe that these nasty, self-centered characters embodied the spirits of my own flesh and blood.

"Hold it!" Pru commanded, capturing the cards in one ferocious clap. "Somebody better tell me what's going on!" The muffled voices of the feuding queens and their king could be heard escaping between Pru's clasped palms. She looked at Annie and me. "Out with it!" she demanded.

Talking at once, we explained what had transpired.

"Oh my," she said. "That does put us in a bind. We need the antidote, but we also need the cards." A small diaphanous arm wormed its way out of Pru's grasp and pinched the soft skin along the inside of her thumb.

"Ouch!" Pru slapped the cards together more vigorously, forcing the ghostly appendage back into the magical card.

A nearly inaudible voice said, "You're going to need us to cooperate. Let us breathe and maybe we can figure this out."

Pru caught my eye. Her expression asked, *What do you think?*

I nodded. Annie exhaled. Pru carefully plucked the cards one by one and laid them out on the table.

Molly O'Malley, the queen of diamonds, spoke up. "I'm thinkin'—if I was picked, what would be in it fer me? Nothin' except the possibility of learnin' something about the treasure." She glared at her two rivals. "Information I wouldn't be sharin' with either of you!"

"What makes you think the fairy would know about that?" Pru asked.

The queen of diamonds shrugged. "These kinda fairies live for ages. Love sparkly things, inhabit the same realm as leprechauns—gold-digging opportunists, all of 'em. They inhabit the underground world where witchery reigns. And they're sneaky. See without bein' seen." She pointed a chubby finger at Edward, the king of diamonds. "One of their ilk could've been watchin' ya. Might know whatever it is you ain't sayin'."

Edward shifted his eyes back and forth. Mary Maude Lee raised her eyebrows, considering. "I'll go," she said.

"Ye will not," Molly retorted. "I'm goin'!"

"First nobody wants to go," Annie said, "now both of you do?"

Edward piped up. "I'll go. Save the, um . . ." He cleared his throat. ". . . ladies, if I may use the term loosely."

"Forget it!" the queens shouted in tandem.

"Let's make a deal," I said. The three face cards floated before me, suddenly attentive. "The one of you who can find out the most *and* that I can trust to pass along whatever you learn gets to go. But you have to prove you're the best candidate."

"But wait," Pru said. She picked up the queen cards. "You have no use for the treasure now. Why do you care so much?"

"I think I can speak for both of us," Mary Maude Lee said. "We both want to find out what this no-good traitor did with the treasure. All the trouble goes back to him!"

"Hmph . . . ," Molly said. It was as close as she'd get to agreement.

"Then, which of you promises to tell us everything you learn from the fairy?"

"No promises," said Molly, "until you can guarantee an eventual rescue."

"She's right," the queen of spades agreed. "Why should we tell you anything if you leave us in the fairy den for all eternity?"

"I've got it!" I said. "We offer both queens to the fairy. She can choose between you. Be as charming as you can and the one who impresses her the most wins the opportunity." I grinned at them. "And then, after you see what you can learn, we share the information with the queen who *wasn't* chosen, and trade in King Edward for the return of the chosen queen."

The king of diamonds flipped up and viciously sliced the air in front of my face. "Entirely not acceptable!" he shouted. *"Not acceptable!"*

"I think it's a grand scheme," the queen of spades said merrily. "Don't you, Molly?"

"Indeed I do!" Molly reached off her card and she and the queen of spades shook hands. Great-grandfather Edward threw a tantrum, pounding his fists, puffing his cheeks, a stream of curses exploding from his lips, sending his card reeling through space and onto the floor, where Annie promptly stomped it into submission.

Pru laughed heartily and grabbed my hand. "Lucy, my dear, you are a genius! I'd say we have our plan! Hold on to these cards to ensure that none of them disappear during dinner. And then we'll make the exchange!"

I took a deep breath and gathered the cards, hoping against hope that my wager would pay off—the antidote for Walter, and another possible clue for me.

18

I retired to my room before dinner, exhausted from the events of the day. My head was still spinning. Frustration with Walter propelling me into a stroll with Seamus, sharing the bough of a tree with him, and—my heart raced at the memory of it—a kiss! No time to even reflect on that before accidentally eavesdropping on Marni and Miss Oonagh, hearing Marni's desperate desire to learn about her long-lost son—to no avail. Trailing her to the workhouse, then discovering Annie with the fairy, making a deal, and coming home to find Brigit and Patsy. And still Marni hadn't returned.

I flopped back onto my bed and stared at the ceiling. I was still angry at Walter. And there was something else. How dare he flirt so shamelessly with Brigit! He made a fool of himself fawning over her. And she, over him. My thoughts skipped to Seamus—his blue eyes and dark lashes, his smile, his lips. . . . "Stop it!" I said aloud, my hands flying to my cheeks, which felt hot beneath my fingers. He was so charming, but I was startled to realize that I didn't completely trust him—why was that? Had I been influenced by all of Walter's chiding?

I grabbed a towel and headed to the bath, ran the water, and sat on the edge of the tub as the room filled with steam. Stripped off my dirty clothes and sunk in for a soothing soak. I closed my eyes and let the water envelope me. Dozed off dreaming of Marni holding hands with her blond-haired boy, Miss Oonagh blowing a smoke ring that settled like a lasso around Walter and Brigit. The talking cards taunting me, until the Grey Man slunk in, everyone disappearing in his midst. And a voice: *Find the treasure or the sea will find you!*

Suddenly I was surrounded by water, choking, thrashing.

I awoke with a start, the bath overflowing, brackish water pouring full force from the tap. I reached for the handle, turned it one way, then the other.

Hopelessly it spun. The bathwater turned dark, ominous—I could no longer see my body beneath the surface. I yanked the stopper. With a huge sucking sound the water began to swirl down the drain, the force of it pulling savagely against my toes. I attempted to climb from the tub, but was pulled back by the force of the current. I slipped and fell, a mysterious undertow sucking me beneath the surface. Salty as the sea, it was. My eyes stung. I coughed and choked, spitting the briny water from my mouth.

A knock on the door. "Lucy—are ye all right in there?"

"Addie," I sputtered, hands gripping the edge of the tub, hoisting myself up.

"I heard a terrible thunk, I did, worried ye slipped in the bath. Ye been in there quite a time!"

I pushed the dripping hair from my face, and looked down—not a drop of water was left in the tub. I stepped out, the floor beneath my feet cold, but completely dry.

"Are ye all right then?" she called.

"I . . . yes, Addie," I managed. "I'm drying myself off."

"Well, hurry up then dinner's close t' servin'!"

"I will." I listened to her retreating steps, staring at the dripping tap . . . *bloop* . . . *bloop* . . . *bloop* . . . the water taunting me.

I wrapped the towel around me and hastily escaped to my room. Sitting on the edge of my bed, I shivered. It was one thing for the sea to threaten me while sailing—it was another for it to pursue me on land. Suddenly the queen of spades, Mary Maude Lee, rose from the place where I'd placed her atop my bureau and hovered before me. "Remember," she hissed. "I'll do my part. But ultimately it's you who needs to find the treasure—or the sea *will* find you!" She narrowed her eyes. "Never underestimate me! Now, get yourself prettied up and get on with it!"

She floated off and settled facedown next to Molly. With trembling hands I attempted to drag a comb through my wet hair, and instead grabbed a ribbon, gathered the salty, tangled mess into a thick column at the nape of my neck. I pulled a simple frock from the armoire, yanked it over my head, and slipped the cards into my pocket. Glancing in the mirror as I headed for the door, I stopped and stared at the young woman looking back at me. But who I saw was Brigit. Unencumbered by a curse, carefree in a way I'd never known. Her blue eyes so much more arresting than my green, her silky, honey-colored hair curving in around her chin and falling gracefully to her shoulders. I'd always thought of myself as comely, in my own way, but next to Brigit . . . and it was clear Walter felt the same way. And on top of it I couldn't even dislike her!

Downstairs Addie and Patsy were laying out a feast—a ham, sweet with brown sugar, an Irish stew of lamb, potatoes, and carrots, applesauce, a pot of creamy potatoes and cabbage. The table was set for a crowd, and it seemed everyone was in the kitchen, sneaking a taste of this, a scrap of that. There was an air of festivity and anticipation that almost made me forget about my disheveled appearance.

"Oh, Lucy! There ye are!" Bridget said. "Been waitin' fer ye, we have. Now maybe we'll have time t' get t' know one another better!" She smiled, took me by the hand, and pulled me toward the sidebar. "Have a taste of me mam's ham! I saved ye the crispy edge, all crusted in sugar!"

The capt'n sounded the dinner bell. "Everyone's place is marked with a name card," he exclaimed. "Let's take our seats, all of us!"

A quick scan of the table indicated fourteen places set, each with a small folded card, our names scrolled in Addie's lovely script. There was Seamus, his hair slicked neatly back in beautiful shiny waves, looking scrubbed and fresh. He nodded at me, the edges of his mouth teased by a smile. Pulled out my chair and waved me toward it in a courtly manner. I blushed and slid into my seat. Old Peader found his place and plunked down, Rosie collapsing at his feet beneath the table. He tucked his napkin at his throat, eagerly clutched his fork and knife in fisted hands. Georgie and Annie sat on either side of the capt'n, Walter beside his brother. Brigit had been assigned directly across from Walter. Grady and Miss Oonagh shuffled in, with Pru behind them, all *ooh*ing and *ahh*ing at the table, complete with flowers and candles.

Despite all this I had the peculiar feeling of missing someone. Of course—Marni. There, beside me, was her name card, but her seat was empty. I sighed. It seemed that I was always waiting for the day she wouldn't return, my anxiety commensurate with her restlessness.

The capt'n stood beside his chair at the head of the table, and Addie at the opposite end—a pair of smiling bookends. Patsy, her white apron tied snugly, gestured with wooden spoon in hand. "That's the way, all of ye's seat yerselfs and I'll be doin' the servin.' Oh, thank the good Lord, there's Miss Marni now, just in time!"

Relief flooded over me. My shoulders relaxed and I was finally able to enjoy the delectable smells and lovely atmosphere. Marni slipped in quietly beside me and gave my hand a squeeze. She leaned over and whispered, "What a lovely piece." I followed her eyes beyond my knife and spoon. My mouth dropped open. I reached for the finely carved statuette that fit in the palm of my hand. The tree was unmistakable, its low, graceful boughs, two birds nestled in the branches, breast to breast. One's head was tilted toward the other. The larger bird had one wing extended, as though shielding its mate. I looked up at Seamus, speechless. But the expression on my face must have told him how moved I was by the beauty of the work and the memory of the moment. It was his turn to blush. He nodded, ran a hand through his curls, and looked away, smiling with half of his mouth.

"The wine is poured, unless ye prefer an ale . . . ," Patsy began.

"Sit, Patsy, please. You may serve if that's what pleases you, but first, as host, I would like to make a toast." We started to stand, but the capt'n motioned us to our seats.

"Oh boy, here it comes!" Miss Oonagh warned. Grady poked her with his elbow.

The capt'n cleared his throat, held his goblet high.

"Often, life can seem rather ruthless. I daresay everyone around this table has suffered some grave loss—the loss of loved ones, of a home, perhaps of a dream, a relationship."

The room was suddenly very quiet, the ticking of the clock marking the inventory we were all surely taking of the forfeitures we'd faced. It seemed the ghosts of those losses gathered about the table with us—my mother and father, Marni's son, Pru's brothers, Walter's mother and father, Miss Oonagh's Daniel, Old Peader's homestead. And, of course, the wife and daughter Capt'n Adams had lost all those years ago while away at sea. The capt'n waited. "Therefore, first I toast to all that's been taken from us, because we've been defined by what we've loved and let go of. And, it is, in many ways, our losses that have brought us together."

A lump grew in my throat. Marni fingered her locket. Annie, Walter, and Georgie held hands. A tear trickled down Old Peader's face.

"Let's get t' the good part already!" Miss Oonagh cackled, the heaviness of the moment lifted.

"So, I toast to a bright future," the capt'n continued, "to the hope life affords, to the power of love to restore and renew us."

"Here it comes!" Miss Oonagh shrilled.

"Yes, here it comes, indeed." The capt'n's eyes twinkled, and he walked around to the opposite side of the table, stopping beside Addie. "Miss Addie, here in the midst of all those we both have come to love and treasure, I have something to ask of you.

As a man who's been around the world and back, I see life as a journey." He dropped to one knee and took Addie's hand in his. "Would you travel on with me, as my first mate?" Her free hand flew to her mouth and tears sprung from her eyes. The capt'n's eyes brimmed as well. "What I'm asking is for you to be my wife. Addie, sweet, will you marry me?"

She flew to her feet and threw her arms around the capt'n, upsetting the glass of wine he still held in one hand. Suddenly both their faces disappeared in a long and passionate kiss.

Addie came up for air, turned to all of us, and shouted, "Yes, I'll be 'is first mate and wife, I will! Yes!"

We jumped to our feet, clapping, shouting congratulations, making our way to Addie and the capt'n, surrounding them in a huge collective embrace.

"Wait!" the capt'n shouted. "There's one more thing that needs doing!"

Miss Oonagh interrupted. "What needs doin' is passin' the ham and taters!"

"We'll get to that, I assure you!" Capt'n took Addie's hand, brought it to his lips, lowered it, and slipped a beautiful sapphire-and-diamond ring on her finger. She held it out to a chorus of *ooh*s and *ahh*s.

"Back t' yer seats so's we can drink t' the happy couple!" Patsy said. We took our places, lifted our glasses, and drank to Addie and the capt'n. "And now, in honor of me sister and future brother-in-law, I'll serve the engagement supper, I will!" Patsy announced.

"Hallelujah!" Miss Oonagh exclaimed as Patsy heaped the old woman's plate. The dinner erupted in a flurry of happy conversation. In seconds we were digging in, enjoying the delicious hearty fare, everything on our plates that much more delectable for the occasion it marked.

As I swabbed a piece of soda bread across a trail of gravy, cleaning off my plate, a flash of light caught my eye. Annie's mouth full of mashed potatoes dropped open and she pointed her fork at me. In all the excitement we'd forgotten about the antidote!

I gave Pru a kick under the table and nodded toward the blinking beacon under the cupboard. Her eyes opened wide as she pushed back her chair and stood. "Shall we retire to the parlor?" she suggested. "Come, come . . ."

"Well, I ain't cleared the plates and such," Patsy protested.

"Oh, I can't allow you to do that," Pru improvised. "Not after all the work you've already done.

No. Lucy, Annie, and I insist on doing that for you. You can serve up some of that famous Bushmill's whiskey while we clean up."

"I'm all fer that!" Miss Oonagh chimed.

"All right then," Patsy agreed. "'Preciate it, I do. Into the parlor!"

With that, the group filed into the next room, Pru shooed the dogs along with them and secured the door while I removed the two queen cards from my pocket. "Are you two ready?"

"Were born ready, the both of us," the jowly-faced queen of diamonds quipped.

"Indeed," the sleek pirate queen concurred.

"Annie," Pru said. "Here. Go ahead."

Pru and I stood back as Annie approached the cupboard. She dropped to her belly and spoke softly.

"Nessa . . . Nessa . . . it's me, Annie."

Nothing.

"I've got the magic cards. Come out."

Again, not a buzz or a flash of light. Annie turned and looked over her shoulder at us.

I whispered, "Try again. . . ."

"Nessa," she began. "I brought *two* cards so you can pick the one you like better! *Queen* cards! You get to pick between two queens!"

A sudden blink. Then another. *Twoqueens!Ohgoodie!*

ButfirstIwanttoseethemagic!

A small flutter, and the clever sprite's face appeared. *Showme!Comeon!Showme!*

"First you have to present the antidote, remember?"

You'rebeingmeanandselfish!

Annie replied, "Oh no, I'm not. You're just impatient. The antidote!"

Ohallright!

In a fluster she disappeared. A moment later she pushed a small, heart-shaped vial across the threshold of the cupboard. Annie reached for it.

Ohno!Don'tyoutouchituntilIseethemagiccards!

I took the cards from Pru and stepped forward. "Okay," I whispered to the queens. "It's your magic contest!" The two cards swooped into a loop-de-loop of flight, dancing in midair. Nessa, who'd been watching from beneath the cupboard, flitted out and, in a flash, took to flight. The three zipped and whizzed in a frenzy of acrobatic antics.

Oh!Ilikethisalready!Fun!Fun!

The queen of diamonds hovered and leaned off her card. "How about this?" she asked. "Magic spit!" She puffed her ample cheeks, puckered up, and spewed a cascade of glitter that swirled around the room in wisps and tendrils.

Ooh!Pretty!

As Nessa flew through the colorful spit cloud, Annie took the vial and handed it to Pru. "Nessa," I asked, "does Walter drink this all at once?"

Yeah,yeah.Allatonceisfine! As she spoke she reached for the queen of diamonds, but, not to be outdone, the queen of spades catapulted between them.

"Spitting is uncouth and lower class," the dark queen said haughtily. "But pirating is an art! Watch this!" She set her sights on a small silver salt spoon on the table, her line of vision apparent through a rainbow-colored beam, like light refracted through a prism. The tiny spoon trembled and rose, and the pirate queen's gaze lifted and directed it through the air and into Nessa's outstretched arms.

Oh!That'stheBESTmagicofall.Ipickthequeenofstealing!

The queen of diamonds pouted and sputtered. "Oh sure, one of ye's as dishonest as the other. Stealin' what isn't yers! Ye deserve one another, ye do!"

"Don't be a poor sport," Annie said. "She won, fair and square. We'll just have to keep an eye on our things!" My first thought was Addie's engagement ring. She'd better not take it from her finger for a moment.

"Okay, it's a deal. But one more thing," I added. "Nessa, if you take good care of the queen of spades, and if the antidote works, we'll give you another opportunity . . ."

What?Whatisthat?

"I have a different card—the *king* of diamonds. So when you're tired of the pirate queen, we'll trade her for the king! He has entirely different powers. How does that sound?"

Good!Good!NowI'mleaving!

The queen of spades floated horizontally toward Nessa, and turned to wink at me before the fairy hopped aboard. I said a silent prayer that the persuasive pirate queen hadn't lost her craftiness— that if there was something to be learned from the fairy about the treasure she'd tease it out of her. As though on a magic carpet they spirited off, doing one figure eight before diving down in a dramatic sweep and disappearing beneath the cupboard.

Pru held up the vial of amber-colored liquid. It glinted and shone. "Excuse me as I make my way into the parlor and pour this into a small jigger glass. Bushmill's for the rest—anti-fairy-dart potion for Walter!"

19

Walter barely got the words "thank you" out before guzzling the little jigger of tonic. His attitude became suddenly conciliatory, and I could see he was embarrassed about the way he'd behaved. I remained as aloof as I could, my feelings still a little bruised. It took several days, but gradually Walter's finger shrunk back to size. The purple discoloration faded to pink and finally to a normal, healthy flesh tone. This only added to the air of frenetic energy in the house, with talk of the upcoming wedding. The date had been set. In two weeks' time my Addie would become Mrs.

Obediah Adams. Always lovely, Addie appeared even more so, her face alight with joy and anticipation. It warmed my heart to see her filled with such happiness, and at the same time I felt an underpinning of loss and fear. Never again would she be *my* Addie in the same way—her life would instead be focused on husband and home.

I held this slight sadness and, I was embarrassed to admit, jealousy at arm's length, and tried to concentrate on my role in planning for the upcoming festivities. All this merriment contrasted with the threat of the curse, which seemed to be gaining strength by the day. Now that I was avoiding the tub, the kitchen sink vied for my attention, a blast of water shooting from the faucet every time I entered the room unaccompanied. At meals I'd wait until a small crowd had gathered so as not to face the watery warnings alone.

On this particular morning Miss Oonagh sat at breakfast with Marni, Old Peader, Brigit, and me, noisily slurping her tea. "Watch out fer the Straw Boys, I tell ye!" Miss Oonagh warned, wagging a bony finger in the air. "Them Straw Boys're up t' no good!"

"Straw Boys?" I asked.

Brigit smiled. "Oh sure, ye know, it's an Irish tradition. At the weddin' reception the local young men don tall pointy hats o' straw. Cover their heads an' faces, maskin' their identity." She passed a plate of scones, clotted cream, and jam.

Patsy nodded and set a platter of eggs and rashers of bacon on the table. "True—they come bargin' in, uninvited, wearin' them hats, drinkin' 'n' carousin', dancin' about. Bring good luck to the happy couple, they do."

Miss Oonagh stood. "Ain't what they seem," she asserted. "I sees it clearly. Trouble beneath them straw hats. Mark me words!"

"Oh, Miss Oonagh, don't be so anxious now," Brigit teased. "It's nothin' but a bit o' fun—a chance fer the uninvited t' take part in the celebration is all."

Miss Oonagh's silvery eyes narrowed. "Shut yer pretty piehole, girlie. I knows what I see. Ain't smart to make light of it!" After speaking her piece she dropped back into her chair.

Brigit's face blushed scarlet, and she lowered her eyes. Patsy pointed her serving spoon at Oonagh. "I know yer a guest here, but I'll not have ye speakin' rudely t' me girl!"

Miss Oonagh paid her no mind, shoveling eggs and bacon onto her plate.

"She *is* rude," Old Peader said, happy to have someone see things his way. "Rude and crude!" As if to prove his point, Miss Oonagh belched loudly and grinned, her gold tooth glinting. I covered my mouth to stifle a laugh.

Marni looked from one to the other, weighing Miss Oonagh's words. "Try not to take offense," she said to Patsy and Brigit. "Miss Oonagh says what she needs to say."

"That I do," Oonagh mumbled through a mouthful of eggs.

Pru strode into the room, map and notebook in hand. She sat, whipped her napkin onto her lap, and heaped her plate. "Today we have work to do. Head off to the Burren to find Molly's Inn. Was still in operation the last time I was here on the Emerald Isle—but that was almost a decade ago. Will be interesting to see what we find." As if on cue the queen of diamonds rose from Pru's shirt pocket and levitated over the table.

Brigit's mouth dropped open in a most unattractive way, revealing what was left of her scone. Her hand flew to catch the crumbs that tumbled down her chin. "What in the world . . . ," she began.

Old Peader shrugged. "After a while, with this group, nothin'll surprise ye." He dug into his eggs and tossed Rosie a piece of bacon. Pugsley barked and without even looking up from his plate, Peader threw another piece that was snapped up in midair.

Pru captured the card and returned it to her pocket. "Unusual cards," she said. "Been in the family for years." As if that explained it, she turned to me. "Molly's excited to give us a tour of the inn. See if we can find out anything that will help us on our quest."

Miss Oonagh straightened up, swiped her mouth with the back of her hand. "An' yer quest," she said to Marni, waving her fork. "Be over soon, it will. Yep."

Marni's eyes turned the shade of the sea on a stormy day. "And will it end well? Will I find what I seek?" Her words, heavy and charged, transformed the atmosphere in the room. Everyone fell silent. The capt'n and Grady both stopped short in the doorway, each with a cup of tea in hand. Even the dogs stood and stared between the two old women.

Oonagh froze, eyes fixed on Marni. For a moment I thought she was suffering a spell of some kind and might keel over, dead. Her lips moved silently, as though restraining rogue words. She finally stilled her face and blinked like an old lizard, her silvery eyes glinting. "A mother's love ain't never wasted," Oonagh said. She got up from the table and shuffled toward the door.

Marni's face sagged and she dropped her eyes to her plate of half-eaten breakfast.

"What kind of an answer is that, I ask ye?" Old Peader shouted. "No kinda answer atall! Poor excuse fer an oracle, that's what I say!"

Glaring at Old Peader, Grady took his mother by the arm.

Miss Oonagh stopped. "Watch out fer the Straw Boys," she cautioned, peering over her shoulder.

"Pay 'er no mind," Old Peader said. "Her an' her Straw Boy blarney!" He shook his head, the wispy tuft of white hair fluffing this way and that.

"It's time to go," Pru said. She stood, collected her plate and cup, and headed toward the sink. "Marni, you're coming. Lucy, find Walter."

"I'd be happy to come along 'n' help, I would," Brigit said, "with whatever it 'tis."

I'll bet you would, I thought, but before I could respond, Pru jumped in. "Thank you, Brigit, but I'm thinking Addie and Patsy might need some help with wedding plans. We can't all desert them, with so much to be done."

"Oh, course, yer right, I suppose," Brigit said wistfully. Pru turned and winked at me.

"Go on, then," Patsy said. "We'll manage without ye's. I've asked Seamus t' stay and lend us a hand. So we'll be fine here, we will." She shooed us out of the kitchen. Walter nodded and smiled, delighted, I'm sure, to leave Seamus behind.

"Wait—Walter's not had 'is breakfast," Brigit called. "Whyn't I pack 'im a scone an' an egg sandwich?" I waited while she scurried about. When she finished, I snatched the cloth sack she'd prepared.

"I'll see that he gets it," I said, making my way to the door. After all, I thought, rolling my eyes, we don't want poor Walter to starve. I trudged to my room to grab a sweater and a ribbon for my hair, and headed outside.

Pru and Marni, Walter, Georgie, and Annie were ready and waiting. Capt'n had provided us with a good-sized wagon and a pair of sturdy donkeys to take us out of town and into the strange land of rocky hills they called the Burren. Pru and Walter sat up front to drive the wagon, and the rest of us climbed in back. Annie and Georgie clutched food sacks as well, probably also provided by the always attentive Miss Brigit. The thought put me out of sorts with myself—Brigit *was* considerate, and Annie and Georgie would have been hungry. It should have occurred to me, but of course, it didn't. It was no wonder Walter thought she was wonderful.

A glance in Marni's direction shifted my attention. Her eyes still had that distant look, and she fingered her locket, as she did whenever she was pensive. "Maybe you needn't take Miss Oonagh's words to heart," I said. "She doesn't know everything."

"And sometimes she doesn't make sense," Annie said.

"It's called seen eye," Georgie said.

"Senile," I corrected.

Marni smiled with only the edges of her mouth, her eyes sad. "I can see the difference between insight and senility. When she's lucid her words ring true to me, even when their meaning isn't clear."

"You never stop looking, do you?" I ventured softly. "For your son."

Marni shrugged. "What was it Miss Oonagh said? 'A mother's love ain't never wasted.'"

I took a deep breath. "I saw you walking the other day—to that horrible workhouse outside of town. . . . You didn't think . . ."

"Not really. But the place was important somehow. I was drawn to it. . . ." Her voice trailed off. "You know, Grady told me Seamus grew up in a place like that—lived there until he ran off and talked his way aboard the Clare Island Ferry. Supported himself there by his wits alone. In many ways Grady helped him, but he actually saved himself. Quite remarkable." Her words took me completely off guard. I knew there was something mysterious about Seamus's past, but I'd never imagined him in a place like that. The very thought rendered me speechless and made me see him in a new light. We sat in silence for a time, the cart bumping over the road, Annie and Georgie gobbling their scones, the town disappearing behind us. The air was misty and cool, the sky white. I hoped the smell of woodsmoke was from the local chimneys and not the scent of the Grey Man, following us from Clare Island. It seemed that life was all about the pursuit of things—Pru and me, our treasure. Marni, her son. Seamus, a place to belong? The sea and the Grey Man, innocent victims . . . I wondered about the mysterious force that drew Marni place to place all these years. Was it misguided? It hadn't delivered the treasure she sought, but it had led her to Walter, Georgie, Annie, and me. But we were the consolation prizes. The thought made me sad. I wanted to be enough for her, as I'd wanted to be enough for Addie.

Soon the hillsides changed from velvety green to a patchwork of strangely shaped, mostly flat gray rocks. They erupted from the fields like puzzle pieces, fitting together in intricate designs. The farther we traveled, the more the green gave way to gray, with crooked channels of wildflowers and creeping foliage between. It became an ever more expansive mosaic of stone, turning the countryside into a harsh and haunting vista. We all fell still, each of us strangely alone together, gazing out over the desolate landscape. Perhaps they were all wondering the same thing as I—why in the world would Molly have come to such a remote place to establish an inn? Maybe that was the point—less chance of Edward finding her and the treasure.

"Look," Marni whispered. She pointed to a massive structure built of four standing wedges of limestone jutting from the ground like pillars, supporting a roof-like slab balanced atop. It resembled a lean-to, constructed of stone. How the builders had hoisted these weighty megaliths was beyond comprehension. "I believe it's an ancient tomb," Marni continued. The whole area had the feeling of a graveyard—still on the surface, with a multitude of secrets concealed beneath.

"Who's buried in there?" Annie asked, her eyes wide. "A giant?" She leaned forward for a better look, dropping her food sack with a loud clunk. "Oh no," she exclaimed, "I didn't mean it! Sorry! Sorry!"

"It's all right," I said. The sack rolled away with the rocking of the wagon. Annie scrambled for it, splaying herself across the floor. "Wait," I said. "What have you got in there?"

Annie grabbed for the sack, but I was quicker. I opened the bag and pulled out a large Mason jar.

Inside, an enraged Nessa pinged against the glass like a moth on a screen, wings fluttering furiously. Her face was red, her hands pressed against the glass.

"Annie! What were you thinking?"

"She wanted to come, but I was afraid she'd fly away. So I put her in—"

"A *jar*?" I shouted. I quickly unscrewed the lid and Nessa shot out, gasping for breath. She flopped onto the bench where we sat, wings wilted, lying on her back, propped on elbows and forearms. Her small chest heaved as she sucked large gulps of air.

Georgie dropped his lunch sack and threw himself into a heap on the floor. "She might shoot!" he yelled, hunkering down behind the seat.

"I didn't think of that," Annie whimpered. "Nessa, I didn't mean . . ."

YouAREmean!IalmostDIEDinthere!

"Oh, please," Annie sobbed. "I didn't mean it!"

"What's going on back there?" Walter called.

"Nothing!" I shouted. The last thing I wanted was for him to have another encounter with Nessa.

"Keep in mind, Nessa," Marni whispered emphatically, "Annie's but a child. She lacks the benefit of age and experience. . . ."

Nessa unfurled her wings that had been pale in color and were now pulsing again with brilliance and vigor. She rose and hovered inches from Annie's nose. Annie stared, her eyes crossed with the effort. Suddenly Nessa leaned to the right, zipped in that direction, and lighted on Annie's shoulder. I contemplated swatting her before she could take her revenge, but she wasn't, after all, a fly. She was human, in some sense, anyway.

"Nessa," I began. "Don't be spiteful. . . . Annie didn't . . ."

OOOHLook! She flew circles in the air above us, pointing toward the ancient lean-to tomb. *Fairies-downthereforsure!ATHINSPACEbetweentheworlds.Gottagothere!*

With that she was gone, a beeline of light following in her wake. We watched the directional beam of energy mark her route above the cart, across the field, under the limestone platform, and into the darkness beneath. "See! I knew I'd lose her," Annie wailed, tears muddying her cheeks.

"Good riddance!" Georgie said. "I'm ascared of her!"

"You're just as dumb as Walter," Annie cried. "Nessa was my friend! My fairy!" Her shoulders hunched up and down with her sobs.

Marni reached for her. "She'll be back—I feel sure of it! Wee folk are territorial. She'll be longing for her cupboard before the day's out."

"And," I added, "she'll be missing you as much

as you miss her."

"Not after you stuck her in a jar," Georgie said.

It took the rest of the ride for Annie to stop sniveling, the sleeve of her dress wet with tears. Pru slowed the donkeys, stopped, and studied the map.

Once again the queen of diamonds bullied her way out of Pru's pocket and floated in front of her. "Over there, for heaven's sake!" She reached off the card, pointing in a westerly direction. "Just beyond that hill."

"Thank you, Granny," Pru said, smiling.

"Don't call me Granny—makes me sound old."

"You *are* old!" Pru teased. We climbed out, hiked across a small hill, and scaled the stone wall.

"Oh my!" Prudence exclaimed. Molly gasped.

A crumbling foundation nosed through sprouts of grass and gorse, the area inside the perimeter void of the rocky puzzle pieces that characterized the locale. It was easy to see where a stairway had stood, and I could make out what must have been the walls dividing the place into a large common room with several smaller quarters behind it.

"It's been abandoned," Pru said, a frown pulling at her mouth. "I'm not sure what we can hope to find here now. . . ."

"Take me out and I'll show ye's a thing or two."

I plucked the card and held it out before me, sweeping my arm from left to right, providing a panorama of the place.

Molly leaned off the card, squinting. "Eyes ain't what they used to be," she complained. "Hold it! There!"

She waved her index finger to the east corner of the ruins, where a huge pile of rubble sat. "Under there—under them rocks! That was where I had the vault built!"

We all attacked the pile, Walter, Pru, and I hauling the larger stones, Marni, Georgie, and Annie the smaller. It was backbreaking work, made even more unpleasant by Molly's exasperated directives. "Move that big one—there, that's it! What's takin' ye so long? Heave ho! At this rate it'll be nightfall before ye're done!"

I looked at Walter, a large dirty rock pressed against my chest, and rolled my eyes. He grinned at me in the way he used to. It was so unexpected I almost lost my footing. Perhaps he'd forgotten that he didn't like me much anymore. I returned the smile, but not quickly enough. He'd already bent to retrieve another stone.

"Look!" Pru shouted.

"Yep, I think ye found it!" Molly whooped.

We circled around Pru and stared at the small

area she'd cleared. Visible below were the remains of a thick, hardwood trapdoor.

"That's where I hid the treasure!" Molly exclaimed. "And that's where it was stolen from!"

"It's worth a good look," Walter said.

We hauled off the remaining stones, slowly exposing more and more of the trapdoor. Most of it was still intact, though parts were worm eaten and weakened with rot. Finally we rolled away the last of the rubble.

"Okay," Walter said. He squatted, positioned one hand in the hole that once housed a handle, and got a good grasp with the other hand. "Here goes," he said. "One . . . two . . . three . . ."

20

The door lifted slowly. There was a flurry of movement in the darkness below. Had it become a den for some wild creature? Walter let go of the door and it slammed shut, sending up a cloud of dusty dirt.

"Could be a bear," Georgie said, eyes wide.

"No," Marni answered. "Haven't been bears in Ireland for centuries. I believe it's something quite tame." Her face had a look of intense curiosity and something like hope. "Open it slowly. We'll all grab hold and throw it back together."

Walter lifted the door just enough for us to curl

our fingers around the edge. We pulled, straining with the heft of the panel, but once it was upright, it pushed back easily. "Oh my!" Annie exclaimed.

Huddled in the back corner was a group of children about Georgie's age. Their faces were dirty and their filthy clothes hung like rags. A red-haired boy, wild-eyed, swift and cunning as a fox, attempted to scurry up the side and away, but Walter nabbed him. In a chorus of protests the rest scrambled out, surrounding Walter, with fists at the ready.

"What're you kids up to?" Walter demanded. The red-haired boy writhed and kicked.

"Let 'im go! He ain't done nothin'!"

"Yeah, we ain't botherin' nobody!"

I stared at a girl with gapped teeth, a headful of tangled, straw-colored hair. She wielded a stick that was not much thicker than her own skinny limbs. Something about her seemed familiar. That's when I noticed the smock she wore—the apron, once white, now gray and yellow with grime, its edges frayed.

"You're from the workhouse!" I exclaimed.

"We ain't goin' back there t' that hell hole," one boy yelled, raising a cheer from the rest. "We'll fight t' the death to stay on our own, we will!"

"We's banded t'gether, and we's stayin' t'gether!"

another hollered. More cheering seemed to bolster their confidence. There were eight of them in all, five boys and three girls, scrawny, scowling waifs. For a moment I imagined Seamus, as a child, among them. Yes, I could see where he got his independent streak, his boldness. It made sense. My heart suddenly went out to this brave, scrappy band of waifs.

Marni's face softened and she stepped toward them. She had a way of reaching out that inspired trust—just like the first time she'd approached me. "No need to worry," she said evenly, taking them in with those sea-green eyes of hers. "We have no intention of harming you in any way."

"Ye ain't from 'round here," the straw-haired girl said. "Ye talk funny!"

Marni nodded. "You, young lady, are very bright and observant. We're from the States, on a quest of sorts. But you needn't worry—our business has nothing to do with you."

I could see the girl immediately warming to her, basking in Marni's compliment. But a pale, freckled boy with jet-black hair crossed his arms defiantly. "Don't listen to her, Meg," he said. "Prob'ly a trick to get us t' trust 'em 'fore they catch us and drag us back there."

Meg chewed her lip. "Rory, ye don't know everthin'. Indeed, she does talk like a Yank."

Rory eyed Walter. "If ye don't mean no harm, let go o' Paddy."

Walter shrugged and released the red-haired boy, who'd been resisting so violently that he fell on his backside with a thump.

Georgie and Annie peered at the motley crew of children, surely appalled by their disheveled appearance. They were like a pack of feral dogs, frightened, hungry, and ready to bite. "What're ye lookin' at?" Rory demanded. He puffed up his chest and leaned toward Georgie. "Didn't nobody tell ye's it ain't nice to stare?"

Pru interrupted. "When was the last time you children had something to eat?" She knelt, removed a package from her satchel, and unwrapped a hunk of cheddar, some soda bread, and a knife. The modest snack became the focal point, the children's eyes and mouths open in anticipation. They inched closer, their small circle tightening, the cheese and bread drawing them like a magnet.

Rory held them back. "We don' need yer food," he said. "We's fendin' fer ourselves!"

The other children looked at him reluctantly, their shoulders slumping. I could feel their hunger in my own gut. Ignoring Rory, Pru sliced the cheese into small wedges, broke the bread in chunks, and arranged it all on a large rock. I glanced at Marni, expecting her to find a way to circumvent their pride so they could accept Pru's offering. But she was staring off to the east, facing the wind, her hair blowing back in a silver stream. Once again she had the look of a greyhound sniffing the air, poised for danger. I followed her gaze and my heart dropped. A cloud of heavy, dark mist was swirling in, gliding across the rocky ground, enveloping everything in its path. The unmistakable smell of woodsmoke pinched my nostrils and burned my eyes. "The Grey Man!" Walter exclaimed. "Quick! Take one another's hands so we don't get separated!"

Recalling our previous close calls, our little group moved swiftly together. Walter wove his fingers through mine and pulled me close. We reached and groped for the workhouse children, to bring them into the safety of our fold, but they scattered like frightened sheep, disappearing into the mist. In the second it took for us to connect, the sinister force overtook us, swallowing everything in its path in a thick, acrid sheath of smoke.

It was far worse than it'd been at Clare Island. We coughed and choked, wretched and gasped for air, only to be further strangled by the poisonous vapor. Still we clung to one another, terrified of being isolated and swept away by the force of the Grey Man's malevolence. We couldn't see one another at all, and if not for the intertwined fingers, I'd have believed I was all alone. Accompanying the physical pain was a terrible, pressing sense of dread, enough to make me want to give up and be overtaken by it. My legs and arms felt heavy, my brain lethargic. My knees folded beneath me. Someone was sprawled on the ground at my feet, but I could not respond to their need. The wheezing and panting of my friends seemed a far-off reality, and I drifted deeper into myself, my life force waning.

Suddenly there was a bright flash of light, a shooting zigzag of color slicing the mist. A buzz beside one ear, then the other. The narrow beams left a trail of color, a mysterious force scribbling in the air around us.

> *Youthinkyoucansuffocatemypeople?*
>
> *Wellyoucan't!*
>
> *Ifanybody'sgonnakillthemit'llbeme!*

"Nessa!" Annie rasped between coughs. "I knew you'd save us! The Grey Man's *nothing* compared to you!"

> *Atleastyou'rerightaboutthat!*

As if in response there was a deep rumbling sound like far-off thunder. The sky darkened ominously.

Nessa's iridescent scribbling dissipated, its color bleeding, tinting, and then erasing small areas of the Grey Man's vapor, creating pockets of breathable air.

BigBLOWHARD!Tryandcatchme! Nessa zoomed in crazy loop-de-loops and figure eights, creating a haze of rainbow-colored light. Her revolutions were so fast that my head began to spin. I had to shut my eyes to control the dizziness.

A clap of thunder, followed by a vicious, jagged bolt of lightning. I felt the hair on my arms stand up, prickling at the vindictive energy. This only seemed to encourage Nessa.

Hahahahahaha!Youdon'tscareme!What'salittlethunderandlightning?! She accelerated her colorful frenzy of flight, orbiting in larger and larger circles, leaving a trail of brilliant hues that steeped, then obliterated, the gray fog. The sound accompanying this feat was that of an entire swarm of bees, an angry, incessant buzz. I closed my eyes and held on tight, Walter's fingers still intertwined with mine on one side, Annie's on the other.

Gradually the buzzing diminished to a faint flutter, and the horrible pressure on my chest lifted. I cautiously opened my eyes. All that was left of the Grey Man was a wimpish curl of mist. A breeze tickled it and carried it off. The others, too, were coming around. I was aware of Walter untangling his fingers from mine, avoiding my eyes. I snatched my hand back and thrust it into my pocket. Nessa dipped in lazy arcs around us, gloating over her success.

Hahahahaha!IguessBIGGERisn'tbetter!

TaughthimaLESSON!

She zipped in front of Annie and hovered there.

NowIneedtoteachYOUalesson!

"Wait!" Annie cried.

Nessa tipped her head, considering.

"Think of the story you'll have to tell the other fairies," Annie continued. "And if they don't believe you, I'll tell them the whole thing!"

HowdoIknowyou'renotlying?

"If I don't do what I say you can shoot me with a fairy dart!"

"Annie!" Walter looked stricken. "You don't know what you're saying!"

"I know I'm telling the truth," Annie replied.

Okay.Okay.AslongasyoutellthemhowGREATIam!

"I will!" Annie promised.

Marni had pulled herself to her feet and stared out across the desolate landscape. "They're gone," she whispered.

My eyes darted from the pile of rubble we'd excavated and out over the rocky terrain, from east to west, north to south.

Marni was right. The ruffians from the workhouse had vanished without a trace.

21

The queen of diamonds nosed out of Pru's pocket. "May have disappeared, but they managed t' make off with the bread and cheese. Crafty ones, them urchins!"

Pru stared into the pit we'd uncovered. From the angle we were standing we had a full view of the chamber in which the treasure was once housed. "Look!" Pru said. The compact space was littered with things the children must have left behind—a small lantern, a bucket, a couple of threadbare blankets, and a pile of hay. "They used this place for shelter. And there—at the back of the vault . . ."

Three of the four stone-and-brick walls were mostly intact—but in the middle of the back wall was an opening, roughly three feet in circumference. "So, that's how they got in and out. . . ."

"Wasn't there in my day," Molly proclaimed.

My eye was drawn to the cornerstone—a huge, block-shaped rock supporting the back wall, just below the hollowed-out place. "What's this?" I murmured, kneeling before what appeared to be an etching. I peered at the design, ran my finger through the chiseled channel.

"Lemme see," Molly squawked, squinting over my shoulder. "It's 'is mark," she said, "the lazy lug who built this place. Dirk was 'is name. Couldn't read nor write, signed everthin' that way. Combination o' the first and last letter of 'is name. D–K."

"Wait a minute," I said. "Did you say Dirk?"

"That's what I said!"

The name was so familiar, but for the life of me I couldn't place it.

"I'm going in!" Walter exclaimed.

Nessa hovered at the portal, peering into the tunnel. *MEfirst!*

With that, she was gone, the light that still radiated around her dimly lighting the passageway. Walter hesitated, a frown forming as he examined his finger.

I gave his arm a squeeze and hoisted myself into the burrow. It had the musty smell of earth, and the air was cool and moist. Strands of invisible webs brushed my face. Crawling along the debris-strewn floor, my palms and knees smarted, but I persisted in following Nessa's lead. So close were the walls that my back often scraped the top, sending down a rain of dirt and pebbles. I had to concentrate on the light up ahead in order to fight off the claustrophobia that set my heart trembling.

Without warning I found myself in total darkness. "Nessa," I whispered. My mouth was dry and I fought the panic rising in my throat. "Nessa?"

Nothing. I considered going back, but it would be nearly impossible to reverse my path through the tunnel. While contemplating this, something skittered over my hand. I recoiled, heart thumping. I thought of Old Peader, buried alive, and shuddered. I had to keep my wits about me. I crept on, the narrow walls forcing me in the only direction I could go. As fast as I could I wriggled along until my head butted a solid wall. The good news was that I saw a bit of light off to the left. In fact, the passageway angled sharply in that direction. I slid through the opening, only to discover that the shaft grew even narrower, requiring me to slither on my belly like a snake. The hint of light was stronger now, perhaps coming from some greater source—hopefully the place where the tunnel ascended to the surface. I dragged myself forward on my elbows, pushing as best I could with my knees. My hands and the earth below them were finally visible, and a small draft of air brushed my face.

Suddenly I felt something tickling my scalp, moving through my hair. I shook my head violently.

HEY!What'reyoudoing?

"Oh! Nessa! Thank goodness! I thought you were a mouse. . . ."

That'sinsulting!

I managed to look up enough to see the shaft giving way to daylight, a circle of white sky, partially obstructed by plumes of grass.

Here'swhereitends!Outwego!

She stayed perched on my head while I propelled myself toward the mouth of the shaft, and heaved myself out. I wiped the dirt from my face, stared at my bloodied hands. My clothes were filthy, my hair surely a sight. I pulled myself to my feet and brushed off my clothes as best I could. The tunnel opened just over the crest of a hill beyond the ruins of the inn, its mouth well hidden. It was easy to see how the children must have entered the burrow from the treasure vault and scooted out the other end, undetected. And how

Dirk could have removed the treasure.

"Over here!" I shouted. I could see our group in the distance, still staring into the pit. In an instant they were running toward me. Nessa performed some fairy acrobatics, showing off what I'm sure she saw as her superior performance within the tunnel.

Walter arrived first, Georgie right behind him. "What did you find?"

Nothin'inthere!

"Besides dirt and bugs . . . ," I added.

"Yeah, but it's a way in and out of the vault!" Walter said.

"Yes," Pru added, "brilliant. The lay of the land and angle of the tunnel enabling the thief to remove the treasure out of view of the inn."

Molly flipped into the air. "Impossible!" she protested.

"Whoever went to that much trouble to dig a tunnel could have just as easily rebuilt the wall behind them," Marni said. "Without you knowing."

"No way the chest could've been spirited through that space," Molly retorted. "Nope. Too small."

"It was a long time ago," Walter mused. "Sections must have caved in. Those kids probably discovered it and dug it out to make it passable."

Pru tossed back her mane of curls and ran her hands through the thick tumble. Her face was still smudged with the Grey Man's soot. "Walter's right," she said. "But that brings us to another dead end. Let's assume Dirk dug the tunnel and was actually able to move the treasure chest through and out the other end—then what?"

We looked across the Burren—miles and miles of the same rocky, treeless countryside. No place to hide. Molly floated up for a panoramic view. "I woulda seen 'em makin' their getaway."

"But you didn't," Pru said.

Nessa flitted before Molly, and took hold of both sides of the card.

"Unhand me!" Molly demanded. "Let go!"

Wouldbenicetohavetwoqueens!

"Oh, no ye don't!" Molly squawked, repelling the hovering imp, the edge of the card straining against Nessa's hands. "You didn't want me before, and ye ain't gettin' me now! A deal's a deal!" Nessa held tight, and the two of them engaged in an in-flight dance, circling and dipping. Molly reached off the card, attempting to pry herself from Nessa's clutches.

Pru nabbed the card, Nessa still clinging to it. "That's enough!" Pru said. "Molly's right. A deal *is* a deal!"

Nessa let go with one hand and rotated toward Pru. *WhatifIknewsomething?*

"Like what?"

Secrethiddenplaces—likewhereyoucouldburyatreasurechest?Or-hideout.Theancientweefolkknowalltheundergroundspaces!

Pru expertly flicked the card, disengaging Nessa's remaining hand.

"Thank you!" Molly said, straightening up and settling back.

Pru held the queen of diamonds before the fairy, just out of reach. There was not a shred of fear or trepidation on my aunt's face, her jaw set, brow creased, gaze steady. "Nessa—tell me what you know, and *if* what you have to say yields some result, the card is yours."

"What are you saying?" Molly yelled. "No fair! I'm your granny, after all!"

Pru ignored her, staring intently at Nessa, willing her to reveal something more.

Ohyesyesyes!

Nessa grabbed for the card again, but Pru withdrew it. "Think about it first, Nessa. Because if you're toying with me, I promise one of us will catch you and put you back in that jar. I'll put some holes in the top so you can breathe, and drop in some bugs now and then for your dinner, a few drops of water, but that will be it."

Annie and I gasped. Walter's face turned white. Nessa's an angry shade of red. In one swift move Nessa reached into a breast pocket and withdrew a glistening hairlike shaft, slipped it into a hollow blade of grass, and brought it to her lips. Pru didn't so much as blink. Again she waved the card in front of her.

Nessa hesitated. *IcouldshootyouRIGHTonthenose.Wouldn't besoprettyTHEN,wouldyou?*

Apparently the thought of a huge purple nose didn't phase my aunt in the least. "Go ahead," Pru said. "What you don't know is that we still have the antidote. Only used a drop for Walter." Annie opened her mouth to correct her, but Walter silenced her with a look.

You'rebluffing!

"Try me," Pru challenged. "Annie, go get your jar from the wagon."

Nessa's bottom lip curled in a pout as she reluctantly lowered the dart.

Iwon'tforgetthis!

"It's good that you remember. You'll think twice the next time you decide to go back on your word, or extort something from us that you decide you want."

"I could say the same thing t' you!" Molly yelled, waving a thick finger at Pru. "Two of a kind, you and that bug of a fairy!"

Pru smiled. "Perhaps," she said. "That's why we understand one another, isn't that right, Nessa?"

Yes!Yes!IfItellyouwhatIknowyou'llgivemethecard?

"*If* what you have to say proves helpful. That's the deal. And if what you say turns out to be nonsense, we'll catch you and put you in the jar. So think carefully before you speak. This will ensure that neither you nor the queen of spades goes back on your word. A little incentive for you to come up with something useful."

Marni looked at Pru, a slight smile playing on her lips. She nodded, almost unperceptively, affirming the plan.

I'lltellyouinafewdays.Haveafewthingstocheck!

"I'm sure you do." Pru turned to us. "I think we've accomplished what we came for, don't you?"

We gathered our things and climbed into the wagon. Pru snapped the reins against the donkeys' rumps, and the cart jolted forward. It bumped over the dirt road, carrying us back toward Ballyvaughan. If we hurried we'd arrive in time for dinner.

As we rode I had the peculiar feeling we were being watched. I glanced over my shoulder as we rounded the bend.

That was when I noticed, just over the crest of a distant hill, eight small figures watching our retreat, their ragged clothes flapping in the wind.

22

Pru, Marni, and Walter headed to the stable with Annie and Georgie traipsing behind. While they unhitched the donkeys, I walked toward the cottage. I could feel the high spirits overflowing from within the capt'n's house as soon as I opened the door. In the front room stood a seamstress's form holding a gown of ivory-colored crochet lace, its intricate design of flowers and delicate vines flowing over a layer of silk chiffon. It had a high neck and long slender sleeves, the skirt gliding over the hips and pooling beautifully against the floor.

"Crocheted most of it meself," Patsy mumbled

through a mouthful of pins held between her lips. She squinted critically at her creation, tucking here, smoothing there.

"It's gorgeous," I gasped, trying to imagine practical Addie adorned like a queen.

"Brigit's in the kitchen, peelin' taters—whyn't ye wash up an' give 'er a hand?"

"I will. . . ." I dashed to the bathroom, hesitating before the sink, its faucet menacing me. Instead I grabbed a damp, rather mildewed wash rag and did a quick scrub of my face, arms, and hands, then rushed to my room to change my dirty clothes. I reached for a clean pair of overalls, then reconsidered. Instead, I grabbed a simple blue cotton frock with a long belted tie that accentuated my waist. I pulled it over my head and fumbled with the row of annoyingly small black buttons that ran up the front of the dress. Glancing in the mirror, I tried to see myself as Brigit would, and frowned. My hair was an unruly fright of dark red curls. I had a scratch across my right cheek, and the sleeves of my dress were a bit short, giving my arms a gangly appearance. There was a perpetual sense of impatience and haste about me, as though I was in a rush to get someplace—which I was. I forced myself to stand perfectly still, to exude the kind of soft, ladylike air that Brigit had—and for a fleeting

instant I caught a glimpse of someone else, someone I thought Walter might prefer.

But who cared what Walter preferred? I tossed
my hair from my face, captured it in a loose ribbon, and started downstairs. Miss Oonagh and Old
Peader sat in the parlor, Old Peader's head thrown
back against the chair, his mouth agape, snoring
lightly. "Catchin' flies," Oonagh cackled. She was
tamping her tobacco, preparing for a smoke. "Better get yer arse in that kitchen," she said, striking
her match, then sucking the flame into the bowl of
the pipe. "B'fore that blondie steals yer beau!"

"Ha," I said. "Walter's not my beau!"

"Ha!" she responded, her face shrouded in
smoke. Annoyed, I made my way past her, toward
the kitchen. Before I even stepped into the doorway
I heard the sound of laughter. Something about it
gave me a peculiar feeling in my gut, and I hesitated for a second before I ventured in.

I stopped short, undetected. Brigit had a half-
peeled potato in one hand. Her other hand lay on
Seamus's arm, a wide smile across her pretty face.
His back was to me. "Watch this, Brig," he said,
expertly juggling two, then three potatoes in the air.

"Oh, Seamus," she crooned, "ye know how t'
make a girl laugh, ye do!" I must have moved, or
perhaps they heard my sharp intake of breath.

"Oh, look—Lucy's here!" Brigit gushed. Was the blush on her cheeks in response to Seamus's attention, or to me catching them at . . . what?

Seamus spun around, and without missing a beat grabbed another potato, adding it to his juggling feat. "Fer you, Lucy—four potatoes!" I forced a smile, but my face felt stiff, Miss Oonagh's words resonating in my head . . . *B'fore that blondie steals yer beau!* I stared at the circling spuds, which he was only able to keep in the air for a second before three of them thunked to the floor. Patsy entered just as the trio of taters rolled across her path.

"What in the good Lord's name are ye's doin'?" she asked, bending down and scooping up the dented spuds. I shrugged, the same question poised on my lips. Patsy wiped the potatoes on her apron. "Been hearin' an awful lotta whisperin' and laughin' in here this afternoon, I 'ave."

I turned on my heel.

"Lucy!" Brigit called. "Wait! Where're ye goin?"

I ignored her, stomping back into the parlor, nearly colliding with Walter. "What's got you all fired up?" he asked. I scowled.

Miss Oonagh chuckled, sending puffs of smoke out of her mouth like an ancient dragon. "When the cat's away, the mice'll play. . . ."

Walter raised an eyebrow and Miss Oonagh

pointed her pipe toward the kitchen. Brigit and Seamus emerged, grinning sheepishly, Patsy's voice following them. "Enough o' yer nonsense!" she yelled. Brigit giggled, but stopped abruptly when she caught sight of Walter.

Hungry as I was, I dashed out of the parlor and up the stairs to my room. Behind my closed door I could hear their muffled voices—Walter's agitated and edgy, and Seamus's laughing. "Hahaha," I whispered bitterly. "Very funny." I picked up Seamus's bird carving that had been gracing my bureau. I had the urge to toss it out the window, but something stopped me. I flopped on my bed, fingering his gift, staring at the ceiling. Tried to refocus on the treasure, or the wedding—anything but Seamus and Brigit flirting their way through the afternoon. With a sigh I pulled the box of clues from beneath my bed, sprawled across the quilt, and spread the papers before me. Our family tree, Pru's careful notes outlining what we knew thus far. The deck of cards, minus the queen of spades. The sight of the *Buccaneer*'s manifest Seamus had torn from the harbormaster's book taunted me. Just as he'd shown off for me, he'd been showing off for Brigit. And then to have the pilfered prize reveal nothing . . .

I unfolded the ragged-edged pages, once again scanning down the familiar script.

But wait. One name caught my eye. I sat up. *Dirk Coogan*. Wasn't Dirk the name of the fellow who had built the vault for Molly? What had she called him? *A lazy lug.*

But if he'd been a crew member on the *Buccaneer*, wasn't it possible he'd somehow suspected what Molly had been transporting, and what she'd be locking away in that vault? And there was something else.

With trembling hands I whipped out the pages Capt'n Adams had snipped from his log. My eyes devoured his careful notes. There it was! Our crew listed by first and family names—*Quaide Coogan*!

I sat back, grasping at the import of this. Finally, the connection between Quaide and the treasure! It had begun with this Dirk, who must certainly have been an ancestor of Quaide's—his grandfather, I'd guess.

A knock on the door interrupted my musing. I quickly stowed the box back under the bed. I couldn't wait to tell Pru what I'd discovered! "Who is it?" I called.

"Addie—heard me girl was out o' sorts. Thought I'd bring ye a little supper."

My stomach let out a huge, hollow growl. "Come in."

Addie pushed open the door and placed a tray

on the foot of my bed. "Brigit didn't say a word at table. Picked at 'er food. You two start off on the wrong foot?"

"No," I said, unconvincingly. "She's really nice . . ." The word *but* dangled silently in the air.

"Waited all these years t' meet ye, she has. I know ye both, and each of ye's so much t' offer the other. Be a shame if ye let some silly boys come between ye's. Told her the same thing, I did."

I looked up. Addie's face was a mix of concern and sadness. Here it was, just days before her wedding, and she was worrying about her two bridesmaids getting along. And instead of helping with the wedding plans my head was filled with thoughts of the Coogans, Quaide and Dirk.

I stood and threw my arms around her. "You're right, Addie. I think Brigit and I could be friends." The words rang false to me, but the way Addie's face lit up reminded me I had to try.

"Grand!" Addie exclaimed. "That's me girl! Patsy's finished dresses fer the two o' ye's. And one fer Annie too!"

The next days were filled with preparations— the flowers and the food, the cake, the cooking and cleaning—all of this difficult for me, trying to avoid any manner of running water. I did my best to ignore the taps that gushed as I passed, but slowing to a dribble as others approached. The threat was always present, casting a shadow of foreboding on what should have been a most happy time. That and the certainty that Quaide would surely surface again. Pru and I were sure of it.

A canopy was raised in the yard, to keep the inevitable shower from wilting the ladies' finery. The pastor of the local parish, Father Lynch, grudgingly agreed to conduct the nuptials out on the farm instead of in town at the church. Lovely as the church was, Addie felt that a wedding should take place where all God's creation could rejoice—exchanging vows to a chorus of birdsong and crickets, sheep dotting the meadow in the distance, dragonflies darting between the guests.

Brigit and I forged a truce of sorts by avoiding any mention of Seamus and Walter. Instead we spoke of nosegays and tablecloths, petticoats, and hair ribbons. All the while thoughts of pirates and the curse swirled inside my head. Walter, Seamus, Grady, and Georgie hauled fifty chairs from the church hall for the wedding guests, and laid out sawhorses topped with wooden planks to serve as banquet tables. As they set them beneath the tent we covered them with linen, lace, and thick, pale pink bows.

I tried to get Annie to help, but she was out of

sorts, cranky, and given to sudden bouts of tears—Nessa had not been seen since we'd returned from the Burren. Annie sulked around Prudence, holding her responsible for the fairy's desertion. "You scared her off with the jar," Annie moaned.

My aunt remained pleasant and patient. "Remember, the jar was *your* idea," she reminded her, chuckling. "But not to worry. The fairy'll be back—when she has something of value to share."

This did little to allay Annie's fears. And with all the hustle and bustle she wasn't getting the attention she saw as her due, so she demanded it in other ways—dropping a glass goblet, traipsing through the mud and tracking it into the house. After a good scolding from Patsy that brought an onslaught of tears, Annie took another tack—hiding here and there in the house, refusing to come when summoned. Walter and Georgie would spend a good part of an hour searching the house and yard, until Miss Oonagh would fire up her pipe, bellow her cheeks, and blow fancy smoke rings—once a zigzag of hazy steps that led them to find Annie huddled under the stairwell, another time a puff that transformed into the shape of a bed. Sure enough, they discovered Annie sprawled beneath Marni's bed, covered in dust balls. Old Peader laughed silently, his shoulders rising and falling.

"Let's ship Oonagh off to the circus," he croaked. "Or the carnival side show. Never seen such a talent fer smoke breathin'!"

As I laughed the old woman reached out and grabbed my arm. Her grip was surprisingly strong. "Don't ferget this," she hissed. She held me with her silvery eyes, inhaled deeply, and formed her lips like the spout of a teakettle. She exhaled in a long, smooth breath, the smoke tumbling into the air between us. Georgie stood gaping alongside me as we watched the vaporous design take shape. It was the same peculiar pattern that she'd drawn on the hearthstone back on Clare Island, the ring with rays protruding like a lopsided sunburst.

"What is it?" he asked.

"Told ye before. That's where ye'll find what yer lookin' fer."

"But . . . ," I began, struggling to grasp her meaning.

"An' beware o' the Straw Boys!"

Old Peader rolled his eyes. "Now she's back on that again. . . ."

Frustrated, I retreated to the kitchen to see what had to be done next. As I entered I saw Marni placing a parcel on the back stoop. Rory, the black-haired boy, and his red-haired friend, Paddy, reached for the brown-wrapped package. Hungrily they untied the string, revealing the food stashed inside. "Let me get you a jug of cider," Marni said. As she turned, they spotted me, and the waifs started to run off. "Wait," Marni called. "You needn't be afraid of Lucy. We're all friends here."

Rory, clearly the leader, shrugged, deciding that the prospect of a jug of cider was too good to pass up. Marni went to the cupboard and I walked to the door. The rest of the children were hiding behind a large outcropping of rock at the side of the pasture. When I stepped outside they scattered like a flock of birds. "Here you are," Marni said. "Come back tomorrow and I'll have something more for you." In an instant the two ran off. Rory whistled loudly, signaling the rest of the group.

"Hunger is a terrible thing," Marni said.

"How did they find us?"

"Likely followed us from the Burren. I saw them scavenging through the compost pile the other day and called them over."

I felt a lump form in my throat at her kindness—the same kindness she'd shown to Walter, Annie, Georgie, and me. Before I could say a word I heard Annie's voice from the parlor—her tone so different from the whining of the last few days.

"I'm going to wear it to the wedding!" she announced. "Over my dress! I'll look like a princess!"

Old Peader muttered something about it not being suitable for a little girl. Oonagh piped in, her voice carrying above the rest. "Some siren's missin' 'er cape," she shrilled. "Like a duck outta water, stuck on land!"

Marni and I bolted toward the door, and there was Annie, the sealskin cape thrown carelessly over her shoulders, its heft dragging on the ground. She pranced about, chin held high. "I'll be the best flower girl in the whole wedding," she boasted, grabbing the edge of the cape with one hand, swirling it in an arc around her. To my chagrin Grady walked in and stopped short, his mouth agape.

Marni's face became a mask of steel, the color draining from her lips. We all stared at her, all the old doubts about her affinity to the water resurfacing. Hadn't Walter's father called her a "sea nymph," a "witch of the sea"? All of those instances of her swimming in the deep, with a strength and stamina not quite human.

Sensing the tension in the room, Annie stopped cavorting, and suddenly the attention she craved seemed too much for her. "I'm going to my room," she said, lifting the cumbersome silvery cloak and marching toward the stairs.

"Wait." Prudence took Annie gently by the

shoulders. "This clearly doesn't belong to you. Where did you get it?"

Annie's bottom lip trembled but she stubbornly stuck out her chin. "I didn't *steal* it," she said. "I found it. I was hiding in Marni's big trunk and it felt soft like a kitty. I just borrowed it. You'll let me, won't you, Marni?" She looked desperately at Marni, who still seemed stricken. Marni lowered herself into a chair, looked away for a second, and sighed deeply.

"I wish I could let you wear it," she said. "But I cannot do that. Please, as Prudence said, return it to my chest."

Annie hoisted the length of sealskin into her arms, her face red with embarrassment, and stomped up the stairs. No one moved until the sound of her steps disappeared, the air in the room charged with questions. Grady pulled one side of his mouth into a grimace and avoided Marni's eyes. "Always knew there was somethin' funny goin' on," he grumbled.

"I know the siren stories," Old Peader said, eyeing Marni suspiciously. "Ye could be one of 'em, if I didn't know better."

"What in God's name is she doin' with that cloak?" Grady demanded, as if Marni was not present.

"Fer her t' know and you to find out!" Oonagh teased.

Marni rose, her eyes fixed on the stairway where Annie had disappeared, and without a word, she followed her up the stairs.

Grady rubbed his chin as if doing so might produce the answers he sought. "Just come back from town," he said. "Down at the pier." He removed his cap, smoothed his hair, and replaced it on his head. "And if it ain't strange enough t' have a lass in a siren's cloak, there's this: way out in the harbor, right on the horizon, I seen two ships." He looked at me and Pru. Nodded. "Yep—the specter ship, and, impossible as it seems, the black ship right behind her."

23

The day of the wedding dawned sunny, the earth green and sparkling with dew. The little wren that lived in the tree outside the cottage warbled a glorious song announcing the festivities. There was a sense of magic in the air, everyone's spirits soaring. I pushed away the sense of foreboding that had plagued me since Grady's announcement about the ship sightings. Had Slash made it back aboard the black ship, sharing what he'd discovered on the *Lucy P.*? Grady, Pru, Marni, Walter, the capt'n, and I'd checked repeatedly with the harbormaster, perused the piers and shoreline, with no sign of either ship. I'd even gone so far as to board the *Lucy P.*, scale the mainmast, and, from the crow's nest, check the seas and shore as far as the eye could see with Father's trusted spyglass.

Nothing.

Grady continued to swear by what he saw, and I wondered if perhaps he had inherited the mental confusion that sometimes afflicted his mother. Sensing my mistrust, he became surlier than usual, but this was easy to ignore.

My dress, of dusty-rose satin, trimmed in delicate lace with beading on the bodice, had been laid across my bed and matching hair combs set out on my bureau. With Pru stationed outside the bathroom door I'd risked a bath, thankfully without incident. Still smelling faintly of lavender and rose water, I slipped into my robe and sat on the edge of my bed, gazing out the window. A sense of unreasonable sadness seized me—while Addie's life was moving along, Prudence and I were still mired in the wretched family curse. Despite our best efforts we still didn't have the answers we needed. We were no closer to finding the treasure. No closer to returning to Maine, to Simmons Point. Perhaps we never would, and, like Marni, spend our days searching for something always just out of reach.

As if my disloyal thoughts had conjured her

up, there was a soft knock on the door, and Marni entered. She smiled gently, immediately sensing my mood, sat beside me, and laid a hand on my arm. "We have to remember that today belongs to Addie alone," she said, fingering her locket. "And continue to believe that our day—yours, and mine— will come."

I turned toward her. "What if they don't? Suppose you never find your son? And I don't find the treasure?" I felt dangerously close to tears.

She sighed. "Then we graciously accept the unexpected gifts. Imagine if I was blind to the blessings handed me—you, Walter, Georgie, and Annie. Addie and Pru. The opportunity to see the world. If I'd been focused solely on my need, look at all I might have missed."

"Yes, but—"

"No buts."

"Marni . . ."

She waited.

"The cloak . . ."

"The cloak." She smiled wryly. "You're worrying about what it means."

"Every time you disappear into the sea I think it may be the last! It's as though the ocean is your calling. I felt it from the first time I laid eyes on you, out there in the harbor in Maine. Then at sea.

On Clare Island. There were rumors. Grady still thinks—"

"That I'm a siren. A merrow." She chuckled. "I'm not. If I had been, and I'd reclaimed my cloak, wouldn't I have returned to the sea long ago?"

"But—"

"My mother, Mary Maude Lee—"

"The pirate—"

"Yes. True, my mother was a pirate. Ruthless. Cold. There was a reason she was fearless at sea. *She* was a siren. My father—your great-grandfather— saw her sunning on the rocks at Clare Island. He captured her and stole her cloak."

I gasped. "How awful."

"All she wanted was to return to the sea. That being impossible, she took to ships, and pirating. She was aloof and cunning, and had a streak of cruelty commensurate with the loss of her freedom beneath the depths."

My heart sank. What a terrible thing for my great-grandfather to do. I thought of a caged bird, a chained dog. "How mean! To keep her prisoner on land just because he wanted her!"

Marni nodded. "Once she had a chance to return to the sea. She'd discovered the cloak hidden in the thatch of Edward's cottage."

"So why didn't she?" I imagined this beautiful

pirate queen, throwing the silvery cloak around her shoulders and diving into the ocean, her legs dimpling with scales as the water rushed over her, feet giving way to a wide, fanned tail.

Marni looked wounded by my indignation. She sighed again. "Because her twelve-year-old daughter found the cloak and moved it where she knew her mother'd never find it."

"Oh!" In an instant I understood. Marni blamed herself.

"She resented me for the rest of her life."

"Marni, I'm so sorry. . . ."

"I'd often wondered if the disappearance of my son was, in some way, my recompense. A rather useless thought."

"You loved her. . . ."

"I needed her. And I kept waiting for her to love me." She stood. "If we don't hurry, we won't be ready in time. Your aunt is already looking like a vision from London, or Paris. . . ."

I looked at my friend, framed in the doorway, her eyes the color of the sea. Half siren, half pirate, but with a heart so much bigger than both of her parents combined. "Marni . . ."

"Yes?"

"*I* love you."

"I love you too."

I stared at the door for a moment after she left, still taking in her story. Then I pulled on my petticoat and dress, buttoned and tied, tugged and primped. Pru arrived and twisted my hair into ringlets, pinning them up in a swirl of graceful swells, securing the coif with the elegant beaded combs.

"Dazzling," she said. "I might need to borrow one of the capt'n's walking sticks to fight off the young men once they get a glimpse."

"Hmph," I said, thinking of Brigit and Seamus. But then I remembered what Marni had said—that the day belonged to Addie. I picked up my skirts and followed my gorgeous aunt out the door.

Downstairs everything was astir! Old Peader stood before a mirror admiring the cut of his clothes—the tall, wiry scarecrow of a man transformed into a gentleman in a vest, a charcoal-colored topcoat with satin lapels, and a black bowtie. Walter, in similar garb, had his dark straight hair slicked back, making him appear years older—and almost a stranger to me. I hadn't remembered his eyes being so dark, his brows so intense. Patsy, making her way through the chaos, giving orders left and right, was gussied up in a many-layered dress with a frilly lace bodice, giving her the look of a determined, pink, ruffled tugboat. Even Miss Oonagh looked lavish, a kimono-style silk print dress hanging on her wiry frame, her head topped with a wide-brimmed hat covered in brilliant iridescent peacock plumes. "One old bird deserves another," Old Peader quipped. "One under the hat, another nestin' on yer head!"

"Shut yer yapper, old man," Oonagh teased, gripping her pipe between her teeth.

Outside, the pasture had been transformed, a cordoned-off area bedecked in garlands of tulle, ivy, and roses. Father Lynch in white and green vestments waved us all into formation, Annie in front with a basket of fragrant rose petals, Georgie behind her in his suit, squirming and yanking at his bowtie, Pugsley and Rosie alongside him. And there was Brigit, a vision in her dress so like mine. But there was a lightness to her, an ease I felt was absent in me. I forced myself to smile, and in a moment forgot it was an effort.

Walter, Seamus, and Grady ushered guests to their seats, while off to the side a bagpiper prepared his strident instrument in a series of droning hee-haws, causing Pugsley and Rosie to whine. The capt'n, in full regalia, stepped up beside Father Lynch, and all eyes turned toward the back door of the house.

The piper began and Annie sashayed forward, scattering handfuls of pale pink rose petals along the path. Georgie tiptoed behind her, back straight as an arrow, balancing a pillow on which sat two rings. Brigit was next, head held high, Walter and I, arms linked, behind her. I ignored Seamus, sitting to my right, despite the fact that he whispered as I passed, "Ye look like me princess, ye do." I raised my chin and marched on. And then there was Addie! Patsy, weeping great tears of joy, had her sister by the arm, but even beneath the yards of delicate veil I could see Addie was smiling, her face alight with joy.

Father Lynch, beaming, wasted not a moment. He nodded for Patsy to lift the veil from Addie's face, the capt'n extended his hand, and Addie laid hers in his and they stepped before the priest.

"Obediah Adams, do you take this woman to be your lawful wedded wife, to have and to hold; for better, for worse; for richer, for poorer; in sickness and in health; to love and to honor from this day forward until death do you part?"

"I do."

Father Lynch turned to Addie. "Addie Clancy, do you take this man—"

Miss Oonagh cleared her throat. "Addie," she whispered loudly. "Ferget the part 'bout 'poorer'! Just skip on past it!" The entire group tittered uncomfortably.

"Shhhhh!" Old Peader scolded, his face aghast.

Father Lynch continued and Addie proclaimed, "I *do*!"

They exchanged the rings and Father Lynch nodded. "I now pronounce you husband and wife!"

Capt'n swept Addie into his arms and tilted her back in a long, passionate kiss. The bagpiper sealed the kiss with joyful strains, and the guests flew to their feet, applauding. Addie and the capt'n turned, beaming, hand in hand, and led us from our outdoor chapel to the tent where the celebration would ensue.

A moment later, the fiddlers rosined up their bows, the libations flowed, and the party began in earnest.

24

"Come on, then, Lucy—stop bein' cross with me!"

I whirled around to find myself face to face with Seamus. He took my hand. "At least save me a dance, then, cross or not!"

A smile slipped away from me before I could catch it. "Maybe later," I said, disappearing into the crowd of regalers dancing and talking at once. The music was wild and repetitive, one young man playing a handheld drum with a small mallet, two more playing fiddles, another a guitar. Men and women gathered in sets of four couples doing some sort of Irish square dancing. As I walked past, Brigit grabbed my arm and dragged me into the dance. "Ye can do it," she shouted over the din, "jest do as I do!" In an instant I was swung around, my elbow hooked with some lad's. Side by side he ushered me briskly around the square before handing me off to another young man. No one seemed to care that I didn't know the steps. The men circled counterclockwise and the women skipped the opposite way, always ending with a new partner. Forward and back we went, bowing and stomping our feet, the circle closing and expanding. As the tempo increased I lost any sense of hesitancy, and threw myself full into it. On and on we went, my heart pounding, tendrils of hair escaping my fancy do, sweat streaming down my back.

A moment later, the set ground to a finish, the guests erupting in applause, crowding around the band. There was Brigit, a fiddle tucked under her chin, tuning up the strings. Seamus was suddenly beside me. "Hear ye play the flute like nobody's seen," he said. "Whyn't ye go and give Brigit a run fer her money?"

I was about to say no when Walter stepped between us. "You never heard anyone play like Lucy," he said. "Look what I have," he whispered, pulling my flute out of his pocket and winking at me. "Brought it just in case. Go on, show 'em." Before I knew it, Addie and Pru were urging me as well, then Annie and Georgie. Old Peader clapped his hands in anticipation of the tune he imagined me playing.

"Give the people what they want!" Miss Oonagh crowed.

Even Marni, supervising her crew of eight recently polished and freshly garbed young helpers, joined in the chorus. Dressed in white aprons, they passed plates of food, helping themselves when they thought no one was looking. "Show us what ye got," Rory hollered. Meg, Paddy, and the other five set down their platters, and wiggled their way to the edge of the dance floor.

I heard a buzz near my ear. *Let'sseeifyou'reanygood!* There was Nessa, flitting back to Annie's shoulder. Leave it to her to show up for the party.

"A reel, key of G'd be grand," Brigit said, her bow at the ready.

The leader counted off, stamping his foot. "One, two, three . . ." The music tumbled forth, and though I didn't know the tune, I placed the flute to my lips, my fingers drawn to the holes. It was as though the spirit of the day flowed from my heart into the instrument, creating a melody that soared over the top of the rollicking ensemble. Brigit and the others provided the rhythm, and together we drove everyone to the dance floor, even Old Peader and Miss Oonagh. As the reel escalated into a frenzy, a puff of colorful glitter gushed from the flute and wafted like a magical cloud among the dancers, only increasing the sense of wild abandon. Finally Walter grabbed me by the hand and pulled me into the dance, spinning and spinning me around until the world became a dizzying kaleidoscope of sound and color.

Suddenly the crowd split in two, and a group of six men burst through the middle. They wore tall, pointy hats of straw that covered not only their heads, but their entire faces, and over their trousers they wore skimpy straw skirts. They danced even more senselessly than the rest, and engaged in general buffoonery. One stood on a chair, flapping his arms like a chicken; another hopped across the table leapfrog style. Addie and the capt'n bowed and curtsied, then joined them in the merrymaking, to the delight of the crowd. Patsy plied the Straw Boys with food and drink, and Grady grinned his approval. Only Miss Oonagh and Pugsley seemed out of sorts with them—Oonagh peering out from under her peacock feathers like an ornery old eagle, and Pugsley taking off after one of the straw-bedecked carousers, snapping at his heels.

"Come on," Walter said, taking me by the hand. Wiping my sweaty forehead with my forearm, I followed him around the back toward the barn, away from the crowd. The sun was beginning to set, the crescent moon rocking lazily against a navy-blue sky. Stars twinkled and crickets chirped. "I was so proud of you up there," Walter said, pulling me in front of him, staring at me as though he'd never seen me before. I felt myself blush and both hands flew to my cheeks. He reached over and pushed a tendril of hair out of my eyes. "Lovely," he said. "I thought so the very first time I saw you."

"Walter . . ." It was almost a question. He leaned forward, his face just inches from mine. Breathless, I closed my eyes.

There was a thud, a groan, a death grip on my wrist. I opened my eyes and screamed.

Walter lay on the ground beside a Straw Boy who held a club in one hand, digging his fingers into my arm, yanking me alongside him. I kicked and writhed but it was no use. He half dragged me, the hem of my frock catching and tearing on the edge of the barn. "Walter," I shouted. But he didn't stir. A thin stream of blood trickled down his forehead. "Help!" I shrieked. "Help!"

"Ain't no one gonna hear ya," came the muffled

voice from under the straw hat. I could smell the spirits on his foul breath.

My heart sank as I thought of Miss Oonagh's warning. I'd know that voice anywhere.

It was Quaide.

25

Quaide whipped off his straw hat, and in an instant tied a gag around my mouth, making it impossible to scream and difficult to breathe. He viciously bound my wrists and threw me in the back of a donkey cart, surely stolen from some un-suspecting farmer. His cohort sat holding the reins. "Make it quick, Quaide," the second Straw Boy directed, "before they miss her and come looking. And there's no need to hurt her. I'll take the reins— you've already had way too much to drink."

Quaide grunted, running a thick arm across his leaking nose, sniffing back the evidence of the effort it had taken to drag me to captivity. He chewed his lip, spit, then secured my ankle to the back of the cart, preventing my escape, and, for good measure, heaved a handful of hay over me.

"Yah!" The second Straw Boy cracked the reins against the donkey's rump and we jolted forward. I could still hear the music and laughter, could glimpse the twinkling lights of the wedding party between the strands of hay. Please, please, I prayed, someone notice I'm missing, someone stroll outside and discover Walter sprawled on the ground, bleeding. . . . Tears pinched my eyes. Why hadn't we taken Miss Oonagh's words seriously? Would whatever power she had send her a message regarding my present fate? And if so, would anyone believe her?

The cart bumped and swayed, the jostling becoming more and more pronounced. I could catch snippets of conversation between my captors, just a word here and there: *outpost . . . treasure . . . what she knows . . .*

Perhaps they would torture me, trying to extricate whatever secrets they believed I held. Well, go ahead, I thought. Even if I had known where the treasure was I would never tell them! *Hmpff!* I groaned through my gag, straining against my shackles. Surely help would come. Other, darker thoughts crept up behind that one, but I pushed them away. I forced myself to calm down, conserve my energy. Who knew what might be required of me when we got to wherever we were going.

The sounds of the party diminished and it was clear I was being taken to a remote place. The air grew chilly and damp, and the silence of the countryside pressed in ominously. Suddenly I heard another sound, a rhythmic clicking and labored snuffling. My heart leaped and as it did, my hope was confirmed. I heard him jump and scramble, felt him wriggle his compact little body up and over the back edge of the cart. "Pugsley!" I murmured, the word strangled by the gag.

In an instant he was covering my face with wet kisses, grunting and wiggling with joy.

"Did you hear that?" the second Straw Boy asked.

Pugsley hunkered down, buried his face in the folds of my dress.

"Don't hear nothin'." Quaide hiccuped.

My loyal dog remained silent for the rest of the journey.

After what felt like hours the cart slowed. Pugsley huddled behind me, beneath the hay, edging into a back corner of the cart.

"Get out!" Quaide ordered, yanking the rope,

heaving me up by the hands. Stay still, Pugsley, I prayed. I could almost feel the bristling of his fur, see his snout curling in outrage.

"Ungag her," came the other voice. "She can scream all she wants—there's no one out here to pay her any heed."

I turned toward the voice of the mysterious Straw Boy as Quaide loosened the gag and untied my wrists. The green-eyed man! He'd removed his clownish hat and we stared at one another, his jade eyes piercing. "So we meet again," he said, his voice velvety with sarcasm.

"Come on," Quaide muttered, his words garbled. "Inside."

It took me but a moment to recognize the peculiar desolate landscape of oddly shaped stones. We were in the Burren, in the middle of nowhere. Just to the right stood an old abandoned cottage and stable, its thatched roof sagging, walls crumbling. As Quaide shoved me toward the sorry structure I caught a glimpse of Pugsley hightailing it out of the back of the cart, dashing down the path we'd taken, a scrap of my frock dangling from his mouth. Go Pugsley, I prayed. Godspeed.

The green-eyed man shoved open the stable door, struck a match, and lit a lantern, dimly illuminating the space with flickering light. They'd set up an outpost, furnishing the shack with three metal cots, a crude table and chairs, and a rack holding clothes and supplies. Oddly, there were craters, gaping holes and rubble around the perimeter of the space. A large rectangular rag rug had been placed in the middle of what was left of the dirt floor.

"Si' down," Quaide slurred, shoving me into one of the chairs. "Almos' forgot my stash," he drawled, a wide grin turning his face into a fat jack-o'-lantern.

The green-eyed man sighed and waved him out with a brush of his hand. "Moron," he muttered under his breath. Oblivious, Quaide lumbered out the door and returned with a large crate full of bottles.

"You stole that from the wedding party!" I cried.

"Wah . . . wah . . . wah . . . so I did," Quaide taunted. "They won' even miss it." He plopped himself in the chair opposite mine, grabbed a bottle, removed the cork with his teeth, and spat it at me across the table. "This calls for a li'l celebration," he hissed.

"Ugh," I retorted, brushing the place where the soggy cork had brushed my cheek. Quaide watched me through narrowed eyes, threw his head back, and poured the amber liquid into his mouth. He chugged, gurgled, and gulped.

"Take it easy, Quaide," the green-eyed man chided. "You're already drunk as a skunk!" Quaide's response was a long, juicy burp. Once recovered from his colossal belch he broke into a jug of ale, smacking his lips between guzzling. I watched him as I might a hog in the barnyard.

"Whatsa matter?" he stammered. "Miss High an' Mighty never seen a man take a li'l refreshment?"

I rolled my eyes. Quaide leaned forward and swatted the air in front of me. "You'd best learn a li'l respect, missy. Had 'nough of you and yours tryin' to cheat me out of what's rightfully mine!"

"Hold your tongue, Quaide," the green-eyed man warned. In response Quaide hiccuped loudly, shoulders bobbing. He wagged his fat sausage finger at me. "You're gonna tell me everythin' you know 'bout that treasure so's I can collect it once and fer all."

"I'll tell you nothing! You've no claim to it!"

"Greedy little wench!" he snarled. "Arrogant, just like yer great-grandpappy. Look where it got him!"

"Quaide," the green-eyed man said, "stop!"

Quaide's eyebrows shot up. "I'm done takin' orders from you, Jack. I'm in charge here now."

I interrupted. "What do you know of my

great-grandfather?"

Quaide smiled. "Not so smart as he thought he was. . . ." He gahuffed. "Never got o'er that my gran'daddy outsmarted 'im."

So I'd been right about Dirk. "This makes you feel entitled to stolen property?"

"May the bes' man win," Quaide slurred. He took another swig. "An' this one here," he said, waving the bottle at the green-eyed man. "Run into him tryin' t' stake 'is own claim. Says the other one's his gra'mother."

"What other one?" I asked.

The veins in the green-eyed man's neck popped. "Quaide! Shut up!"

But it was clear Quaide wasn't listening. The liquor had loosened his tongue. "Pirate queen. Mary Maude Lee. This here's 'er grandson." He hic-cupped again, a high-pitched yelping sound. "We's worked out a deal, splittin' the spoils. He brought the brains, and me the brawn! And so far I ain't seen the brains!"

I stared at the green-eyed man. If that was true, then . . .

The green-eyed man glared at Quaide, his lip curled in disgust. But Quaide's eyelids had grown heavy, his mouth slack, and his chin flopped onto his chest. He snorted and slumped onto the table.

I turned my attention to the green-eyed man. "Your name is Jack?" I asked. "How are you related to Mary Maude Lee?"

"I'll be the one asking the questions," he said, staring with those cat eyes of his. Something about his gaze was familiar. He had an eerie calm about him, something focused and unflappable. For an instant I felt as though I'd been there before, face to face with him. The green-eyed man continued to study me. "You're a wealthy young woman, by all accounts, and so is your aunt Prudence. Why would you risk life and limb to pursue this quest? When is enough, enough?"

I barely heard him. An idea crept into my head and took hold. If he was Mary Maude Lee's grandson, he might be . . . Marni's son! I inhaled sharply, my hand flying to my mouth. Those eyes—of course. They were her eyes too! His manner of composed poise and patience. Of unflustered self-assurance despite Quaide's crude display. I jumped from the chair.

"Who . . . who was your mother?" I asked.

The man's face clouded over ever so slightly. "Never had a mother. She abandoned my father and me when I was just a boy. Didn't have the mothering instinct." His voice betrayed an edge of bitterness. "Then she died."

"No, no, she didn't," I sputtered. "It's all a lie. It was your father who took you away, because . . . because . . . your mother wouldn't have him bringing you up into a life of pirating! She's searched for you, her whole life long!"

"Enough," he said. But his expression wavered.

"She has your hair woven in a locket—she wears it every day. You were towheaded as a boy, weren't you?"

He hesitated. "How would you know my mother?"

"Marni! My friend, the one who took care of me since I lost my family in Maine! She saved me from drowning—twice. She's been with me from the start. Surely you've seen her, accompanying us all over the world! You have her eyes!"

"The old woman with the long silver hair? I'm supposed to believe she's my mother?"

"And not only that! You asked me why Pru and I would hunt down Mary Maude Lee's treasure? Because she put a curse on all Edward's descendants—swore that every male in Edward's line should die at sea. And so far my grandfather, my father, my uncle . . ." I held up a finger for each.

"All died at sea. And not only the males—it killed my aunt and mother. And Marni—she's the daughter of Mary Maude Lee and my grandfather, which means . . ."

"That I'm the next male in line?" He gazed off into the darkness, or maybe into the past, his eyes changing color like the sea on a stormy day. He spoke softly, his words measured. "It's true, the sea's nearly claimed me, more times than I can count."

I nodded. "And me."

He shook his head. "Crazy talk . . ." But something in his demeanor had changed. He was suddenly not so sure of himself. "So, this supposed curse . . . ?"

I slipped my hand into my pocket, pulled out my flute, and put it to my lips. My fingers flew over the holes, the familiar melody pouring out in a stream of glittering mist. At the last note the music continued of its own accord, a haunting interlude that invited me to raise my voice in song. I took a deep wavering breath and began to sing:

> *"This is the ballad of Mary Maude Lee—*
> *a Queen and a Pirate—the Witch o' the Sea.*
> *Tho' fair of face, and tho' slight of build,*
> *many a seafarers' blood did she spill!*

A la dee dah dah . . . a la dee dah dee,
This is the ballad of Mary Maude Lee."

At this, the green-eyed man's eyes widened, perhaps in recognition of the long-forgotten melody he'd likely heard as a boy. I continued on, my voice gaining strength and confidence.

"She fired her blunderbuss, torched their tall sails,
Laughing as mariners screamed, moaned, and
     wailed.
Off with their silver! Off with their gold!
Off with supplies lying deep in their holds!"

Quaide began to snore, so I sang all the louder.

"Her coffers grew fat, till Edward, that gent,
Escaped with her booty, and then off he went."

Here, for emphasis, I hopped onto a chair, slowed the tempo, and enunciated each syllable.

"She swore her revenge against that sorry traitor,
Placed a curse on the sons of the cuss who betrayed
     her!"

Jack stood, and I jumped to the next verse.

"Mary Maude Lee said, 'I'll spit on their graves!'
Then drew back and spat in the white churning
waves.
And each generation of menfolk that followed,
Into the sea they'd be chewed up and swallowed!"

During the interlude I prompted, "Here's the important part!" and sang on:

"The only real way that the curse can be broken
Was revealed in the last words that Mary had
spoken,
If not in my lifetime, then to my descendants,
Hand over my treasure and appease Mary's
vengeance!'"

The glitter swirled around the room and dissipated with the last note of the refrain. "That's why Prudence and I have been searching for the treasure!" I exclaimed. "Not for personal gain, but to end this, once and for all!"

Jack looked between us, Quaide still snoring, his face flattened against the table, a puddle of drool collecting beneath his bottom lip.

"What if you're lying?" Jack said. "I didn't spend my entire life searching for this treasure my father spoke of to be outsmarted by a twelve-year-old."

"I'm almost fourteen!"

Jack scowled. "Twelve, fourteen . . . no matter."

"Look," I said, gesturing toward Quaide. "You heard him. His father was the one responsible for stealing the treasure. Why would you team up with *him*?"

"Because I thought he might know something."

A blubbering sound escaped from Quaide's lips. I might be only thirteen, but anyone could see I'd be a more reliable ally than Quaide. I raised an eyebrow. Jack looked away. I pressed on. "What does he know about his grandfather's role in this?"

Jack met my gaze, considering. "Not a whole lot. He knew about Edward the First. And that, supposedly, Dirk had stolen the treasure, moved the family out here, and later disappeared, leaving them penniless. The fabled treasure had become a Coogan family legend. But since Dirk and Edward were both long gone there was nothing to do but focus on Edward's descendants. Given that your father was a sea captain, it was easy to track his comings and goings. Finally, the path led to you."

"And you joined him in Boston, when we first set sail?"

The green-eyed man looked surprised. "What makes you think so?"

I thought of how, peering through my spyglass,

I'd seen him exchanging money with Quaide, out on the Boston pier. "I know more than you think," I bluffed.

Warily, we studied each other. I so wanted to trust this man with Marni's eyes, but . . . there was too much at stake. I took a deep breath and ventured on. "Listen," I said, "we're related—we share a grandfather—well, your grandfather, my great-grandfather. You're a sort of an uncle to me. What if we were to work together? Who do you trust more—me, or *him*?" Jack eyed Quaide, nearly sucking the table, his eyes half closed, hands splayed, his breath coming in ragged gasps.

Jack stared at me with piercing green eyes. I felt as though he could see clear through to my soul.

"I'll tell you what I know if you promise to do the same." Even as I said it, I knew I wouldn't share everything. Nor would he. This lack of trust felt disloyal to Marni, somehow, but I couldn't take the chance.

Jack rubbed his chin, considering, his face reflecting the same keen intelligence I'd come to trust on Marni's face. "If what you say is true, you and Prudence technically aren't entitled to the spoils. The treasure needs to be returned to the descendants of Mary Maude Lee. Your lineage extends from Edward and Molly, *not* Edward and Mary."

I nodded. He was right. But it was never the money I was after. "But remember," I said, "you're not the only descendant. There's Marni. Once we find the treasure, the two of you can decide how it should be divided. Plus," I added, "I'll lead you to the greatest treasure of all. . . ."

"What would that be?" he asked.

My eyes welled, thinking of my own loss.

"What?" he asked again.

I gulped and looked him straight in the eye. "Your mother," I said. "I can finally give you back to your mother."

26

In a tentative spirit of cooperation we managed to coax Quaide from the table onto his cot, where he lay on his back like a beached whale, his snores erupting in gurgling bursts. He'd be out for the rest of the night, and would surely be sick once he awoke in the morning.

A thought occurred to me. "Is it possible Dirk buried the treasure here?" I blurted. It *was* the perfect spot—out of the way, but not that far from the inn where Dirk had likely absconded with the treasure. And the outpost sat atop a hill—a mountain, almost—where the scoundrel could spot a would-be challenger approaching from any direction.

Jack jutted his chin, indicating the crater-ridden floor.

I persisted. "What about outside?"

Jack sighed deeply and I felt a little foolish. But not enough to abandon the idea.

"See for yourself," he replied, walking me toward the door. It took a few seconds for my eyes to adjust to the darkness. A trench had been dug along the periphery of the crumbling foundation. And the surrounding area looked surprisingly like the terrain around our homestead in Australia—the ground riddled with holes. Two shovels were still planted in a heap of debris, where Quaide and Jack must have left them. My heart sank. The treasure wasn't here. Another thought plagued me—if Quaide and Jack had been seeking, for years, to find the treasure, wouldn't it make sense that others might have been trying as well? Maybe someone none of us knew had discovered the treasure long ago, and made off with it, taking their secret along with the bounty.

I was suddenly exhausted. I yawned, bleary eyed. "Get some rest," Jack said, not unkindly, "before Quaide wakes up."

"And then . . . ?"

Once again his face became guarded. "In the

morning I'll decide." In one fluid move he took hold of my wrists, and firmly wrapped them with a long strip of coarse fabric. "I'm sorry," he said, avoiding my eyes. "I have no choice but to ensure you don't decide to run off during the night." Regardless of how sorry he was, we were back to being captor and captive. He led me, leashed, to my cot, and tethered me there. I said nothing. I'd somehow assumed that once he knew Marni was his mother everything would change—but I'd been wrong. I turned my back to him, my face burning with embarrassment and indignation. I'd revealed too much, and gotten nothing in return.

He extinguished the lamp and the room went black, save for the bit of moonlight shining through the single window. The springs of Jack's cot groaned as he settled himself. In minutes his breathing took on the steady cadence of sleep. Tired as I was, slumber was impossible. It began to rain, a gentle drumming on what was left of the roof. In no time, droplets trickled through the thatch, pelting down until the cot felt like a dirty sponge beneath me. Each drip sounded like the ticking of a clock. Time was running out.

I inched my way as far from the leak as possible, mind racing despite my exhaustion. Thoughts of Dirk, Quaide, the inn, this outpost . . . the futility of the excavations in and around the place.

Drip . . . drip . . . drip.

Shivering, I wondered whether the rain was just another way for the curse to assert itself. If there was a downpour, perhaps it would drown me right there on the cot.

Still . . . there had to be a reason Dirk set his homestead atop this hill, situated like a fort. Clearly, a lookout post offering him views of any treasure seeker who dared approach. There would have been no other reason to settle here—the rocky land was suited neither to farming nor grazing. It was far from town and neighbor. Traveling up and down the mountain was a challenge. The effort it took discouraged both friend and foe. Why, if not to protect the treasure?

Suddenly a thought struck me. Could it be that this hilltop lookout hadn't been situated to provide a view of would-be thieves and bounty hunters scaling the mountain? Rather, might it have been chosen because the panorama allowed Dirk to keep watch over a hidden treasure trove somewhere *below*? If he spied anyone approaching the spot, he could intercede. There were other advantages to this scenario—he wouldn't have had to transport the hefty spoils up the steep side of the mountain, and if anyone traced the missing treasure back to him and searched his property, they'd come up empty-handed. The idea seemed deceptively simple. There had to be a way to see if I was right.

By wriggling toward the top of the cot I was able to loosen my bonds slightly. I writhed and squirmed until I could position my bound wrists beneath my face. By turning my face slightly, the burlap strips brushed my lips. I craned my neck forward and, like a rodent, began to gnaw at the prickly restraints. I ground at the rough cloth until my jaw ached, my mouth filling with an earthy, straw-like taste. The process was painfully slow, but little by little the fibers separated, then split. Finally my hands became free enough to grab the edges of the frayed fabric and yank. One last rip and I was free. I flew to my feet, tiptoed around the holes in the floor, swiped the lantern and matches from the table, and snuck out the door.

The sun had not yet risen, the clouded ghost of a moon still hovered at the edge of evening. But despite the drizzle, a hint of dawn glowed along the eastern horizon. Soon Jack would be awake— I would bet he was the type of no-nonsense man who rose with the sun. There was no time to lose!

I inched along the rim of the hilltop, eyes peeled to the landscape below. I thought of lighting the lamp, but decided against it. Too easy for them to spot me. Instead I strapped it over my shoulder, the matches safe inside. At least this way they wouldn't be able to take advantage of it. Stealing around the perimeter of the craggy summit, I peered into the mist. I didn't know exactly what I was looking for. In an easterly direction, only a jigsaw of rocks and sparse greenery. Off to the right, the meandering road that surely led back to Ballyvaughan—perhaps I should just run in that direction, find my way back to Capt'n Adams's house. But no, if Quaide and Jack spotted me they'd easily overtake me with the cart. I picked my way around the periphery of the steep hilltop, eyes peeled. It was a landscape of natural rubble, spanning as far as the eye could see.

I stopped for a moment. If Dirk had situated his homestead so that he could keep an eye on his treasure trove, how would he have done it? I glanced back at the crumbling structure. There was but one crude window on the southern wall. A logical place to let in light, but what if . . .

I moved along the embankment, aligning myself with the window, in order to afford myself the view Dirk would have had from inside. The sun peeked over the horizon, parting the fog in the valley just enough to expose a portion of stone wall. The mist continued to swirl and dissipate, and as it did, more and more of a snaking border of rocks became exposed. The piled stones had been laid in a geometric pattern.

My heart began to race. I'd seen this configuration before—the lopsided sun with uneven rays was the symbol Oonagh had scratched on the hearthstone back on Clare Island! And what had she said—that this is where I'd find what I was seeking?

I went back and grabbed one of the shovels before scrambling down the hillside. The gravel churned beneath my shoes. Dropping to my backside, I scooted along the steep slope as best I could, until the ground leveled a bit. On my feet, I hoisted my dress, and cautiously trod the rest of the way down the hill using the shovel like a walking stick. It was rough going. But the mountainside wouldn't be my greatest challenge—at least the angle of the hill might prevent them from seeing me. Once I crossed the valley to get to the stone formation, I'd be completely exposed.

When I reached flat ground I began to run. From atop the mountain the shape of the rock formation had been clear, but the closer I came, the harder it was to distinguish.

I began to comb the perimeter as well as the length of each jutting ray, searching for some clue, any hint that might be useful. As I headed in an easterly direction the wind whipped up, bringing with it another rain shower. In minutes my dress was soaked, my hair clinging to my neck in wet strands. I reversed direction so that the wind was at my back, and the rain slowed to a drizzle.

Puzzled, I turned eastward and again, the rain came down in earnest, the wind blowing it toward me in punishing sheets. The ground became saturated, my shoes hopelessly muddied. The farther I inched forward, the harder the rain fell. I slogged on, the torrent of the rain forming a thin stream that trickled down from the mountain. The waterlogged ground sucked at my feet until I was ankle deep. I'd been so intent on locating a clue that I hadn't really thought about the curse—how the water had become my enemy, even when far from the sea. Once again I stepped back and the rain subsided. I closed my eyes for a moment and heard: *Press on, darling. . . .* Was it my mother's voice?

In response, the stream gushed around my ankles and the sod grew spongy beneath my feet. Shielding my face from the downpour, I spied an area of drenched ground that dipped ever so slightly along the base of the wall—a small circular area that appeared to be sinking due to the deluge. Or perhaps something was buried there! Heeding my mother's words, I stepped forward, shovel at the ready, positioning my foot on the blade. Then

I threw my full weight into it. A portion of ground gave way; I scooped and lifted, once, twice, three times. A stream swirled into the hole, like water down a drain, drawing even more of the surrounding turf into the expanding cavity. The torrent gushed around my feet and into the pit. I lost my balance. Dropped the shovel.

The ground gave way, swallowing me whole.

I plunged into darkness.

27

Down, down I slid into a musty, muddy chasm, water nearly enveloping me. I choked and gasped, spewing muddy water. The lantern I'd strapped over my shoulder banged against my ribs, rocky outcroppings bruised my arms and legs. My screams echoed against the walls of the abyss.

Finally my feet hit solid ground. It took me a moment to realize I was alive, and basically unhurt. Save for a thin ray of gray light shining down the shaft, it was pitch-black. I fumbled for the lantern, its glass dome still somehow intact, and with trembling fingers probed for the matches I'd dropped inside.

The first match I lit was promptly blown out by a gust of air from above. The next was damp, sputtered once, and went out. I slowed the panic that rose in me, the feeling of the cave walls closing in. "Slow and steady," I whispered. I took a deep breath, felt for the match, struck it, cupped my hand around it, protecting the wavering flame, then eased the flickering light toward the wick. I held it there for one second ... two ... three. ... Just as it began to singe my fingers the flame caught. I lifted the lantern, a low glow infusing the space. At the far end of the narrow corridor of rock was an opening into a larger chamber. Strange formations of stone hung from the ceiling and grew from the floor like huge icicles, water drip-dropping into luminous pools that had never seen the sparkle of the sun. I inched forward, treading carefully down a natural staircase of craggy rock. As I descended, the air became cool and clammy, turning my skin to gooseflesh. A steady stream of water splashed over my feet, leaving the floor dangerously slick.

Finally the shaft leveled off and I inched forward, back to the wall, to ensure I wouldn't step off a blind precipice. Gradually another sound became audible—a constant tumultuous churning, like the rushing of a river. I carefully rounded a bend, and an enormous waterfall became visible, several stories high, a glassy stream plunging into the pool below. I inched along the rim, shivering in the spray kicked up by the crashing water. The ledge was a mere six inches in width. A seemingly bottomless chasm loomed beneath it. I stopped and toed a small stone over the edge. One second, two, three, four seconds before I heard it splash. One false move and a person could disappear without a trace.

Slowly, but not too slowly came a familiar voice inside me. The same voice that had instructed me so often at sea.

"Father?" I asked. The word echoed eerily—fath*er . . . er . . . er . . . er . . . .* I felt hot and cold at the same time, sweat trickling down my back, my arms shivering.

Too much thinking can spook you. Sidestep. Move by feel, not by sight.

Ready now, left foot, together—STEP! That's my girl!

I edged my way around the underground pool, until finally the ledge widened. Catching my breath, I started through a short passageway that opened to an expansive chamber. I raised the lantern and gasped.

The chest was the size of a large coffin, its lid flipped back, revealing stack upon stack of gold and silver coins and thick, brick-like bars of precious metal. In between were stuffed bulging canvas bags tied with drawstring, some of which had split, spilling the glittering contents into and over the sides of the chest. Gemstones, pearls, perhaps diamonds, and sparkling crystals. Even beneath more than a century's worth of dust and debris the priceless plunder twinkled and shone like stars in the night sky. Beside the treasure lay two skeletons, both clad in the remains of their disintegrating clothes. I tiptoed closer. One of the dead men, a giant of a man, lay on his back, a large sword wedged between his ribs. What was left of his ragged clothes clearly belonged to a laborer, the remains of a coarse woolen jacket still covering the arms.

The other man, a gold tooth glinting from his jawbone, lay on his side, a fierce dagger jutting from the vertebrae of his throat. A decaying topcoat clung to his ribs and arms, remnants of its fancy trim work scrolling around the cuffs and lapels. I crept closer, drawn to the gold ring surrounding his bony finger. I held the lantern high and leaned forward for a better look. The ring's flat oval face was engraved—I knew even before I read the inscription what it would say: E.S.

Suddenly, a scuffling sound. I scrambled to my feet, holding the lantern high. At the same time a trickle of water seeped around my feet.

A flash on a distant wall, a flickering light. The sound of footsteps. I considered snuffing out my lamp, but once I did that the chances of relighting it would be slim. I'd never find my way out in the dark. And dying alongside my great-grandfather was not something I cared to do. Better to face Quaide and Jack.

I hunkered down. Closer and closer came the shuffling footfall, the light of a lamp bobbing against the stony walls. But wait . . . I'd stolen their lantern. . . . Had they had another, stashed away?

I peered into the dim light, waiting for them to appear.

A small whining sound. A low growl. Panting. Rhythmic clicking. I flew to my feet. "Pugsley? Pugsley, is that you!?"

A flurry of yips. The sound of his nails on the stone floor meant he was running toward me.

"Be careful!" I shouted. "Slowly, Pugsley!" My warning boomed back at me.

"Lucy," came a voice from the distance. "Where are you?"

My heart stood still. "Marni?"

"Yes! I'm coming for you. . . ."

Pugsley bound in and leaped into my arms. I hugged him tightly and rushed toward Marni, just emerging from the treacherous corridor. She raised her lantern and devoured me with her eyes.

"You're all right," she said, the deep line between her brows easing.

"How did you . . . ?"

Before she could answer she caught sight of the treasure. Her eyes became clouded with a faraway look. The echo of Jack in her features was unmistakable. "Oh my," she whispered, stepping forward. I followed her, watching her take it all in—the decadent riches, the evidence of greed and unbridled desire, and the legacy of revenge surrounding it. "Generations of pain and loss—all for this?"

"It's almost over." I placed my hand on her shoulder and wondered how to tell her about Jack. I wanted to be able to say that he was eagerly awaiting her. That he was kind and noble. But I wasn't sure of any of that. That he was smart—yes. That he had her eyes. And if he would only allow himself to let his guard down . . .

Instead I asked how she'd found me.

"The search teams had already left by the time Pugsley came hightailing it home. He led me toward that mountain, and I thought for sure that's where they'd taken you. But when we passed this ring fort, he put his nose to the ground and brought me on a wild-goose chase."

"Ring fort?"

"Mysterious ancient stone structures—associated with fairies and the like . . ."

I remembered then what Nessa had said that day in the Burren. She'd talked about these "thin spaces between the worlds"—places where fairies sometimes gathered.

"Pugsley tracked you to the mouth of the cave," Mari continued. "It took me a while to navigate, but I knew enough to follow him."

"Marni," I began. "There's something else . . . the Straw Boys . . . they did take me up the mountain, to a hideout there. One was Quaide."

"That much we all suspected. He didn't hurt you . . . ?"

"No, but—"

Suddenly Pugsley began to growl, a low rumble that raised the hair along his back. Then we heard it too—the shuffling of feet. Muffled voices.

Instinctively, we drew together, eyes riveted to the entrance of the chamber.

Quaide burst in, his face screwed up in rage. But then, as he caught sight of the dazzling treasure, he gasped, his small beady eyes flashing, his fleshy mouth dropping open, eyes wild. He tramped around both skeletons and knelt beside the chest, filling his pockets with coins, lifting handfuls of jewels and letting them flow through his fingers like pebbles. "Oh!" he yelled. "Ohhhhhh! Finally, the payoff! I'm gonna be the world's richest man!" Over and over he pawed at the booty, running a coin across his lips, lowering his head toward the bags, inhaling deeply. He was possessed by the lavishness of the spoils, like a cat in a field of catnip. "Yes!" he wheezed. "Hit the jackpot! No—not the *jack*pot! Jack'll be getting *nothing*!" He laughed maniacally. "Not after he let the little missy run off!"

As if responding to his name, Jack appeared in the entranceway. In an instant he took in the scene, then locked eyes with Marni. I felt a jolt of energy, a stream of silent words exchanged. One hand flew to her cheek, the other to her locket. Her bottom lip began to tremble.

"Yes, Marni," I said. "That's what I was trying to tell you. . . ."

"Shut up!" Quaide growled. He yanked the sword from between his grandfather's ribs and swung it fiercely over his head, setting off a storm of flapping. Hundreds of startled bats pelted our faces, pinged off our bodies. I ducked, shielding my head. When their frantic retreat was past I looked up to find Quaide peeling several from his shirt, another from his hair. He waved us into the corner. "Sit there an' don't move," he ordered, brandishing the blade.

"Put it away, Quaide," Jack said, laying a hand on his mother's arm. "Nobody's threatening you. You're wasting precious time." He glanced my way. "Why don't we work together, all of us? Figure out a way to get this treasure out of here. You can't do it alone."

Quaide screwed up his face. "Suddenly you're a do-gooder, Jack? First ye let Lucy run off, now ye're protectin' old ladies?" He grunted. "Here's how much I trust you." He drew back and spit. "Here's how much I trust *any* of yous. Who's gonna be the first to go?" He pointed the sword toward Jack's throat.

"Stop!" Marni yelled, lunging between Quaide and Jack.

Quaide savagely swung the cutlass. Blood gushed from Marni's shoulder. Jack caught her as she fell.

"You monster," I shouted. I knelt beside her. "Don't die!" I commanded through clenched teeth. "Do you hear me? You. Can't. Die."

Jack ripped off his shirt and pressed it into Marni's wound to slow the bleeding. Marni was pale, but conscious.

"Everything's all right now," she whispered, smiling weakly. "But a little more time would have been nice."

There had to be a way to stop Quaide. To get Marni to safety. If he didn't have the sword we might overpower him. . . . Quaide wiped the bloody blade on his trousers, leering at us. "I guess we know who's in charge now," he said.

Suddenly a deafening whooshing sound filled the chamber. Torrents thundered over the waterfall. Murky water roiled up and out of the pool in the adjoining chamber. Rippling and churning, it surged around our ankles, lapping against Marni and Jack.

Wild eyed, Quaide wielded his weapon. "I'm ending this once and for all!" he shouted, charging at me through the rushing water, the sword held over his head. There was a flash, and then another.

Notsofast!Thesearemypeople! Nessa appeared, a queen card tucked beneath each arm. She soared toward Quaide, a blade of grass poised at her lips.

TherecouldbeanotherREWARDinthisforme!Thekingcard ANDsomegold!

Quaide swatted wildly, splashing and flailing, but Nessa persisted. The hairlike projectile blew from her grass dart gun in a barrage of sparkling light.

"Aghhh! Ow! Aghhh . . ." Quaide writhed about,

his nose growing bulbous, cheeks inflated like two maroon balloons. He tottered side to side, still grasping his weapon.

This was our only chance. I threw myself full at him, thinking of nothing but knocking the sword from his hands.

He faltered. Lost his balance. Staggered backward toward the precipice, his long, diminishing cry echoing through the cave. We froze. A few seconds later there was a thump and a splash. The water receded, its trickling music echoing off the cavern walls.

And then all was silent.

28

As we prepared to carry Marni up and out of the cave, we were met once again by the sound of footsteps.

"Nessa, where in the world did you go?" came an exasperated voice.

My knees went weak with relief. "Aunt Pru," I shouted, "we're in here!"

Pru and Walter appeared in the entranceway.

Ledyouhereandthat'sthethanksIget!

Pru swatted Nessa out of the way and they both rushed in, eyes darting between me and the treasure. But at the sight of Marni and Jack they stopped short.

"It's you!" Pru cried. "Let go of her! Oh, good Lord, she's bleeding!" Walter grabbed Jack by the arm, eyes flashing.

"No! No, it's all right," I exclaimed. "I'll explain— after we get her out of here!"

Walter eyed Jack warily and reluctantly released him. Then our eyes met. "Quaide?" he asked.

"Gone." I fought a wave of tears. "He stabbed Marni, I went to knock the sword out of his hands, and . . ."

"It's all right," Walter said, taking me in his arms. "Whatever he got, he deserved."

Carefully, we carried Marni back up the way we came. As we inched along I related the story of my capture, how I figured out Jack's identity and the secret of Dirk's lookout post, and the most challenging part of all—how the closer I came to the treasure, the more threatening the water had become.

"And still you pressed on." Walter shook his head. "Is there anything you're afraid of, Lucy P.?"

I shook my head. "I'm always afraid," I said, "but like Nessa, I persist." She still hovered around us like an annoying hornet, pestering us for a piece of silver or a nugget of gold.

"Not now," I shouted as we settled Marni in the back of Pru's wagon, Jack by her side. Walter took the reins.

"Hurry," Jack said. "She's pretty weak." While his voice did little to betray his feelings, his face was tense. He was clearly a man accustomed to keeping his emotions in check. Something, I realized sadly, that most motherless children learn to do.

Walter looked at Pru and me. "You'll follow in the other cart?"

"We'll be right behind you."

Walter snapped the reins against the mule's flank. "Yah!" And they were off.

In a last-minute flash of intuition, Pru and I descended once more into the cave. I said a prayer for Marni's swift recovery as I slipped the ring off Great-grandfather's finger and onto my own. Together Pru and I removed the dagger that was lodged in Edward's remains, wiped it clean, and sliced our index fingers—just enough to draw a few drops of blood. This we mingled and dripped on the chest of spoils—a symbol of the Simmons women having fulfilled their obligation.

Finally we climbed out into the light, disguising the mouth of the cave as best we could. We got in the cart and headed back to Ballyvaughan. Now all that was left to do was to determine the best way to deliver the treasure back to its rightful heirs. And then it would be finished.

29

"**B**est thing fer ye would be t' have a little smoke," Miss Oonagh urged Marni. "Calm the nerves, clear out the lungs." The two sat side by side in the parlor where Marni was recuperating.

"What a crock o' blarney," Old Peader muttered. He wagged a finger at Oonagh. "And don't ye even think of lightin' that confounded pipe near our patient."

Marni smiled. "I have everything I need for a full recovery," she said, gazing at Jack. "And I'll pass on the tobacco."

"Suit yerself then," Miss Oonagh retorted.

In the two weeks since the stabbing, Marni had been showered with care. Patsy plied her with food and strong, brisk tea. Pru and I read her poetry. Annie brought flowers. Georgie tried to offer her a toad from the garden, but Old Peader stopped him. "Last thing she needs is warts," he grumbled. Addie dressed her wound, applying a potent fairy salve, compliments of Nessa. Seamus provided entertainment—jokes, juggling, and the like, and also carved a small mermaid figurine that he left on the table beside her. The orphan children, suddenly shy, brought bunches of wild flowering weeds and small interesting stones from the Burren. Mostly they just sat by her feet, watching anxiously to be sure she was recovering from her wound. Pugsley and Rosie too stood watch, as if guarding her convalescence.

Of course, Brigit excelled in nursing Marni, providing blankets and broth, a cheerful fire in the hearth, all with a gentle touch, which, surprisingly, I hardly resented at all. After being so graced with the discovery of the treasure, and the joy of Marni and Jack's reunion, I found myself much more generous of spirit.

But it was sitting beside Jack, the two of them talking softly, filling in the bits and pieces of their lives, that had the most therapeutic effect.

As soon as we could, we'd returned to the cave and, with Walter and the capt'n's help, transported the treasure to the cottage, where it was stored under lock and key. It had taken us three strenuous trips, lugging it out of the cave and onto a cart, our priceless cargo covered with hay and a large tarp so as not to raise any suspicion.

Then came the task of determining how to repay those who had helped. Jack, following his mother's lead, had divided the spoils, gifting some to Pru and me, and smaller sums to Walter, Georgie, and Annie. Grady too was rewarded for his role, as was the capt'n. Seamus was another story. When Pru had suggested that we gift him with a little something Jack had hesitated. "I doubt he'd accept," Jack said, without explanation.

Strange too that since Jack had arrived Seamus had made himself scarce—his excuse was that he'd taken a job at the town pub, waiting tables, earning some good tips. After two weeks of this he turned up and offered Jack a fat envelope of cash. "To repay ye what I owe," Seamus said.

Jack hadn't seemed surprised. "It's true, you never really delivered the goods. Lucky Quaide never caught up with you."

"What are you talking about?" Walter asked.

Jack patted Seamus on the back. "He has a

good heart. Quaide tried to buy him off back on the island, but I guess once he met all of you . . ."

"Take the money, please," Seamus urged. "Almost sold me soul fer the price of a new set of oilskins to take sailin'. And then I went back on me word, though it was the right thing t' do." He looked my way. "Lucy—cross me heart an' hope t' die, had I known ye well and what Quaide was up to I never woulda . . ."

"I knew it!" Walter said. "The night you were supposed to keep watch over the harbor at Clare Island . . ."

"I did the right thing in the end, I did. Just slipped up a bit at first. But I made it up t' ye's, haven't I?"

Walter nodded grudgingly. In the end, at Seamus's insistence, Jack took the money, they shook hands, and all was forgotten.

Finally there was only one thing left to do. Pru and I had vowed to return to Simmons Point in Maine, to walk the place where our house had stood, to commemorate it in some way, as a tribute to Mother and Father.

"So," Addie asked at dinner that evening, "how will ye know if the curse is finally broken? Shouldn't there be a sign or the like?"

I too craved some kind of validation. Some

insurance that we'd successfully fulfilled our obligation.

Just then Nessa flew in on her triple-card glider made of both queens and Edward's card, the king of diamonds, still gloating over her role in the drama.

Ideservesomegoldandjewels!Givemesome!

Pru narrowed her eyes. "A deal's a deal, Nessa. You agreed to share information in exchange for the second queen card. And correct me if I'm wrong, but aren't those the two queens in your hands? And then we gave you the king card besides!"

Youtrickedme!SoonasIledyoutothecavethecardsstopped talking!Stoppedflyingtoo! Nessa hovered before us, thrusting the cards under our noses. The images stared blankly, their poses static and stiff.

Theyusedtobemagiccards!

"Spirits finally settled in their graves where they belong," Miss Oonagh rasped. She drew on her pipe and exhaled a white cloud of smoke that rapidly dissipated. "Gone, jest like that. Their work is done."

"And that means the curse has been dispelled?" Jack asked.

Oonagh shook her head. "Ain't no curse no more."

"Thank the good Lord," Old Peader said, blessing himself.

Nessa tossed the cards on the ground. *What goodaretheythen?*

Jack chuckled. "They didn't come with a guarantee. But because I'm generous, and no longer cursed, I'll give you this." From his pocket he pulled a string of the tiniest pearls. "Here. Your just reward."

Nessa grabbed the strand, examining it closely, running them through her teeth to test their quality. *Good.Nowhowaboutsomegold?*

"Nessa . . . ," Pru warned, pointing to the jar on the shelf.

Allright.Allright!

Throughout this exchange Marni gazed out the window, a faraway look clouding her sea-green eyes. "There's something I need to do," she said softly. "To ensure that all my mother's affairs are properly laid to rest. Lucy—might you help me?"

All eyes were on us. "Of course," I said, wondering what in the world was left to be done.

"Meet me at the harbor, beyond the dock, where the water laps against that thin strip of sand."

My heart began to race. "Why don't we go together, Marni?"

"You go ahead. I'll be there shortly."

I dabbed my mouth with my napkin, stood, and headed outside. All the way to the harbor questions plagued me. What unfinished business could there possibly be? I had a vision of her walking calmly into the water, as I'd seen her do in Maine, and be completely enveloped by it. Is this how she would leave me after all?

I reached the spot, leaned against a large boulder, and gazed out to sea, the *Lucy P. Simmons* in the distance. In minutes I heard Marni's footsteps on the path. She sidled up beside me, a good-sized parcel in her hands. "Sixty years ago I should have done this. But it's never too late to do the right thing. Help me, Lucy."

Together we unwrapped the bundle, gently tearing back the paper to reveal the sleek silver fur. The cape unfurled, draping across our arms and onto the sand. I watched Marni run her hand across it, eyes brimming. "Forgive me, Mother," she said quietly. I followed her lead, gently carrying the sealskin mantle toward the sea. We knelt, lowered it into the surf. It shimmered as the water flowed across it, rippled for a moment in a kind of undulating dance, and then was carried off by the current. We both stood and stared at the place where it had been just a moment before.

Suddenly Grady appeared. He removed his cap. Cleared his throat. "The *Lucy P.*'s all shipshape and ready to sail. I say we start to load 'er up. Sail to

Galway tomorrow to hire us a crew."

Together we walked back to the house. Walter and the capt'n had agreed to sail along as far as Galway to help hire the sailors who would get us safely home. After that brief voyage they'd head back to Ballyvaughan by land, and Pru and I would sail home to Maine.

"America." Seamus sighed. "Always wanted t' see Lady Liberty."

"When d' we sail?" Miss Oonagh asked.

Grady sighed. It appeared Miss Oonagh saw the Galway excursion as an attractive outing. Grady looked at Pru and me. "Up to you."

The capt'n placed one hand over Addie's and the other over mine. "Are you sure you can't be convinced to stay?"

I thought, again, of Simmons Point, where Mother, Father, and I'd been so happy. I'd been so sure that returning would somehow fill the empty space in my heart that their absence left. Suddenly I wasn't so sure.

Annie and Georgie looked longingly at me. "Why can't you stay?" Georgie pleaded. Annie wrung the handkerchief between her fingers and chewed her lip. My heart was torn. I'd never really thought much beyond finding the treasure—hadn't considered what leaving would entail. Nor had I considered the possibility of the children finding a place for themselves here. Laying down roots where they'd begun to finally grow and thrive—without me.

It took the rest of the day to gather my things, to reacquaint myself with the nooks and crannies of the ship. Once aboard it began to feel a little more like home, but as I leaned on the rail, gazing upon the emerald shore, something tugged at my insides. What did home mean, anyway? Was it a place or a state of mind? Did it have to do with memories or the people you loved? The ship's bell clanged, calling to mind the days when it had sounded outside my home in Maine. Why did it feel as though I was leaving home rather than returning?

That evening we shared a quiet dinner, everyone trying hard to remain in good spirits, putting our best faces forward. Despite our good intentions, the meal was steeped in an unspoken sadness, the clink of utensils filling the silences between the words we struggled to say. Even the dogs were distressed—Pugsley nosed nervously around Rosie, who slunk off by herself and collapsed in a resigned heap.

"The only thing separating Ireland and America is the Atlantic," the capt'n said, in what was intended to be a bright voice. "A good sail once in a while is a grand thing!"

Old Peader sniffed and wiped his eyes. "This'll be the last time I lay eyes on ye's," he whispered. "Next time ye come t' me grave I won't be risin' from it!"

Marni placed her hand on his shoulder, but didn't correct him. We all knew he spoke the truth, hard as it was to hear. I almost couldn't bear to meet Marni's gaze or to actually consider life without her. Walter stared at me throughout the meal. He'd wanted to sail all the way back to Maine with us but couldn't possibly leave Annie and Georgie. I picked at my food, unable to swallow for the longing that gripped my throat. "Nothing is forever, Lucy," Marni said softly. "A decision you make today can be undone tomorrow. Or a year from now. Remember that." I looked up to see Pru eyeing me intently. "Marni's right, Lucy. We don't have to . . ."

"It's all right," I snapped, then focused my attention on my plate, afraid that if I met their eyes or said another word the tears would begin.

We lingered at table until well past ten, no one wanting the day to end. The conversation slowed, and finally, one by one, everyone slipped away until the only ones left were Walter, Seamus, Brigit, and me.

Walter stood. "Best to get a good night's sleep," he said to me.

"I know," I managed. Walter looked from Brigit to me and paused. "Well, good night then."

"Guess I'll be goin' then too," Brigit replied. She turned to face me. "Never met anyone like ye, Lucy. Wish we'd had time t' be the friends I know we could be." We embraced, she turned, and was gone. I wondered who would win her heart—Walter or Seamus. I shoved the thought away.

So, that left Seamus and me, still trying to figure out who we were to each other. He smiled. "Brigit's right," he said. "Never met anyone like ye."

I reached out and took his hand. "Seamus . . . ," I began.

"Don't go sayin' g'bye yet. See, I always wanted to go to America . . . I . . ."

"Ireland is in your soul," I said. "You could come, but we don't even have a plan for our life back there. I'm not too sure where we'll live, what we'll do. . . . I just need to get back to Simmons Point. For my mother, my father . . ."

"It's all right," Seamus said. "Jest hard to say g'bye, it 'tis." He pulled me close, his hand under my mane of hair, drawing my head against his chest, my face nestled against his throat. I could feel the beating of his heart. We stayed like that for a while before we both slowly backed away and said our good nights.

I lay in the darkness of the room I shared with Pru, wondering how I could have accomplished everything I'd set out to do, and end up feeling so bereft. It was a long time before I fell asleep—perhaps because I didn't want the day to end.

The morning didn't dawn as much as it grumbled its way out of darkness. The sky was white, the air heavy. A distant thunder rolled across the Burren, perhaps protesting the fact that we'd removed the treasure from its bowels. It was not the kind of day a sailor welcomed. At breakfast Grady paced before the window, scratching his head and scowling. "Shouldn't sail today," he said. "It don't bode well. . . ."

The capt'n agreed. "No reason you have to leave now. Tomorrow will likely be better."

Miss Oonagh raised her fork, a piece of bacon wagging from its tines. "No! Today's the day; I feels it in me bones. The sea calls. Yep, I hears it!"

"So now you're a sailor, Mam?" Grady barked. "I think I know best when to sail and when not."

Oonagh stood, waving the bacon like a battle flag. "Ye think ye know everythin'," she said. "Well, ye know only what ye sees in front o' yer face. Me, I sees the other side. And I sees we're t' sail today! Couldn't be clearer!" The bacon flipped off her fork and Pugsley snapped it out of the air.

"I don't think—" the capt'n began.

"Don't think then!" Miss Oonagh cried. She hobbled from the kitchen, still clinging to her fork. "I'm gettin' me bag and headin' toward the ship. Who's comin' with me?"

Grady sighed and shook his head. Pru peered out the window. A shelf of gray clouds pressed in from the west. Marni had that faraway expression I knew so well—Jack wore the same look. They were a pair of bookends, at opposite sides of the table. "I share Oonagh's feeling," Marni said. "As unlikely as it looks, today seems to be the day."

Pru nodded. "Miss Oonagh's more than earned my trust. And I'd place my bet on Marni's instincts any day."

"We only go as far as Galway for now," Walter reasoned. "Not much of a sail."

So it was agreed. There were tears and long embraces. Old Peader wept openly, embracing Pru and me. When he reached for Oonagh, she smacked him on the arm. "Dry up!" she scolded. "I'll be back this evenin'!"

Addie hugged me close and whispered in my ear, "You'll come back t' me someday?"

"You know I will."

Marni left Jack's side and grasped me by the shoulders. "Trust that things will turn out as they should," she said. "They always do."

"I love you," I whispered.

"And I, you."

We marched to the dock in a solemn bon voyage procession. Halfway to the harbor Walter took me by the arm, gently pulled me aside, and waited for the others to pass. Dreading our farewell, I pulled away. "I can't . . ."

"Leave me," Walter whispered, finishing my sentence. "You can't leave me. We've been together since the beginning." His eyes were darker than usual, his face more angular in his intensity.

"I know, but . . ."

Walter glanced over his shoulder, stepped toward me, kissed me full on the lips. "Don't go," he whispered into my hair, his breath tickling my ear.

From a distance I heard Grady call, "She's ship-shape and Bristol fashion, all standing and ready to launch!"

"I have to go," I mumbled, pushing past him so he wouldn't see the tears welling in my eyes.

We boarded, and in no time fell into our old natural rhythm, hoisting her sails and guiding her out of the harbor. I couldn't bear to meet Walter's gaze or to watch the emerald shore shrinking. Instead I trained my eye on the horizon, gauging wind and water, looking forward, not back. Our graceful vessel rolled over the waves, out toward the open seas. I drew Father's spyglass from my pocket and squinted into the lens. It felt weighty, tingling against my skin, pulling to starboard. The sensation traveled through my fingers and hands, up my arms until the hair on the back of my neck prickled. My body was alive with this nervous energy, as though an electric current flowed through my veins, my senses charged and twice as sharp.

I knew what I was going to see before it appeared, and still I was surprised. The specter ship skimmed the top of the waves—a shimmering phantom in the distance, bearing down on us at a supernatural speed. The water before it and the clouds above it whipped into a funnel of such power that in an instant the boundary between sea and sky became indiscernible. Grady saw it and let out a cry, alerting the rest. The wind suddenly rose up and assaulted us with the force of a locomotive. Lines were ripped from our hands and whipped about like giant snakes. The sails billowed and puffed before splitting at the seams and tearing to shreds. We held on to her masts for dear life—all except Oonagh, who stood at the prow, white hair streaming wildly behind her, one hand raised as though in tribute to this terrible god of the sea.

The ship nosed up on the crests and plummeted, drenching us in black, salty sheets of water. Had we been too quick in believing the curse had been broken? Only one other storm had risen up so suddenly and violently—the hurricane back in Maine that had lifted my house from its foundation and heaved it into the sea.

Despite the tumult of water and onslaught of wind the specter ship continued its advance. Another wave crashed over us, sending me sliding across the deck. I grabbed hold of a line just as the phantom ship glided beside us. There was a split-second lull, like the eye of a storm, through which I could clearly see the deck of the other vessel. My heart began to race as their familiar forms took shape. "Mother," I whispered. "Father . . ." I felt their silent voices reverberate in my heart—*Lucy—the magic of love always overcomes the power of evil. And home is where you're loved.* For a brief, shining moment their vaporous forms glowed, and I took in the image of their faces, the love reflected there. Then they and their ship disappeared.

A bolt of lightning flashed, striking our main-mast, sending a sizzling green wave of fire down its length and through the ship. Her timbers shuddered and groaned. A seismic wave swelled against the portside, knocking the ship over, sending us tumbling into the sea. Her bow split in two; the stricken mast toppled in an explosion of flames. I gasped as the water pulled me under and dragged me into the depths. I broke the surface, lungs nearly bursting. I watched the *Lucy P. Simmons* shatter into a million pieces, her bell still clanging. A wall of water bore down on me and the raging current catapulted everything in its wake toward shore. Struggling to stay afloat, I watched her bowsprit shoot past like a spear, her rudder flip and disappear under the surface. A ragged chunk of her hull splintered against the rocks. I splashed past a section of rail, the figurehead bobbing aimlessly beside me. The sizzling mast burst into a million colors, sending a whirlwind of glittering mist over and around the carnage of our ship. Waves of sparkling vapor enveloped the wreckage, whipping it into a tempest of swirling debris, hurling it onto the rocky shore. The cyclone spun in frenetic circles, creating a maelstrom of color and light. The sea reared up and I was spit out of the ocean. I hit the ground hard, the air knocked out of me. I choked and wheezed, coughing up briny water and sand. There was a deafening explosion, a blinding flash. I covered my face with my hands.

A second passed. Then another.

An eerie silence ensued. The water lapped gently against the shore; a seabird called. I lifted my head, opened an eye. Pushed myself up on my elbows, chest heaving. Pugsley licked my face, nudged my arm with his wet snout. He was safe! And, miraculously, there was Pru, stumbling to her feet, Walter and the capt'n beside her, staring out to where the ship had been just moments before. Grady hauled himself up and lifted Oonagh from the ground. The old woman's silvery eyes glinted with excitement, her hair in a wild, tangled nest about her face.

What was left of the swirling mist had wafted over the headlands beyond where the sea had dropped us. The brilliantly hued vapor parted and rolled back, revealing a glimpse of a large structure. I recognized the familiar roofline, and as the mist continued to dissipate, I spied the leaded-glass windows, the ornate gingerbread trim. Wicker chairs lined the porch as they had when Mother, Father, and I used to sit there and read. The ship's bell hung beside the door as it always had back in Maine, the nets strung along the trellis laden with climbing roses. I moved toward the house—*my* house—the house that had been thrown into the sea, that had been transformed, that had carried me to my destiny.

Over the crest of the hill they ran—Addie, Patsy, and Brigit, Seamus and Old Peader. Georgie, Annie, Marni and Jack. I could only imagine their horror standing on the dock, watching the storm overtake us, their terror at the sound of the explosion, their concern propelling them along the shore to the inlet where our crippled ship had been thrown aground. Addie stopped short, her hand flew to her mouth—such was her astonishment at seeing the home of her former employ reincarnated along her own emerald shore.

In a moment we were all together on the porch, in an ocean of kisses and embraces, everyone talking at once. Their fingers ran along our cheeks, hands ruffled our hair, the gift of touch ensuring that what they saw was true and real. The hum of gratitude and awe faded as I heard Mother's and Father's voices once again: *Lucy—the magic of love always overcomes the power of evil. And home is where you're loved.*

It might not have been the family I'd planned on, but in them I'd discovered a treasure greater than any. I looked from my beloved aunt Pru to Marni, and then at these people thrust into my life, seemingly by chance. Walter and the children. Grady and Oonagh, Brigit and Patsy, Seamus and Jack. Old Peader, still dabbing his eyes and shaking his head. And, of course, my ever-faithful Mr. Pugsley.

I knew then that this voyage was complete and that finally, at long last, I was truly home.

EPILOGUE

"Wherever ye go, ye take yerself with ye!" Addie exclaimed this often as our lives on the emerald shore unfolded. We all remained true to who we were, falling into the routines and following the inclinations we'd had before the voyage that brought us together.

Grady, Oonagh, and Old Peader settled in a cottage with a view of the sea. Marni and Jack chose another thatched house nearby, reminiscent of her bungalow back in Maine. Walter, Georgie, and Annie took the cottage on the capt'n's property as they had before, affording the children the feeling of home that the capt'n and Addie had provided. Brigit and Patsy returned to Dublin, and Seamus to Clare Isle to keep an eye on Grady's property there, but the three were regular visitors. Pru and I adored living in the Simmons house, the presence of Mother and Father powerfully felt.

In light of our newfound lives the treasure had lost much of its appeal, even for Jack. So no one was surprised when Marni used a good portion of the spoils to fund the construction of a large country manor, designed to house the lost children she had always been so drawn to. Soon Rory, Paddy, Meg, and their gang of foundlings from the workhouse had a roof over their heads and food in their bellies, and they became the next generation of recipients of her extraordinary care.

And there were other surprises as well. Right after our ship's reincarnation Rosie disappeared for more than a week. Old Peader was inconsolable, Pugsley depressed. So you can imagine the celebration when Rosie reappeared with four pups scrambling behind her. They were a peculiar mix of pug and border collie, with all the personality of both. One went to Georgie, another to Annie, a third to Old Peader, and a fourth to Marni's Ballyvaughan Home for Adventurous Children.

The last of the fortune was spent building two

ships—one for Pru, Walter, and me, the other for Jack. While finding a home was the greatest gift of all, traveling the seas was in our blood. Remaining anchored to those we loved the best had always provided the courage to voyage into the great mysterious world—a world of magic, of challenge, and of hope. And so we christened two new ships—ours named *Nearest and Dearest* and Jack's *Treasured Heart*.

There would be many voyages yet to come.

ACKNOWLEDGMENTS

Many thanks to Katherine Tegen, Claudia Gabel, Melissa Miller, and the entire HarperCollins team for launching Lucy's incredible voyage, and to my writers group (my ODE friends): Pamela Bramhall, Anne Dichele, Lisa Fiedler, and Dianne Schlosser, for being on board with me the whole way!

Set sail with Lucy P. Simmons!

Dazzling magic, swashbuckling adventure,
and good, old-fashioned heart!

 KATHERINE TEGEN BOOKS
An Imprint of HarperCollins Publishers

www.harpercollinschildrens.com